CW01346168

# GHOST SONG

MARK L'ESTRANGE

Copyright (C) 2019 Mark L'estrange

Layout design and Copyright (C) 2019 by Creativia

Published 2019 by Creativia (www.creativia.org)

Cover art by Cover Mint

Edited by Felicity Hall

This book is a work of fiction. Names, characters, places, and incidents are the product of the author's imagination or are used fictitiously. Any resemblance to actual events, locales, or persons, living or dead, is purely coincidental.

All rights reserved. No part of this book may be reproduced or transmitted in any form or by any means, electronic or mechanical, including photocopying, recording, or by any information storage and retrieval system, without the author's permission.

*To my LRU Family: Rebeccah, Claire, Namita, Alisha, Laura, Sarah, Chandrika, Dele and Rob.*

*Thank you for putting up with the madness.*

# PROLOGUE

Spaulding Hunt stood on his gravel driveway smoking an after-dinner cigar, as was his usual habit. He was very much a man of habit, and always had been. At the age of eighty-four he felt entitled to indulge in whatever took his fancy, without feeling the need to justify his actions to those around him.

In truth, the confirmed bachelor had never allowed the concerns or wants of others to cloud his judgement. He had very much lived his life according to his own code of conduct.

Expelling a huge ring of smoke into the night sky, Spaulding turned at the sound of footsteps behind him.

Mr and Mrs Jarrow climbed down the stone steps which led to the gravel drive, before wishing their landlord and employer a good night.

Spaulding acknowledged their departure with a slight nod of his head and the merest hint of a smile.

The Jarrows had worked for Spaulding in several capacities for over twenty-five years.

Mrs Jarrow acted as house-keeper, cook and cleaner, whilst her husband took on the duties of gardener, handy-man and chauffeur.

They lived in a modest cottage in the grounds of Spaulding's manor house and even though he charged them a peppercorn rent for their accommodation, the meagre wages he paid them meant that they both had to secure alternative employment on a part-time basis.

Jack Jarrow worked three mornings a week in their local sorting office, whilst his wife covered three afternoon shifts as a barmaid at their local.

Had Spaulding been willing to pay a proper wage, the Jarrows could easily have made looking after him and his crumbling manor a full-time occupation. But as it was, the middle-aged couple did what they could in the time that they could spare.

Emily Jarrow ensured that Spaulding's breakfast was on the table at 8 o'clock promptly every morning, including weekends, and that his dinner was served at 9 o'clock each evening.

Spaulding insisted on a full English breakfast consisting of porridge, egg and bacon, toast and marmalade and a pot of tea - every morning. His lunch was invariably a sandwich and a pint or two, served by Emily more often than not at the local.

For dinner he insisted on a four-course fare starting with soup, followed by a main, dessert then cheese. Dinner was always washed down with a full bottle of claret, and usually a glass or two of port to compliment his cheese.

Unlike many octogenarians, Spaulding's appetite had not diminished with his advancing years; yet even now he managed to maintain a relatively proportionate build for his height.

He watched as the Jarrows climbed into their car and pulled out of the driveway.

The second that they were out of earshot the singing commenced, as Spaulding knew that it would.

It was the same every night.

Once he was alone his torment would begin!

First came the singing. That sweet, gentle voice seemed almost as if it were carried on the wind, as the strains of the heart-wrenching lullaby filled the air surrounding him.

*"As the waters run deep, so my soul yearns to soar.*

*On the wings of an eagle, I'll wait nevermore.
In the arms of my true love, I will pause for my time.
So, hold me forever, until you are mine."*

Try as he might, Spaulding was unable to block the sound out. Even by sticking a finger in each ear the lullaby managed to pervade his defences.

It was almost as if the music were emanating from within him, a cry from his soul.

He knew the voice!

After so many years it was completely plausible that he would have forgotten it by now were it not for the fact that it visited him each night, and often during the day if he was alone.

He had no control over it, and no way of stopping it.

From a combination of disgust as well as frustration, Spaulding threw down his half-smoked cigar and stormed back into the manor.

He slammed the door behind him and stood for a moment with his back against it.

As he expected the singing had crossed the threshold with him, and now that he was inside the lyrics echoed throughout the manor as if they were being sung in each room simultaneously.

Spaulding slapped his palms against each ear in a futile attempt to drown out the sound.

Taking several paces forwards into the great hallway, he lifted his head and screamed out at the top of his lungs.

"Enough! I can't take this anymore! What do you want from me?"

In response to his yelling, several of the doors to the upstairs rooms began to open and slam shut, one after the other.

As if on cue, the downstairs lights began to flicker and fade until eventually they went out altogether, and the only illumination came from the roaring fire in the dining room which cast eerie shadows through the open doorway to where Spaulding was standing.

The upstairs doors continued to open and slam shut, but the noise they made did little to drown out the singing which still seeped out of every room inside the manor.

Spaulding walked over to the foot of the sweeping staircase and gazed up into the darkness of the upstairs floors.

"Why can't you just leave me in peace?" he screamed, into the blackness.

> *"Cry for me my lover, 'til the seas have run dry.*
> *Never seek answers, and never ask why.*
> *The path I am destined is not paved with gold,*
> *But the warmth of your love, keeps out the cold."*

The words of the lullaby which he had long ago learned by heart, in spite of himself, echoed down to him as if to taunt or goad him into action.

Slowly, using the bannister for support, Spaulding began to make his way up the winding staircase. "What can I do?" he yelled once more, keeping his head raised as if expecting someone or something to suddenly appear in his line of vision.

As a sharp wind whistled down the staircase, the old man clung onto the bannister for dear life. The force of the gust rocked Spaulding as if he had suddenly been caught up in a vortex, almost knocking him off his feet.

The sheer audacity of the attempt to prevent his ascension made Spaulding all the more determined to complete his task.

Taking a deep lungful of air, he pushed on ahead, refusing to submit.

As he reached the halfway mark, Spaulding could feel a tightness in his chest.

Before he had a chance to respond to his plight his left hand began to go numb, and it took a supreme effort for him to tear it away from the bannister.

Spaulding stood for a moment on the stair, unaided, as he proceeded to rub the pins and needles from his hand. But before his efforts bore fruit, a sharp, stabbing pain accosted his left side as if someone had thrust a knife into him.

Grabbing his left shoulder with his right hand, Spaulding felt the ground beneath him give way.

He was faintly aware of the singing still resonating through the air as he tumbled head-over- heels down the stairs until he finally ended up slumped in a heap at the bottom.

As the life left his aged body, the singing stopped and the lights in the manor came back on.

Spaulding stared ahead with dead eyes, unable to witness the ghastly apparition which loomed above him from the top of the stairs.

# ONE
## PRESENT DAY

Meryl Watkins carried a tray of drinks over to one of the many tables surrounding the stage at the far end of the pub that she ran with her husband Mike.

The bar was heaving, even more so than it usually was on a Friday night. Meryl put it down to a combination of the snow that had fallen the previous evening and which was now lying several inches deep on the ground, and the fact that once a month she and her husband played host to a live band at the pub.

Tonight, they had a folk group consisting of four cousins. One man was on drums with another playing guitar, then there was one girl on the flute with another on guitar. The one playing guitar was also the lead singer.

They had never had this group in before, but they came with a recommendation from a couple of other landlords who Meryl and Mike knew through the industry.

They were Romany travellers who performed all over the world, and although they had never released any albums they were always asked to perform again by their hosts when they were next in the vicinity.

Meryl rushed back over to the bar where there were already at least five customers waiting to be served, on top of the ones that her husband and their two other barmaids were in the process of seeing to.

The players were already setting up their equipment on the tiny stage, and the two girls had already received several wolf-whistles from some of the males in attendance. Meryl did consider whether she needed to make an announcement to keep them in order, but the two girls appeared to appreciate the attention and responded by blowing kisses out to the crowd.

The performance was due to start at nine-thirty, and just before the long hand on the clock reached the six Meryl felt an icy blast as the outer door to the pub opened and one of their regulars shuffled in from the cold.

The old man had been in every night at the same time for as long as Meryl could remember.

He never spoke to anyone other than to say please and thank you when paying for his drink, and he always sat in the far corner away from the other patrons to enjoy his ale in peace.

Meryl noticed the shocked look on the old man's face when he realised how crowded the bar area was. For a moment he stood in the doorway gazing around at the packed interior, and Meryl was convinced that he was contemplating venturing back out into the cold without his usual two pints inside him.

On an impulse Meryl handed a customer their change and apologised to the next one in line as she made her way around the bar, and she grabbed the old man by the arm just as he was turning to leave.

The man looked up with a mix of shock and confusion on his face until he realised just who his assailant was.

Meryl smiled broadly. "It's a bit busy in here tonight," she explained, "but there's an empty table at the back, just for you."

With that, she carefully guided the old man through the crowd until they reached their destination.

Once he was seated, Meryl offered, "The usual, is it?"

The old man smiled, "Yes please," he answered, and Meryl patted him on the arm as she went back to the bar.

Having served a couple of her regulars, Meryl returned to the old man with his usual pint of strong ale.

She placed it on the table in front of him and as he opened his wallet to pay, she held her hand over his. "First one's on me, today," she said with a wink.

The old man thanked her, politely, and Meryl left him to go back to the bar.

The band introduced themselves and began their set.

Their music covered an eclectic mix of tunes but they had arranged these so that they all stayed within the folk/country genre they had promised, and by the end of their first set the crowd were all joining in with all the well-known songs they covered.

When the band took their break, there was a sudden surge of revellers aiming for the bar to replenish their drinks.

In between listening and serving Meryl kept an eye on the old man in the corner, and as he drained the last gulp of his pint she began to fill his next glass.

She managed to make her way through the crowd just before the old man was about to rise to try and fight his way to the bar. His face lit up when he noticed Meryl approaching his table, and he slumped back down in his chair and began counting out his money in anticipation of her arrival.

"Oh, thank you so much," the old man sighed, "I was dreading fighting my way through that lot to get to the bar."

Meryl laughed. "I don't blame you," she replied. "I'm just glad that I'm on the other side of the bar, we're really busting tonight."

The old man nodded and handed over the correct change for his pint. "They are very good," he remarked, nodding towards the empty stage.

"Yes," Meryl agreed, "first time we've had them here, but it won't be the last. I'm glad you are enjoying their performance."

"Oh, I am, very much so," the old man smiled.

"Well, I had better get back to the bar before there's a riot, the band will be back in a minute to complete their set. I hope you'll stay until the end."

The old man nodded. "I will, thank you."

After a ten-minute break the band returned to the stage amidst tremendous applause and more whistling.

The lead singer acknowledged the crowd's appreciation, and before they started their second set she took a few minutes to introduce the individual members of the band. The girl on the flute was her cousin, and the two men were both her brothers. They all acknowledged their appreciation for the crowd as each one was cheered in turn.

Their second set went as well as their first, with the audience equally enamoured by the band's performance and willing to participate. Although the alcohol had convinced some participants that they could sing in tune the truth was very far from it; but everyone was enjoying the evening which was the main thing as far as Meryl was concerned.

At the end of their second set, the band laid down their instruments and all took centre stage to receive their much-deserved standing ovation.

As the audience called out for more, Meryl rang the bell for last orders.

The lead female vocalist looked over at the bar owner and held up her index finger by way of asking if there was still time for one more song.

Meryl nodded her response and proceeded to organise a tray of drinks for when the band had finished.

"Ladies and gentlemen," began the singer, once the cheering and clapping had died down. "We would like to do one last song for you this evening." A cheer went up. "Thank you," the girl smiled, appreciatively. "This is an old Romany lullaby which most of us learned from our mothers when we were still in the crib. We hope you all like it."

Meryl glanced over at the old man in the corner.

His glass was already empty, and Meryl decided to offer him another pint on the house. She had often watched him when he came in for his usual Friday night visit. It was obvious to her that he did not know any of the other patrons, and he always made a point of sitting as far away from the crowds as he could.

The pub had its share of single older regulars, but they all seemed eager to jump at the chance of becoming involved in someone else's conversation - often attaching themselves onto groups of complete strangers.

On some occasions the drinkers made it plain that they did not appreciate the intrusion into their private discourse, and Meryl always felt a twinge of sadness for the lonely individual who would inevitably shuffle away in search of company elsewhere.

But in all her time there, Meryl had never once seen the old man so much as try to strike up a conversation with anybody; staff or punters.

On a couple of occasions Meryl herself had tried to drag some form of dialog out of him while she was pulling his pint, and although he was always extremely polite and courteous, he managed to halt each attempt she made with single word answers.

As she made her way over to the old man with his fresh pint, the singer began her final song.

> "As the waters run deep, so my soul yearns to soar.
> On the wings of an eagle, I'll wait nevermore."

To Meryl's surprise, the old man suddenly jerked his head round towards the stage. His movement was so abrupt and unexpected that he sent his empty pint glass scudding across the table, and he just managed to grab it in time before it tipped over the edge and smashed on the stone floor.

The old man's hands began to shake, uncontrollably, and as Meryl reached his table she gently leaned over and placed her hand over his in an attempt to steady him.

In the background the singer's voice carried over the bar and throughout the pub.

The rest of the band played softly, as if to ensure that they did not interfere with the singer's melody.

Meryl placed the fresh pint down in front of the old man.

When he looked up to meet her gaze Meryl could see tears brimming over his eyes, leaving twin trails down his cheeks.

Meryl suddenly felt an overwhelming compulsion to put her arms around him and tell him that everything was going to be alright. In truth, she had no idea what had caused the old man to become so upset in the first place.

Instead she decided that hugging him might draw too much attention, and the last thing Meryl wanted was to cause the old man further embarrassment, so she grabbed a couple of paper napkins from a pocket in her overall and handed them to him so that he could wipe his eyes.

Choking back his tears, the old man thanked her for her kindness.

Meryl felt compelled to stay and find out what was wrong. Mike was forever having a go at her for taking on the troubles of the world, but she could not help herself.

For the sake of a few kind words and a little comfort, she was more than happy to see if she could do anything to ease the old man's grief.

Meryl sat down beside him and angled his pint so that the handle was towards him.

"There's another one on the house," she whispered, so as not to disturb those around them listening to the singer.

The old man turned to her once more and thanked her through his tears.

Meryl held his gaze for a moment.

There was something in his eyes which conveyed a sadness that was almost palpable.

As the girl finished her song the audience began to applaud, loudly.

The rest of her band joined her once more in thanking everyone in attendance for their appreciation, and promised that they would return there the next time they were in the vicinity.

This announcement received an even greater cheer of delight.

As the band began to clear away their instruments, Mike carried over the tray of drinks Meryl had just prepared for them. She caught Mike's eye on his way back to the bar and signalled that she was staying put for the time being.

Mike immediately put two-and-two together and realised that his wife was once again attempting to share the burdens of the world, and playfully shot a glance up to heaven.

Meryl stuck her tongue out at him in response, which caused him to start chuckling as he reached the bar.

Meryl turned her attention back to the old man beside her.

He had managed to wipe away the last remnants of his tears, but the effort had left his eyes puffy and red-rimmed.

He put his hand over his mouth as he cleared his throat.

"Take a swig of that," Meryl encouraged him, nodding towards the pint she had just brought him.

The old man thanked her again and lifted the glass to his mouth, taking several gulps.

When he replaced it on the table, he continued to dab his eyes with the napkin.

Watching him, it appeared to Meryl as if he were about to burst into tears again at any moment.

"Is it something you want to tell me about?" she asked, softly, "a problem shared, as they say."

The old man stared straight ahead for a moment, looking in the direction of the band who were now seated at a table in front of the stage, enjoying their drinks.

After a moment's silence, the old man replied. "It's that song!" he announced.

Meryl looked towards the band, and then quickly back to her guest.

It took a moment for his words to sink in.

Finally, Meryl thought that she understood. "Oh, I see, does that song hold some treasured memories for you, something from your childhood perhaps?" she enquired, pleased with herself for managing to engage the old man in an actual conversation.

To her amazement the old man jumped up from his seat, this time almost knocking his full drink flying.

"I have to go!" he stated, his voice starting to crack as if the effort were too great for him.

Meryl rose next to him.

She could see from the state he was in that he was in some distress, and she could not help but feel as if it was somehow her fault although she could not put her finger on the cause.

Meryl watched as the old man shuffled around checking his pockets to ensure that he had all his belongings before he left.

Although he was turned away from her, Meryl could see that he was still having to wipe his eyes so she suspected that fresh tears were brewing.

As Meryl was blocking his exit from one side the old man attempted to walk around between the table and the wall, but the gap was too small and he only succeeded in banging his leg on the edge of the table.

His failed attempt at escape only succeeded in making the old man more agitated, and when he turned to leave and found Meryl still blocking his path his frustration caused yet more tears to trickle down his face.

Even though Meryl could hear Mike's voice in her head telling her not to interfere, she decided that she could not allow the old man to leave in such a state. Above all, she did not want to feel responsible for him leaving the pub in haste and slipping on the ice on the way home and having an accident.

Steeling herself, Meryl placed a comforting hand on the old man's shoulder and offered him a reassuring smile. "Do you mind me asking you your name?"

The question obviously took the old man by surprise, and for a moment he appeared to visibly calm down.

"It's Jonathan," he replied, stammering slightly as if he were trying to force the words out. "Jonathan Ward."

"Well, I am Meryl Watkins, and that man behind the bar is my husband Mike," she held out her hand towards the old man, "and I would like to formally welcome you to our pub, with apologies for not introducing ourselves to you at an earlier opportunity."

Jonathan Ward clasped Meryl's hand, almost as if on instinct, and squeezed, gently.

Regardless of the fact that mere seconds before he had been intent on leaving the bar as quickly as possible, he could not be so rude as to refuse a handshake from his host.

The pair of them shook hands, and the old man seemed to relax visibly during the process.

Convinced that the exercise had accomplished the required effect, Meryl indicated for Jonathan to re-take his seat.

The bar was starting to empty, and most of the patrons finished their drinks and made their way out into the cold night air.

Still with some hesitation, Jonathan acquiesced to Meryl's suggestion.

Once they were both seated, Meryl spoke. "I am very sorry if I upset you Jonathan, I assure you that was never my intention."

The old man shook his head. "Please do not reproach yourself," he assured her, "you weren't to know."

Looking past her, Jonathan glanced over to where the Romany band were still enjoying their well-deserved drinks.

He turned his attention back to Meryl. "It's just that song you see, I haven't heard it in nearly fifty years, and I hoped that I would never hear it again for as long as I lived!"

Meryl was confused by the old man's words, and her expression illustrated the fact.

She desperately wanted to ask the old man to explain but she bit her tongue, conscious of the fact that she had already managed to upset him once this evening and she did not relish repeating the experience.

In the end, she did not have to.

The old man could see the bemusement etched into Meryl's face, and that, combined with the kindness she had shown him, gave him the courage to face up to something which had haunted him for most of his adult life.

In that moment, he decided it was time to lay his own personal demon to rest!

Once and for all!

# TWO

Once Jonathan informed Meryl that he had decided to confide in her, she excused herself for a moment so that she could pour herself a drink, say goodnight to her staff, and thank the musicians for playing such a marvellous set.

Jonathan sipped his drink, nervously, and watched while Mike showed the bar staff out and locked the main door behind them.

The band finished their drinks and walked over to the bar to leave their empty glasses.

As Meryl showed them to the door, Jonathan called out to the lead singer.

"Young lady," he stood up to catch her attention. "I was wondering if I might have a quick word with you before you leave?"

The girl smiled and walked over to the old man's table, closely followed by the rest of the band. "Yes," she said, cheerfully, "what can I do for you?"

Meryl suspected that Jonathan was about to ask the young singer about her encore, so she came back over and stood next to the old man.

Jonathan was visibly shaking so he tried to steady himself by holding onto the back of his chair, but Meryl grabbed his arm and insisted that he sit back down before he started to speak, so the old man complied with her wishes and re-took his seat.

"I was just wondering…about that song you sang at the end of your concert…you mentioned that your mother taught it to you when you were a baby."

The girl smiled. "That's right, it's a bit of a staple amongst the Romany clan as it's usually the first song we're ever taught. Why do you ask, have you heard it somewhere before?"

Jonathan rubbed his hands together as if to ward off the night cold when in truth it was still quite warm in the bar, and the log fire which Mike had been replenishing throughout the evening was still blazing away across the room.

As he opened his mouth to answer, the words caught in his throat. Jonathan turned his face away and held his hand to his mouth to clear his throat, once more.

When he turned back, Meryl was holding up his glass as if to encourage him to take a sip before he continued. Jonathan thanked her and took a long swallow before replacing the glass on the table.

The young female singer leaned over the table and rested her hand on Jonathan's sleeve. "I'm so sorry," she said, softly, "I didn't mean to upset you."

Jonathan waved his hand as if to dismiss her concern. "Not at all, young lady," he replied, "you didn't upset me, it's just…" He paused, as if unable to find the words he was looking for.

He turned to Meryl, as if for inspiration.

Meryl, sensing the old man's discomfort, decided to intervene.

She called over to her husband to fetch everyone a drink, and invited the artists to take a seat. "Let's all get comfortable," she suggested, cheerfully. "We'll have ourselves a little lock-in, just an informal gathering between new friends. Something to keep the cold at bay for a little longer."

While Mike fetched the drinks and the band made themselves comfortable, Meryl took the opportunity to discreetly whisper into Jonathan's ear- just to make sure that he was comfortable relaying his tale in front of everyone.

She was starting to feel a little guilty that she had put him on the spot, even though he was the one who had called the band members over to join them.

Regardless of how much her husband teased her, Meryl was not one to pry into someone else's business. However, she had the distinct impression that the old man was carrying a burden which he desperately needed to share.

Once Mike had brought over the drinks and everyone had taken their seats, Meryl raised her glass. "Cheers everyone," she offered her glass up for the others to clink, and once the wishes had been passed, they all took a drink.

Jonathan knew that everyone was waiting for him to answer the young singer's earlier question, so he decided it was best just to pitch in without over-thinking it. Otherwise he was afraid that he might back out, and part of him was determined that the time had finally arrived to tell his story.

Taking a deep breath, he began. "Now then young lady, you asked me if I had ever heard your song before…"

"It's Melissa," the singer informed him. She turned to the rest of the band. "This is Julie, Fred and Barry."

They all waved and nodded their acknowledgement, and Jonathan reciprocated.

"Well, the truth of the matter is," he continued, keeping his voice low as if he were afraid that someone outside might overhear him, "many years ago, long before any of you were even born, I went through a terrifying experience which will haunt me for the rest of my life."

The gathering all exchanged glances at the old man's revelation.

Their expressions showed a combination of shock and anticipation.

Finally, Melissa spoke up. "And what you went through, it had something to do with the song we finished our set with?" she asked, curiously.

Jonathan nodded. "I realise it must sound ridiculous that such a beautiful song should cause me so much distress, but if you'll allow me to explain the circumstances to you then perhaps you will understand why my memory of it is so disturbing."

"Of course," Melissa responded, soothingly. "I think you've got us all intrigued now."

There were several nods from around the table.

The old man knew that he had passed the point of no return, and now - even though the mere thought of it sent an ice-cold shiver down his spine - he felt compelled to tell his story.

He considered for a moment what might be the worst-case scenario under the circumstances if he told those gathered his account of what had happened to him all those years ago.

As far as he was concerned, his life was all but over anyway.

Death was just a waiting game for him, and so it had been for more years than he could remember.

The old man rubbed his eyes with his thumb and forefinger, as if to symbolically clear away any doubts which lingered to prevent him from speaking.

He was ready!

"It's hard to know where to start," he said, almost in a rhetorical fashion, not looking at anyone in particular. "I don't want to bore you with my life story - you know how some old people love to ramble on about the good old days, and what they did and did not do."

He looked up, and was encouraged by the fact that everyone seemed to find his last statement amusing.

"I met my wife Jenifer in the late sixties at a pop festival, if you can believe it. It was during the summer in a large field where everyone had to bring their own tents and sleeping bags, unless they were happy just sleeping on the ground under the stars.

"The air was charged with flower-power and free love, and there were several people experimenting with pot and various other forms of recreational drugs."

He looked up. "Not me, you understand, I was way too boring and straight-laced for all that."

There was a smattering of laughter in response.

"At the time," he continued, "I was working in a bank in our local high street, so I had to ensure that I did not let myself go too much. In those days you could find yourself being handed your cards for the slightest thing, if it was considered unbecoming behaviour by your employers. Especially when you worked for such a conservative organisation as I did.

"I remember that it was the second day I was there. The weather had been gorgeously hot, and like many in attendance I was completely caught up in the romance of the spectacle.

"Some of the bands seemed to play throughout the night, so that whenever you dropped off there was still music when you woke up.

"There were caravans and stalls selling fish and chips, hotdogs, doughnuts, candyfloss and all manner of treats, so the air was permanently infused with the smell of tempting food wafting across the field, which in turn made you feel hungry even when you weren't.

"I'll never forget the first time I laid eyes on my wife. It was late afternoon on the second day, and suddenly the whole world seemed to stop as this vision of loveliness walked by, right in front of me. Her beauty was captivating. She had the face of an angel and skin the texture of porcelain, with lustrous flowing blond locks cascading down around her shoulders. For a moment I could no longer hear the music or the shouts and chants of all those around me, and it literally felt as if the breath had been sucked out of my body.

"I turned to watch her walk away, and in that instant I felt compelled to follow her wherever she was going. Bear in mind I had no idea what I was going to do when she reached her destination; I wasn't the type of bloke who felt comfortable just walking up to a girl and starting a conversation, especially not with one who was as pretty as her. But something spurred me on. Something told me to persevere and let fate take its course, so on I went.

"The way she managed to weave through the huge crowd with such grace and elegance was in complete contrast to my clumsy attempt at following her without making it appear too obvious. I lost track of how many times I tripped and stumbled over bodies writhing on the floor. Fortunately for me, most of them seemed so lost in the spirit of the moment that they didn't appear to notice my clod-hoping attempt at dancing around - rather than on top - of them.

"Eventually, I caught up with her standing in a queue to buy candy floss. I waited a few feet behind her feeling completely inadequate and disappointed with myself for not being able to approach her. Furthermore, being this close to her, I knew that if she saw me when she turned around there was no way that I could continue to follow her without causing her alarm, and that was the last thing I wanted.

"As luck would have it, fate stepped in for me. As she turned around having just purchased her treat, a young couple, both clearly high on something, careered into her and sent her flying off her feet straight towards me. The whole scene could have ended very messily, but as it was I managed to catch her and stop her from falling; although her candyfloss ended up on the grass.

"The couple who had caused the accident were totally oblivious to what they had done, and continued to veer across the field bumping into everyone in their path.

"Jenifer was clearly miffed at the fate of her candy, but once I let go of her she turned around to thank me for saving her from falling. I made some joke about not being fast enough to save her candy as well, and she laughed. There was obviously no point in going after the couple as they were now lost somewhere in the melee, so instead I offered to buy another candyfloss.

"At first, she protested and said that she couldn't let me, but before she could stop me I had my money on the counter and I had placed her order.

"When I handed over her new stick, Jenifer leaned in and kissed me on the cheek. I know that I must have blushed because I could feel my face burning."

"Well, it's so nice to see that chivalry is alive and well," she said, trying not to laugh at my reaction to her kiss.

"We introduced ourselves to each other, and without even realising it I guided her over to a much quieter area of the field so that we could sit on a bench and talk. I was desperate to know everything about her: where she lived, what she did, what ambitions she had, what her hobbies were, and in the end, I managed to bombard her with questions for so long that the next time I looked up, the sun was starting to set behind the field.

"Of course, the bands were still playing and the crowds in the field were in no way ready to wind down, but when Jenifer put her hand in front of her mouth to stifle a yawn I realised that I had monopolised far too much of her time, and that it wasn't really fair of me to keep her there any longer.

"The worst part was that even though we had been chatting together for so long, I still did not feel sufficiently confident enough to ask her out on an official date. With a heavy heart I remember mumbling something about letting her get back to her friends who must be worried not to have seen her for so long. But to my surprise, not to mention delight, she announced that the group she had come with had agreed to all do their own thing once they arrived, and that in fact she had not clapped eyes on several of them since they had got there."

Jonathan could feel his throat beginning to become dry, so he leaned over and lifted his glass to his lips and took several good swallows to lubricate his vocal chords.

"Anyway," he continued, "as wondrous as this news was to hear, I still felt completely inept at trying to contrive a feasible excuse to keep Jenifer in my company.

"I remember there was a very awkward moment's silence while I was desperately trying to think of what to say next. Jenifer didn't help matters by just sitting there gazing around at the field, looking almost good enough to eat.

"In the end I think I asked her if she was hungry, which she wasn't. So next I offered her a drink, but again she replied that she was fine. The feeling that I was fast losing her interest in me was almost tangible as I continued to wrack my brains to think of what to say next. Finally, just as I thought that all was lost, she laid her head on my chest and gently snuggled into me as if she were about to go to sleep.

"To say that I was taken-aback would be an understatement. I remember feeling completely numb as if I had been shot by a stun-gun, or something equally as ridiculous, and for a moment I could not will my body to respond to Jenifer's action. Fortunately the effect was merely temporary, and slowly I moved my arms up and around her so that I could hold her properly.

"We stayed like that for ages. It was wonderful, and I for one did not want the moment to ever end. But the sun had well and truly set, and with the darkness soon came the cold. Even though it was the middle of summer the wind soon picked up, and Jenifer only had on a thin blouse so it wasn't long before I could feel her shivering in my arms.

"Sadly, I didn't even have anything over my shirt to offer her to ward off the chill, so after a while we were both sitting there, literally shaking from the cold.

"It sounds so ridiculous now, especially saying it out loud, but at the time and given the circumstances, I was so afraid of shattering the magic of the moment that I tried to ignore the fact that we were both freezing, preferring instead just to try and ignore the sensation and pretend as if it were not really the case.

"But, eventually, Jenifer could stand it no longer. She eased herself away from me and wrapped her arms around her shoulders, rubbing them vigorously to try and re-start her circulation. In that split second, I was afraid that she was going to make her excuses and that I would never see her again. The fact that we had enjoyed a cuddle together meant nothing at the time, as everyone was experimenting with being more open with their feelings and women especially seemed less afraid of being given a derogatory label for being too tactile.

"But as it turned out, my fears were erroneous."

"Well I don't know about you," she began, "but I need something more than just your arms to keep me warm tonight."

"Before I had a chance to respond, she kissed me gently on the cheek and skipped off the bench."

"Why don't you go and get something warmer too?" she suggested, "and we can meet back here, afterwards."

"To some, her words might sound like a brush-off, a polite way of making an excuse to leave with the intention of never returning. But as I gazed into Jenifer's eyes I somehow knew that her words were being spoken in earnest, and that she had every intention to keep to her promise to return to our bench.

"We set off in our different directions and within five minutes I had collected my jumper and jacket from my tent, and was back on our bench.

"I waited for what seemed an eternity but in reality, it was probably no more than half an hour, before I saw Jenifer re-emerging through the crowd and heading towards me, bundled up in an oversized tan jumper and a padded overcoat with a beaming smile on her face.

"We spent that night snuggled together on that lonely bench, far enough away from the crowds to feel as if we were in our own space but not too far away to hear the music from the various stages dotted around the field.

"I had never believed in love at first sight, until that night. By the morning I found myself engulfed by an overwhelming wave of emotion, and before I could stop myself I blurted out my feelings to Jenifer like some infatuated teenager with a schoolboy crush."

Jonathan looked around the table at his audience. He wanted to glean from their expressions whether he was boring them to death or not.

It struck him that this was the first time he had ever reminisced about his wife to a stranger, let alone a group of them, and he was surprised by how effortlessly the words were flowing out of him.

There were so many wonderful things about his wife that he longed to divulge, but he knew that this was not the correct forum and definitely not the right time.

Those assembled had only stayed because he had piqued their curiosity concerning his recollection of having heard their song all those years ago, and why the very sound of it now brought back such terrible nightmares. Nightmares which he had lived with for over fifty years, too afraid to so much as share his experiences with another living soul.

But now, it appeared, the time had finally come!

"What was Jenifer's reaction to your outpouring of affection?" It was the other female band member who asked the question.

Jonathan smiled. "Fortunately for me Jenifer was not only wonderfully kind, but also sensible, and she told me in no uncertain terms that although she was very attracted to me, she needed to know me a lot better before contemplating falling in love with me."

"Sensible woman," Meryl observed, shooting her husband a knowing wink.

"That she was," Jonathan agreed. "Sensible, beautiful, caring, compassionate…I could go on forever bestowing her virtues. But unfortunately, the story I have to tell you has little to do with the happiness my wife brought me, and more to do with the terror I was yet to suffer at the hands of another.

# THREE

"It all began for me in September 1970. Jenifer and I had married in the June of that year, and as money was a little tight we decided to wait until we could afford a proper honeymoon abroad. One day a letter arrived from a solicitor, informing me that I had inherited a house from a distant relative - who prior to that moment I had never even heard of.

"Apparently, I was subsequently informed by the said solicitor, he was a distant cousin on my father's side and according to the terms of his will I was eventually traced as his only living male relative, and as such I was his sole beneficiary.

"My parents had both been killed in a car accident the year before I met Jenifer, leaving my younger sister Jane and I to fend for each other. Jane was only nineteen when they died, and she had just gone away to university. Our parents' death left us both shattered and she ended up taking a year off, fully intending to start again the following September.

"We both inherited our family home, and at the time neither of us had any intention other than to live in it together for the time being to help keep some stability in our lives. We had always been close, and both took great comfort in the other's presence in the house to help us through the darkness of the early days after the funeral.

"I was already working at the bank so at least we had the stability of a regular wage coming in, but after a couple of months at home Jane started to feel guilty about not contributing to the household kitty. Even though I kept telling her not to worry herself about it, in the end she found herself a position at a hotel through a local temp agency just to keep herself busy until she returned to university.

"As things turned out, whilst working at the hotel she met her future husband Neil who was the assistant manager there; and although I was a trifle concerned that their relationship smacked of being a 'whirlwind' romance, who was I to talk?

"The bottom line was that Jane never did return to university, but she was, and still is for that matter, very happy, and Neil has always been a good husband and father to their three children, so in the end everything worked out for the best.

"Once Jane and Neil decided to buy a place of their own together, I re-mortgaged the house so that Jane could have her share. I did consider selling and starting again, but I had such happy childhood memories there and even though under normal circumstances the re-mortgage would have been beyond my pocket, as I worked for a bank they offered me a special rate so it was just within my budget.

"I had only had one experience of dealing with a solicitor before, and that was when I had to see to the probate of my parent's will. The solicitor on that occasion was a dour-faced, sullen individual, with extremely poor customer service skills, as well as a very bad case of body odour. Not that I would automatically tar every other solicitor with the same brush, but the memory of that initial encounter still resonated in me while I was speaking on the telephone to the solicitor for my recent benefactor's probate.

"The property that I had inherited was in Northumberland, which to my memory I had only travelled to once before, during a family holiday when we went to visit my father's older sister. My father was a very late child so there was thirty years difference in their ages, and from what I understood they were never that close.

"Both Jenifer and I were understandably very excited to go and view our new acquisition, but as fate would have it we were desperately short staffed at the bank and I had already taken a week off for our wedding, so, when I approached my manager with my annual leave request he made a point of reminding me that loyalty and dedication were the key qualities he looked for in an employee who, one day, wanted to move up the managerial ladder, as he was well aware that I did. As it was he agreed to allow me to take a second week off, but only after a couple of my colleagues had returned from their leave. So, I just had to be patient.

"Jenifer was naturally disappointed, but she fully appreciated my situation at work so she too just accepted it. Throughout the next couple of weeks, the house in Northumberland was all that we could talk about. The solicitor had very graciously sent us some details concerning the property, and when we excitedly opened the envelope neither of us could believe our eyes.

"The description of the property, along with the drawing of the layout and its adjoining land, made it look enormous, and the grandness of the structure reminded us of some of the stately homes we had visited on Sunday outings, with the national trust organisation.

"The building itself, according to the documentation, had been built in the eighteenth century. It was set in its own grounds and boasted three levels, four if you included the basement, which housed the kitchen and scullery. The front entrance was housed in a massive arch, which was supported by two concrete pillars, with a couple of stone lions standing guard at the bottom of the stairs.

"According to the description the property needed some considerable repairs, but my father's cousin had lived in it his entire life so at least it had to be habitable. Not that we were considering moving to Northumberland! Jenifer was extremely close to her parents and I knew that she would never consider relocating so far away from them. She also worked for her father in his photographic studio, and over the years he had come to rely upon her more and more. She had confessed to me that in many ways she felt obligated to stay, as she was not sure how well he would cope on his own. Added to which she did actually enjoy her job, and she loved dealing with people of all kinds who came in for portraits or to arrange to have their weddings and other special events recorded for posterity.

"Now given half a chance, Jenifer would have loved nothing more than to work on the manor house herself. She wasn't just a terrific photographer; she could turn her hand to almost anything artistic whether it was painting, drawing, needlepoint, fashion design, upholstery, DIY - almost whatever she tried. She would gush for hours after dinner about how she would design matching curtains and fabric covers for the furniture, as well as what colours she would paint each room, or what wallpaper would suit which walls best.

"Although I have never had any kind of artistic talent myself, it was easy for me to be swept away by her enthusiasm for the project and sometimes, if she was really excited about a particular idea, the time would just slip away until it would be midnight before we looked up and realised how late it was.

"But for all her eagerness and passion, we both took a very pragmatic approach in deciding what we would, in fact, do. Our plan was that once we had settled the death duties which the solicitor was in the process of calculating for us, we would sell the place and hopefully, if there was enough left, pay off our mortgage. It was still a windfall and a very pleasant surprise, but we were realistic enough to consider the fact that although such a lavish property might make a fortune in London, it was not going to be the same story in its present location.

"Also, according to the solicitor's description, there was the state of the property to take into account plus, besides the death duties, the solicitor had mentioned that there might be some outstanding debts courtesy of my benefactor.

"But with all that, nothing could quell our excitement. We further discussed the possibility of being able to give Jane part of our windfall. Jenifer understood how close we both were, and what's more they had grown quite close too. Therefore, we both agreed that we would look at the state of our finances once the dust had settled and see where to go from there.

"But the overall fact was that we were still incredibly thrilled about the future, especially with regards to our latest acquisition.

"The days at work leading up to our big adventure seemed endless, and for the first time in my life I actually considered how tedious and boring my chosen profession could be. I began to watch the second hand on the clock as it slowly mocked me for my impatience.

"With less than a week to go before we set off on our quest, Jenifer's father was offered an extremely lucrative contract for a large fashion house which was just about to branch out into selling accessories as well as clothes. He had been offered the work as a result of a wedding that he and Jenifer had covered a couple of months earlier, which quite by coincidence was attended by one of the directors for the chain that was launching the new collection.

"Under normal circumstances Jenifer would have been just as excited as her father for the upcoming event, as it would be a tremendous opportunity for them to showcase their talent which might in turn lead to future bookings with the same company.

"Typically, however, the booking was planned for the week that we were going away to Northumberland to visit our new house. Naturally there was no point in asking the fashion house if they could postpone their shoot, as it would doubtless have meant that they would just go somewhere else and Jenifer's father would lose his commission, not to mention the chance of any future work from the same organisation.

"Jenifer was torn. On the one hand she was desperate to come with me and see the house, but on the other hand she appreciated how desperate her father was to take on this new - and very influential - client, and there was no way that he could have handled the project on his own. He had often commented that if it had not been for Jenifer's passion for the business he would have either had to scale down the operation or possibly even sell it off altogether.

"Jenifer and I spoke at length about what we were going to do about the situation, but we both knew that the pair of us would feel far too guilty to leave her father in the lurch. I even considered asking my manager if I could postpone my holiday for a week, but after the fuss he had created about my initial request we both decided that that would not be a viable option."

Jonathan smiled up at the group seated around the table.

"Back in those days a job in banking was about as good as it could be for man with my qualifications, and the law did not protect the employee as much as it does now. I had seen colleagues dismissed on the day for the most minor of indiscretions, so I knew that it was not in my best interests to rock the boat.

"So, in the end we decided that the best course of action was for me to travel down to the house as arranged, and with any luck Jenifer could join me before the week was out, depending on how things went with the fashion shoot. If push came to shove we could always take a trip up there over a weekend, it was just a shame that we had missed the last bank holiday weekend for the year. It would be a tiring journey driving all that way for one night, but if it meant that Jenifer could see the house it would be worth it. Also, the bank was always closed over the Christmas period, so that might give us another opportunity to visit if Jenifer could wait that long.

"As much as she refused to let her parents see her disappointment, the closer my date to leave grew the more down-hearted Jenifer became. I knew instinctively how hard it was going to be to leave her behind when I set off, but our hands were tied.

"Eventually, the weekend before my trip arrived. Had we have been going together, we would have left first thing on the Saturday morning. But as I was going alone, I decided to postpone my departure until the Monday so that we could spend an enjoyable weekend together, and I could spoil my wife a little as recompense for her disappointment.

"We spent most of Saturday in the west end, shopping. The deal was that as it was part of Jenifer's treat I would not complain. I had always hated clothes shopping, right back from when my parents used to drag Jane and I up into town when we were small. As much as I loved my wife's company, it made little odds when she was darting in and out of boutiques and I was made to spend what seemed an eternity sitting outside changing rooms whilst she tried on every dress in the place. Especially when she ended up buying the first dress she tried on!"

There was a smattering of titters from a couple of the men, including Meryl's husband who received a well-aimed elbow in the ribs for his cheek.

Meryl did not wish to disturb Jonathan while he was speaking, so she mouthed a silent instruction to Mike to replenish the glasses for everyone.

Jonathan continued. "We dined that evening at our favourite restaurant, and on the Sunday, as the weather was uncommonly pleasant for the time of year, Jenifer suggested that we spend the day by the seaside. We had always shared a love of the sea, and never needed an excuse to visit one of the many resorts accessible within a few hours' drive from London.

"On this particular day, we chose Brighton as our destination as we had not visited it for a while. Being so late in the season we made very good time, and even managed to find a place to park along the front.

"The minute we both stepped out of the car our senses were infused with a heady combination of the usual seaside fare and treats being peddled by the seafront traders. As was our usual habit when visiting the seaside, we both had a modest breakfast so that we could look forward to overindulging in fish and chips, doughnuts, toffee apples, and naturally Jenifer's favourite, candy floss.

"Jenifer had always been a marvellous swimmer, and her penchant for the sea was quite overwhelming so she had brought her costume so that she could have a dip before we ate lunch. I, on the other hand, was more than happy with our local pool, so while she stripped off into her costume I set out a couple of towels on the beach so that I could watch her swim.

"Jenifer would always swim out too far for my liking but she was not in any way reckless, so she made sure that she did not go out any further than the buoys that had been placed there as a marker. I watched from the beach, squinting into the sunlight until her tiny form almost disappeared from view. I would often catch myself holding my breath until I could see her on the return journey. But I never told her so because I did not want to spoil her fun.

"After her swim Jenifer towelled herself off and changed in one of the toilets along the front, and then we lay in the early afternoon sun for a while to top up the tans we had acquired during the summer. I managed to doze off, but fortunately Jenifer woke me up before I burned. Her swim had given her quite an appetite, so we made our way to a small fish restaurant we knew down one of the lanes where we had always managed to secure a table.

"We decided to walk off our lunch by taking a stroll along the front. As usual we planned on visiting the arcades and funfair later, so we initially headed out in the opposite direction, allowing ourselves plenty for the return journey.

"On our way back, as the pavement was growing more crowded with the arrival of latecomers, we decided to walk along the beach instead. The journey back took far longer than the journey out, mainly because there was a plethora of small craft shops at beach level and Jenifer could not resist stopping off to buy anything unusual that happened to catch her eye. I would always liken her to a child in a sweet shop whenever she was around craft stalls at fairs.

"As we approached the pier, I suggested that we use the next ramp to take us back up to street level. We were about to turn off when something else caught Jenifer's eye and she began to pull me along, gesturing excitedly towards what appeared to be an old wagon further along the beach. It looked like something from an old Western film which should have had a horse attached to the front of it. The panels - unlike the canvas ones generally seen in the movies - were made of solid wood, and they were decorated with incredibly detailed and ornate paintings of various animals, forests, planets, and the like.

"As we grew closer, I saw the sign outside the wagon which had caused Jenifer to grow so excited. It was an advertisement for a gypsy fortune teller, promising, for a small fee, to reveal your future. Personally, I had never believed in fortune tellers, and table rappers, and people who claimed to be able to speak to the dead. The entire lunatic fringe, as far as I was concerned, were there merely to part gullible individuals from their money."

Jonathan suddenly slammed his hand across his mouth, and his face grew red.

"I am so sorry," he said, apologetically, looking at the individual band members. "I did not mean any offence towards any of you, or your traditions. Oh, how stupid of me!"

Melissa leaned over the table and placed her hand on his arm. "Please don't reproach yourself," she offered, comfortingly. "We know that you didn't mean anything by it; please continue with your story, I'm fascinated to know what the fortune-teller told you."

The others in the band all nodded their agreement and smiled at the old man, as if to convey their agreement with Melissa that they had not taken offence.

Jonathan took a sip of beer to clear his throat before he continued.

He was grateful for the band's understanding nature, but he still felt foolish that he had allowed his words to slip out without considering their feelings.

"Now," he continued, "where was I?" Jonathan took a moment to catch up with his train of thought before he continued. "I could tell from Jenifer's eagerness that she was intent on visiting the wagon. Instinctively I began to pull back as we approached. Sensing my reluctance, Jenifer turned to me with that excitable look on her face that she always wore whenever she wished to convey to me that she desperately wanted to try, or buy, something which she knew I did not share her enthusiasm for. By now I had stopped dead in my tracks, refusing to play along. But, as usual, once Jenifer altered her expression to that of a pleading child, complete with pout and sad eyes, desperate to get her own way, I crumbled.

"Madam Zorha, according to the sign outside her wagon, had travelled the world reading the fortunes of everyone from kings and queens, to film and pop stars, and as a result she was in great demand, which sort of made me wonder why she was reduced to telling fortunes from an old cart on the beach. However, I did not share my concern with my wife. My guilt at having to leave her behind the following day as I set off to Northumberland would be eased, I reasoned, by allowing her this small indulgence without too much complaint on my behalf."

## FOUR

"Once Jenifer realised that I had relented, as she knew that I would, I was dragged by my sleeve to the door of the wagon. Naturally it was left to me to knock, which I dutifully did by climbing up the short wooden steps which led to the arched door. We did not have to wait long before we were 'invited' to enter the inner sanctum when the occupant yelled back at us with an unceremonious, 'Yes'.

"Leading the way, I tentatively pushed open the door and peered inside. The interior was very badly lit, which I believe was done on purpose to help create a suitable atmosphere. The tiny space was cluttered with all manner of different sized chests and boxes, brimming over, in most cases, with what appeared to be bolts of different coloured cloth. The containers had been arranged in such a way as to allow anyone entering a clear path to the other end of the wagon.

"The lighting, such as it was, was subdued to say the least, and my nostrils were immediately assailed by the scent of incense sticks permeating the air. In the far corner there was a small area which had been curtained off but the fabric used was so thin that it barely concealed anything behind it, and squinting through the darkened haze I could just about make out the figure of a small woman seating on a wicker chair, behind a small, oval table.

"I remember turning back as Jenifer gently squeezed my hand, as I was not initially sure if her signal meant that she still wanted to venture in or for us to beat a hasty retreat. As it was she gestured with her head, instructing me to go forward, so I turned back around and called out to ask if it was alright for us to come in. I could just about make out through the misty atmosphere the woman signalling with her hand for us to join her. I gently pulled Jenifer towards me so that she was clear of the door as it slowly closed behind us.

"It might sound a little odd, but as we carefully manoeuvred through the gauntlet of trunks and boxes I remember thinking that the wagon seemed to be emanating a strange aura which immediately made me feel slightly uncomfortable. At the time I put it down to whatever we were inhaling from the incense, but when I spoke to Jenifer about it later that evening, she confessed to having had the same impression upon entering.

"We made our way steadily towards the flimsy fabric which acted as the partition, and once we were close enough to be able to see the woman behind the curtain properly I felt obliged to ask again if it was ok for us to be there. Once more the gypsy gestured without speaking for us to move forward, and once we were both through the curtain she signalled towards the two chairs which were placed opposite her for us to sit down.

"As we took our seats, Jenifer and I quickly shot each other a nervous glance. It was very easy within the confines of that wooden sarcophagus to forget that we were actually at the beach on a bright and sunny day, and that just outside there were throngs of happy revellers enjoying the lovely weather. For the fact of the matter was, once the door had closed behind us, all sound from outside was completely eradicated.

"The woman who by now, as we were so close, we could tell looked extremely old and wrinkly, one might almost say wizened, closed her eyes and began muttering to herself as she gently rocked back and forth in her chair. We both sat there in the brooding atmosphere for what seemed like an eternity, neither of us feeling confident enough to dare disturb the old woman's incantations. Eventually she stopped speaking and looked up at us both before holding her hand out.

"I took the hint, and retrieving my wallet from my back pocket I took out a pound note and placed it squarely in the centre of her palm. There were no prices advertised anywhere inside or out, so I presumed that a pound should cover our session. But when the old gypsy kept her hand out without even acknowledging the money I had given her, I realised that I had been mistaken.

"I considered placing a ten-shilling note over the pound in her palm but decided instead that another pound should seal the deal and if it did not, then I would speak up and ask outright how much she demanded for her services. Although I knew how excited Jenifer was about having her fortune told, I also knew that if the cost was too exorbitant that she would not insist that we stay.

"Luckily, the old woman closed her hand around the notes and placed them securely in a pocket in her skirt. I must admit, I did breathe a silent sigh of relief that we were not about to enter a bartering contest with the old woman.

"The old woman reached back over the small table and held both her hands out, palms up. Jenifer and I both took the initiative and placed our right hands, palms-up, in one of hers, respectively. She studied our palms for a couple of minutes without speaking. We just sat there, trying our best to keep still, even though to me especially the situation was starting to resemble something from a television comedy sketch.

"Finally, the old woman started to speak, although she kept her gaze firmly locked on our hands which I must admit felt a little odd, but I played along for Jenifer's sake more than anything."

"You are both share good health," she announced, in her broken English, "and there is happiness in your hearts."

"Then she paused for a moment as she continued to study our palms."

"One of you work not good, dull, no excitement."

"At this point she looked up at me, and pointed with her index finger."

'You do not enjoy occupation as much as you hoped, but you work hard."

"She then glanced over to Jenifer."

"Your work artistic, good for you, but you also have talent to expand your success into other work you have not discovered yet".

"We both exchanged glances. The gypsy woman was spot on as far as I was concerned. My position at the bank had grown increasingly tedious over the past year, but just as she had stated I could not afford to leave and wait for something else to come along, and by that same token I had no idea what else I might want to do instead anyway.

"As for Jenifer, again the old lady was right on the money. She loved her job working with her father, and she had already demonstrated her aptitude for turning her hand towards most things artistic. Therefore, it was perfectly plausible that in time she might discover other strings to her bow, which in time could prove to be even more lucrative that her photography.

"I confess that by this point I was beginning to grow a little more intrigued by what the gypsy had to say. I was impressed by the fact that she had not asked us any questions about our circumstances before launching into her incredibly accurate description of our domestic lives. It was possible, of course, that she was exceptionally observant, and having noticed the wedding ring on Jenifer's finger and seeing the two of us together she managed to hazard a guess that we were both very 'happy' and 'healthy'. But her reflections concerning our employment could hardly have been gleaned from our appearance or demeanour, so she deserved at least a modicum of kudos for that alone.

"The old woman continued in much the same vein for a little while longer. She picked up on the fact that my parents had both passed on and that I had a sibling, whereas Jenifer was an only child. She even manged to describe with some accuracy the place where we first met, right down to the fact that we first spoke to each other about 'something sugary', which I took to mean Jenifer's candy floss and the incident at the concert.

"After a few more minutes the old woman released our hands and we both retracted them, simultaneously. It was odd, but for a couple of seconds I could feel a strange tingling sensation running through my fingers so I instinctively started to shake my hand and make a fist to try to relieve the feeling. Jenifer too, I noticed, commenced a similar action with hers, although she was far more discreet about it than me.

"The gypsy turned in her chair and, with a slight strain, lifted a cloth-covered object from a nearby stand and placed it in the middle of the table. She muttered a few incomprehensible words under her breath, and then she whipped off the cloth to reveal a large spherical glass ball lodged in what appeared to be a metallic claw-like holder.

"Jenifer and I both exchanged a furtive glance. As impressed as we both were with the old lady's predictions thus far, the sudden introduction of a crystal ball into the mix seemed to give the proceedings an air of pantomime. Jenifer managed to keep a straight face; nonetheless I received a sharp kick under the table as I struggled to supress a laugh.

"The old gypsy either did not notice or just chose to ignore my schoolboy antics, as she kept her gaze focused on the glass sphere. Once I had managed to subdue my juvenile behaviour we both sat in silence once more, awaiting the next instalment from our host.

"I watched intently as the old woman squinted into her crystal ball, the expression on her face etched with a combination of curiosity and profound wisdom. She cupped her hands around the sides of the glass orb, but kept them just far away enough so as not to actually make contact with the surface. She stayed like that for several minutes, her focus completely transfixed by whatever she could see in the crystal.

"Suddenly her hands sprang away from the glass orb as if some immense heat was emanating from it, and she threw herself back into her chair. She moaned out loud, almost to the point of screaming, and clamped her palms against her ears as if to try to block out some unearthly sound.

"Jenifer and I looked at each other in bewilderment. I must confess that still being somewhat sceptical about the entire episode I began to wonder if this was some well-rehearsed kind of confidence trickery, designed to make us leave without receiving our money's worth. But my cynicism was soon erased when the old gypsy thrust her hand into her pocket and retrieved the two pounds which I had paid her earlier, before flinging them across the table towards me."

"There's nothing today! You go, please, no more today, go, go!"

"As she spoke, she indicated with her hands so that we were in no two minds that she wanted us gone. For a moment Jenifer and I just sat there in stunned silence. The thought crossed my mind that perhaps the old gypsy was annoyed because I had seemed amused earlier when she first produced her crystal ball, but then I reasoned that if she was truly annoyed with me she would not have wasted so much time studying the ball before insisting that we leave. Furthermore, the fact that she had returned our money seemed an odd thing for her to do if her reason for wanting us out was because I had not shown her the necessary respect.

"The old woman rose from her seat in such a hurry that the movement sent her chair falling backwards behind her. This sudden feat spurred Jenifer and I into action, and we both stood up together and turned to leave. I wanted to stay long enough to apologise formerly just in case I had actually said, or done, something to upset the gypsy, but Jenifer grabbed hold of my hand in such a way that I knew instinctively that she wanted to leave at once.

"After we took a few steps towards the door we heard the old woman calling back after us. I ushered Jenifer in front of me, almost as if to protect her from the shouting woman as I turned back to face her. To my astonishment the old gypsy had crept right up behind me without me even realising it, and there she stood, thrusting my money back into my face.

"I held a hand up as if to convey that she could keep the money, but she virtually forced it into my jacket pocket before she turned and shuffled back towards her upturned seat.

"Once outside Jenifer and I both looked at each other, neither quite sure what to say on the subject. It had certainly been an experience, but one that neither of us was in any great hurry to repeat. The atmosphere inside the wagon, possibly due to the cramped surroundings, had been very claustrophobic, and I believe that Jenifer was even more glad than I was to be back out in the fresh air with the rest of the crowds.

"We decided to put the experience behind us and not let it spoil the rest of our day. We ate fish and chips for lunch on the beach while we watched the various families in attendance enjoying the beach. After lunch we walked along the coast in the opposite direction to that which we had taken earlier, and finally made our way onto the pier. I waited until Jenifer had to use the toilet before I changed up a bag of pennies for her to use in the amusement arcades. This was an activity that she had enjoyed since she was old enough to see the bright lights and magical designs on the machines. Jenifer had often told me how when she was a child and her parents would take her anywhere that housed such contraptions, she would beg and plead with them to allow her to play until they finally gave in.

"Fortunately, even at a young age, Jenifer knew from the outset that she was never going to win anything, and whatever she did win always went straight back into the machine. Personally, I had never shared my wife's unvarnished rapture at giving away hard-earned money to a metallic bandit, but when I witnessed her squealing like a kindergartener at the sight of the bag of pennies I was holding up it sort of made it all worthwhile.

"I spent the next half hour or so following Jenifer around as she decided which machines to play on, and even joined in her excitement whenever she hit a jackpot. Once the money was gone, we moved onto the fun fair at the end of the pier. This was yet another of Jenifer's favourite pastimes, so whenever we visited one of the many seaside venues within driving distance we had to make sure first that it had a fair. Fortunately, Brighton was one of the destinations which we knew kept its fair all year round.

"Apart from all the usual rides we had experienced on previous visits, it appeared that there was a new addition in the form of something called the 'Sky Rocket'. It was an awful-looking contraption which appeared to consist of an extremely rickety track which climbed even higher than the 'Big Dipper' and moved faster than the cars on the 'Waltzer'. What made it even worse was that the organisers had elected to plant this monstrosity at the very end of the pier, so that when the cars reached their apex it appeared as if the riders were about to be launched straight out to sea.

"This, naturally, made the ride far too enticing for Jenifer to miss out on, and ignoring my pleas and protestations she dragged me excitedly towards the queue. As we waited in line I watched the cars going up and down with my heart in my mouth. The closer we grew to the front of the line, the faster I could feel my reserve ebbing away. I knew full well that there was no way that I could ever talk Jenifer out of riding on the confounded contraption, but by the time we were close enough to be part of the next group allowed on my nerve snapped and I informed Jenifer that, all joking aside, I could not face the ride.

"I could tell right away that she was disappointed by my reluctance, but realising that I was not cut from the same cloth as her she reluctantly agreed to ride alone.

"That was, until she saw the sign at the front which stated that each car had to have two riders, so no one could ride alone. Jenifer's face dropped a full mile, and a subtle whine of despair escaped her lips before she had a chance to prevent it. She looked back at me with her bottom lip protruding, her eyes conveying a plea of longing which she had never hit me with before, as she assured me as best as she knew how that she would look after me and that we would both be back on solid ground before I knew it.

"I almost caved in, such was the passion with which she entreated me, but just then a group of young girls in front of us all turned in unison and one of them asked if Jenifer, very politely, if she would mind riding with her, as she too was without a companion to share her cart. The idea seemed to solve all our problems, and I must admit to feeling a tremendous rush of relief once I realised that my presence was no longer required.

"I moved out of the queue and stood back several paces so that I could watch Jenifer and her newfound friend from a safe distance.

"Once everyone, including Jenifer, had piled on the ride and been strapped in by the operator, I waved them off as the gigantic piece of apparatus whirred into life.

"The late afternoon sun was on its decline, and a chill wind shot through me causing me to shiver involuntarily. Just at that moment, I felt a hand tug at my jacket sleeve. I looked down, and standing there, right next to me, was the old gypsy woman from the beach. I was so taken aback by her sudden appearance that for a moment I fancied that she had sought me out to demand her fee back.

"The situation appeared quite comical to me at that moment, because within the confines of the wagon I had not realised just how short the woman was. She barely reached above my waist, and from a distance it must have looked as if a child was pestering their parent for something.

"All the same, the chill I had just experienced from the wind picking up was nothing compared to the sharp, icy-cold feeling of dread which overtook me as I stared down into her malevolent eyes. She wore a black scarf which covered her head and most of the lower portion of her face, and in the encroaching darkness the balls of her eyes appeared to be quite black.

"I had to make a distinct effort not to yank my arm away from her; such was the immediacy of the terror the old woman caused in me. Instead I took a deep breath and attempted a smile of sorts, before asking her how I could help her.

"Her tiny fist had a tight grip on my sleeve, and as small as she may have been in stature I felt that it would have been nigh on impossible to prise her away from me, even if I had been desperate to do so. As it was I leaned down so that she could hear me over the noise from the fair, but before I had a chance to speak she wagged her index finger at me."

"Don't go…Don't go…You, no go!"

"She made it sound more like a command than a request, her voice rising in volume in competition with the fun fair. The entire situation seemed so surreal to me at the time that I found myself unable to stifle a smile as I tried to reply. The old gypsy obviously took my expression as an indication that I was not taking her warning seriously because the next thing I knew she began to shake me with all her might, to the extent that I was convinced that she was about to tear my jacket.

"I could see others around us starting to take notice of what was going on, and for one terrible minute I was afraid that someone would think that I was trying to mug the old woman, such was the ferocity with which she was struggling with me. I tried my best to calm her down, but my efforts were in vain. As her voice rose in volume she was almost on the verge of screaming at me, and I could not help but notice the look of sheer terror in her eyes.

"At that moment, from out of nowhere, a young girl appeared and gently pried the old gypsy away from me. She spoke to the old lady in a language I did not recognise, and I could tell by her gesticulations that the old woman was not at all happy with the girl's interference.

"I waited until there was a lull in their conversation before I spoke up. I asked the girl what the problem was, and tried to explain what had happened at the wagon, and that I would be more than happy to reimburse the old lady for our reading if that was what was bothering her. At first, I was not altogether convinced that the girl understood what I was saying, or in fact that I was even addressing her, as she kept her focus on the gypsy.

"The young girl finally managed to calm the old woman down, and once she had, she turned to me with a half-smile.

"Sorry," she said, apologetically. "It's alright, I'm sorry for my grandmother's outburst, she has not been well".

"I smiled back my acknowledgement and once more offered to pay the gypsy for her time, but the young girl assured me that the money was not the issue and wished me a pleasant evening as she tried to veer the old woman back in the direction she had just come from.

"Although the old woman still appeared adamant in her refusal to move away without a fuss, the young girl had definitely taken charge of the situation and eventually the old woman allowed herself to be led away.

"I stood there for a while, watching their receding figures as they began to dissolve into the crowd. My concentration was such that I did not notice Jenifer sidle up beside me until she linked her arm through mine. 'What was all that about?' she asked, curiously. I shrugged my shoulders and told her how the old gypsy just turned up and started chastising me for leaving the wagon, presumably because we had not paid. 'But she insisted we take back our money,' Jenifer reminded me, 'did you try and give it back again?'

"I assured my wife that I had, but that the young girl had assured me that it was not necessary. 'Odd,' was all that Jenifer had to offer, and I concurred, absolutely."

# FIVE

"Odd though it might sound, especially in this day and age, but when it finally sunk in the following morning that Jenifer and I were going to be away from each other for an entire week, we both found ourselves a little tearful. The fact was that since we had been married we had not spent so much as a single night apart. Even when she was still living with her parents a full week had not gone by without us seeing each other at least two or three times. So, as it turned out, I found myself heading down the motorway with a heavy heart, when I should have been more excited at the prospect of finally viewing my inheritance.

"I had arranged an appointment for that afternoon with my benefactor's solicitor, explaining that I was driving down and so hoped to be with him by early afternoon. As I was negotiating unchartered waters I did not want to make a firm time for our appointment, and the solicitor, a Mr Ralph Peterson, seemed perfectly satisfied with my estimated scope of arrival.

"In those days the concept of satellite navigation had not been thought of, at least not for the motorist anyway, so I had to navigate my way with the assistance of road signs and an atlas of Great Britain which I had purchased specifically for the occasion. Jenifer and I had spent the best part of an entire evening trying to plot my route, and although once we had completed the task the journey seemed fairly straightforward, on the day I still managed to lose my way. At one point I pulled over at a petrol station to check my bearings, only to discover that I had been driving in the wrong direction for over twenty miles.

"To make things worse several of the roads we had plotted were 'A' and 'B' roads, most of which had virtually no signposts whatsoever, and just to add salt to the wound, they were plagued with tractors and various other forms of farm vehicles, all of which seemed incapable of travelling at anything above ten miles per hour, and due to the narrowness of the side-roads it was virtually impossible to overtake them. The other problem, which I must admit that I had not considered prior to leaving, was that I was driving my father's old Granada which had definitely seen better days. The car was one of my parents' possessions which I had been reluctant to part with, due mainly to all the happy memories I had of the four of us travelling in it on days out. My father was a dab hand at motor mechanics and he was proud of the fact that he completed most of the maintenance and repairs to his car himself. I, on the other hand, knew next to nothing about cars other than where to put the petrol, and I kicked myself for my lack of enthusiasm whenever my father offered to show some of his maintenance tricks of the trade.

"Without my father's attendance to the vehicle, I had sadly allowed it to run down to the extent that it was now long overdue a good service. I was reminded of this lack in my routine whenever I drove over a pot hole, or took a corner too swiftly on my way to the solicitors, and some of the noises the car was making made me wonder if I was actually going to be able to complete the journey in one piece.

"Fortunately, I eventually arrived in the small town of Briers Market still intact, although far later than I had initially anticipated. Mr Peterson had given me directions to his office, which were fortunately straightforward and easy to follow. I managed to find a parking space across the street from his office, and checked my watch as I crossed the road. It was now almost five o'clock and the shops and offices along the high street all had their lights on as the daylight was fading.

"Once inside I was confronted by a stern-looking middle-aged lady who, once I introduced myself, peered at me over the rim of her spectacles with a distinct look of disdain."

"Mr Peterson was expecting you some hours ago!"

"She made no attempt to disguise the contempt in her voice, as if I had only come from the other side of town rather than having driven all the way from London. I made my apologies, although I felt that she was being unduly harsh with her criticism. Her expression softened somewhat when I confessed that my journey had taken far longer than I too had anticipated, and she gestured for me to take a seat while she informed Mr Peterson of my arrival.

"The office was rather small and cluttered if I am being honest, with bundles of papers tied together with ribbon, stacked on top of each other all over the place, including some on the floor which had been rammed into corners and alcoves so as not to become trip hazards. Having just met Mr Peterson's secretary it surprised me that someone who appeared, on first impression, to be so punctilious, was happy to work in such haphazard surroundings.

"My train of thought was derailed by the re-appearance of the solicitor's secretary. She did not bother to walk back over to me, but instead elected to stand at the far corner of the office, having just emerged from what I took to be Peterson's inner sanctum, and bellow across the room in her haughtiest voice that Mr Peterson was ready to see me. She made me feel like an errant schoolboy who had been summoned to the headmaster's office.

"As I approached Peterson's door his secretary stayed in situ, which, by the time I reached the door, made me realise that I did not have enough room to squeeze by her in order to enter the room. I stopped once I was immediately outside the entrance and smiled at her, weakly, hoping that she would take the hint and move for me. But alas my subtle gesture was to no avail. Instead she made a point of re-announcing me to her boss before finally moving to one side to allow me to pass.

"Peterson was a good deal younger in person than he had sounded on the telephone. He jumped up from his desk as I entered his office and offered me his hand. While we were shaking he signalled for me to take the seat opposite him."

"Could I tempt you to have a tea or coffee?'

"As he made the kind offer, he glanced over to his secretary who was still loitering in the doorway. But, when I looked over at her, I could tell immediately from her demeanour that she was in no mood to be acting the part of hostess so I politely declined his offer, although in truth I was gasping as I had not had anything since breakfast. Once his secretary had closed the door behind her I apologised to Peterson for my tardy arrival, and explained about my lack of a decent sense of direction, as well as the various hindrances I had encountered on some of the smaller roads. Peterson laughed, good-heartedly."

"No problem, Mr Ward, I began to think that you had decided to stop off somewhere en route and complete your journey down tomorrow."

"I agreed that in hindsight that this might have been the wiser option, but my overwhelming compulsion was to arrive sooner rather than later as I was very keen to see my inheritance. As it was by the time I arrived the light was already starting to fade, so I knew by that point that I would not be able to see it in daylight until the following morning. But I was still excited by the prospect of seeing it in the flesh, so to speak, that evening.

"Over the next hour, Peterson painstakingly went through all the formalities concerning my inheritance. At my request he kept the language in layman's terms so that I did not have to keep stopping him repeatedly mid-point to ask him to explain something. The solicitor had a large manila file containing, what appeared to me to be, several hundred documents and individual sheets of paper, some of which had started to yellow with time.

"It became apparent to me during the course of our conversation that my benefactor's side of the family had relied upon Peterson's family practice for generations, and some of the documents within the folder were dated from the previous century."

"I took the liberty of sending away the deeds to your new property for re-registration; although I am quite sure that you will be looking for a buyer for the property, it is always best to keep everything up to date. I'm sure you understand."

"I explained to Peterson that Jenifer and I would be making the final decision together, regarding what we would eventually do with the property. To this Peterson gave me a very curious look, and proceeded to explain to me that in his opinion the cost of renovating the manor house and the subsequent upkeep would far outweigh the saleable value once the work was completed."

"Of course, I am speaking as your late relative's solicitor now, as I realise you have not engaged me in any official capacity. But I feel that it would be remiss of me not to give you the full facts, as our firm has had several dealings with the previous owners concerning the property over the years."

"I thanked him for his candour, but re-iterated that even if the property were a crumbling ruin that I still would not make any decisions without Jenifer at least having a chance to see it. Peterson seemed to understand this, and continued with our interview. I was signing so many different papers that, after a while, my hand started to throb. Things seemed far easier and more straightforward when Jane and I inherited our parents' house. But still I persevered, as I reasoned with myself that once our meeting was over, everything would be settled to our mutual satisfaction.

"As time wore on and the seemingly endless drafts and papers continued to be laid before me for ratification, the toll from my journey was starting to show itself, and I even had to stifle the odd yawn, with apologies to my host. Finally, when the mantle clock which sat on one of the bookshelves behind the solicitor struck the hour, Peterson turned in his chair as if to confirm the time, and before he had a chance to turn back to me there was a knock on his office door.

"The solicitor bid his secretary to enter, which she duly did, and slipped me a quick scowl before reminding Peterson of the time."

"Yes of course, thank you Ruth, you may leave for the day, I'll lock up."

"With that she bid him goodnight, and favoured me with an almost non-existent nod of her head. Once she had left us Peterson and I continued with our meeting, until the clock behind him informed us that another hour had passed. At this point the solicitor looked at his wristwatch and thought for a moment before announcing:

"Mr Ward, due to the lateness of the hour may I suggest that you book into your hotel and we can finish this all off in the morning?"

"He realised immediately from the expression on my face that he must have said something untoward. The fact was it had never occurred to me that I might need to arrange accommodation. I fully intended to stay at the manor, regardless of what condition the property was in. I explained my situation to Peterson, and he stroked his chin as he pondered my situation. After a moment or two Peterson placed his elbows on his desk and made a steeple with his fingers, before advising me that, in his opinion, it would be far more practical if I were to see me new property in daylight, rather than stumbling around it at night.

"He confirmed for me that my late relative's housekeepers, the Jarrows, lived on the estate, but that his understanding was that they both held down separate jobs in which, since my benefactor's demise, they had increased their hours to include evenings, so neither of them would be home until late. Peterson also made it clear that he too had plans for the evening which he was already running late for, so he would also be unable to show me around.

"I assured him that I did not wish to be a nuisance, but the fact of the matter was that, because I had not anticipated having to book a hotel or guest house, I did not have enough money in my wallet to afford to pay for a night's lodgings, and due to the lateness of the hour all the banks in town would already be closed.

"Peterson told me not to worry, and that he could sort everything out for me. With that he picked up the receiver of the phone on his desk and dialled a number into it, which he obviously knew by heart. I could hear the faint dialling tone from the other side, and after a few rings the call was answered."

"Jerry, Ralph Peterson here…look I need a favour, a client has just arrived in town, far later than anticipated, and he needs a room for the night and some supper…I knew you would, the only thing is the banks are all shut, but I'll vouch for him that he'll pay you first thing tomorrow, once they open…Wonderful, thanks, Jerry…His name is Jonathan Ward…Thanks again mate, I owe you one."

"Peterson looked very pleased with himself when he came off the line."

"There you are Mr Ward, everything has been taken care of. You will be staying at the 'Wild Boar', one of our finest hotels, and you can settle your bill in the morning once the banks open."

"Peterson escorted me out of his office and into the street. Night had crept over since I had first entered his office, and now the sky was completely black. We stood outside his main door as Peterson gave me directions to the hotel. The Boar had a car park, so the solicitor suggested that I drive there rather than leave my car out in the street overnight. I thanked him for all his help and we shook hands before we parted. As I crossed the street to my parked car the wind was starting to whip itself up, and I found myself having to dodge a couple of flying newspapers and a discarded carrier bag.

"The journey to the hotel took less than ten minutes in the car, and on the way I noticed a local branch of my bank which I was extremely relieved to discover. Now at least I knew that I could pay my bill in the morning. I parked in the car park and collected my suitcase from the boot, before heading into the main reception area. The hotel, according to the poster in the foyer which was taken from an old newspaper headline, was in fact a converted coaching inn, dating back to the seventeenth century, and, judging from the décor, the owners had obviously tried to keep the overall feel of the place exactly how it must have been when originally built.

"I made my way to the main reception area, and was just about to ring the bell when a corpulent man, with a ruddy face, and a big, bushy moustache appeared and introduced himself as my host."

"Ralph explained your predicament to me on the phone, Mr Ward. No need to worry, we'll see you right for tonight."

"I was very grateful to hear his words, for I realised that had something gone astray in the arrangements between the hotel proprietor and Peterson, it would doubtless be too late by now to get back in touch with the solicitor to straighten things out. But as it was I was shown to a very comfortable double room, with a view of the high street from the window.

"Once I had unpacked and laid out some clothes for the following day I made my way back down to the main bar for my supper, stopping off at the pay phone in the lobby to call Jenifer. The phone rang almost a dozen times and I was about to replace the receiver and try again later, when it was suddenly snatched up and I heard my wife's sweet voice on the other end.

"I filled Jenifer in on my horrendous journey down, and brought her right up to date regarding my meeting with Peterson and my subsequent change of plans for the night. Jenifer sounded more disappointed than I was by the fact that I hadn't so much as set eyes on our new property, as of yet. I explained that due to the length of my meeting with the solicitor and the lateness of the hour, that at best I would only have been able to see the manor in shadow. But Jenifer informed me that had she have been with me she would have insisted on seeing the property that night, regardless of the hour, and I believed her. We talked until my change had run out, and I promised her that I would call again the following evening.

"I sat down to a very welcome sumptuous dinner of thick soup, pork chops with real mashed potato, peas and onion gravy, followed by a sticky toffee pudding with custard made just the way I liked it. I washed this all down with two pints of local ale, which had a much stronger kick than what I was used to in London. After my long drive and the fact that I had not stopped anywhere for lunch, this meal tasted better than anything else I had ever eaten.

"Once I had finished my dinner, I took myself up to bed and it was only a matter of minutes before I had drifted off in the arms of Morpheus. I slept right through the night and was woken the following morning by my landlord's wife knocking on my door, informing me that it was eight o'clock. I quickly showered and changed before making my way back down to the reception.

"As I was not able to pay my bill right away, I was not sure whether or not the landlord would want to keep hold of my belongings until I returned with some money. But I need not have worried, as he was as charming that morning as he had been the previous evening. He assured me that there was no rush to pay my bill, and insisted that I sit down to a full breakfast before I left for Peterson's office.

"After breakfast I packed my bags and drove out of the carpark, heading back into town towards the solicitor's office. When I arrived, I was met once more by Peterson's stern-faced receptionist, who informed me that her boss was with a client in town, and would not return to the office for another hour. I thanked her, politely, and used the time to visit the bank, before driving back to the hotel to pay my debts.

I remember thinking at the time as I drove back and forth across the town, just how beautiful the day was. It was one of those crisp, sunny, autumnal mornings, where the strength and the brightness of the sun belies the cold wind which cuts through to your bone if you fail to protect yourself with enough layers."

Jonathan leaned forward on his elbows and placed his face in his hands, rubbing his skin with his rough palms, vigorously, as if trying to clear away something which was stuck to his face.

Before anyone from the group around the table had a chance to ask him if everything was alright, he lifted his head once more.

"If only I had known then what I know now, I would have turned my car around and headed straight back to London and my lovely wife!"

## SIX

"By the time I made it back to the solicitor's office, I was relieved to see that Peterson had returned. This at least meant that I would not have to spend any time alone with his unwelcoming secretary.

"Peterson smiled broadly as he ushered me into his office, apologising for the fact that he had forgotten to mention his earlier appointment yesterday before we parted. I assured him that it was of no matter, and we sat down to finish going through the last of the documents which I needed to sign.

"Once we had finished, Peterson suggested that we use his car to drive out to my new property. He explained that the roads en route were a trifle awkward to negotiate for someone who was not used to them, and it was his opinion that it would be best for me to experience the route without having to concentrate on driving it."

"I spoke to Mr Jarrow this morning and explained the situation. He and his wife will meet us there to show you around the property, and when you are ready, Jarrow will drive you back into town to collect your car. You should hopefully be familiar enough with the route by then."

"Peterson's suggestion did seem a little strange to me, as I would have thought that following him to the manor in my car would have been far more practical. But I acquiesced to his recommendation, primarily because he seemed quite set on the matter, and after all he had done for me I did not wish to appear ungrateful.

"It took us about fifteen minutes to drive through the centre of town, after which we turned off the main road leaving the traffic and crowds behind us. Although Briers Market was a relatively small town, certainly compared to London, it still seemed to have its fair share of congestion. As we left the town behind us the roads became much narrower, and the white markings which normally ran through the centre were nowhere to be seen. The offices and shops gave way to houses and cottages, and the further away we drove, the greater, it appeared, was the distance between each dwelling. I began to lose myself in the magic of the scenery, forgetting for a moment that I was supposed to be memorising the route.

"Peterson suddenly broke the silence of our journey, with an announcement which I wondered if he had been reluctant to broach after my conviction from the previous evening that I intended to hold on to the manor and not make any decisions regarding its sale, until after Jenifer had seen it."

"I feel that it is my duty to inform you, Mr Ward, that the client I was visiting this morning has asked me to make you aware that he is willing to make a very generous offer for your new property."

"Peterson kept his eyes fixed firmly on the road ahead while he spoke, which in itself did not seem at all odd as the road was both narrow and full of potholes. But all the same I could not help wondering if, for some reason, he was doing it on purpose to avoid my gaze. I thanked him for the information, but reiterated my intentions from our previous meeting."

"I quite understand, Mr Ward, my other client only wished me to make you aware of the situation. He owns the land adjacent to your house, you understand, and he is eager to expand his holdings. Just something to bear in mind should the occasion arise."

"We drove on a little further until there was nothing on either side of us but trees and grass. As we motored along I noticed that the trees up ahead appeared to be closer together so that their branches leaned in to form a kind of tunnel over the road ahead. Once we were in the makeshift tunnel the road weaved first one way, then the other, and after a while it grew so dark that Peterson had to turn his headlights on so that we could see where we were going. When we emerged from the tunnel of trees the road began to climb steeply, causing Peterson to drop a gear in order to keep the car moving at a decent pace. At the crest of the hill the road veered off to the left, and out of sight, and as we approached the turn, Peterson slowed right down and began beeping his horn. I looked around to see who he was signalling to, but we appeared to be the only ones on the road.

"The solicitor pulled over to one side, and pressed his horn once more. Just as I was about to enquire as to why he was acting in this manner, I heard another, much louder horn, responding. Peterson gave one more short pop on his, and seconds later a huge articulated lorry came around the corner. The driver acknowledged our perseverance with a wave of thanks, before driving past us. I looked down to my left, and saw to my horror that the road quickly gave way to a slope which led down a grass verge for some thirty feet to a line of trees. It concerned me how close Peterson had driven to the verge, but I then realised that if he had not pulled over so far that the passing vehicle would not have been able to squeeze through.

"Before moving off again, Peterson gave another sharp honk. This time, as there was no response, he carefully edged his way around the bend until he could see that the way ahead was clear. The entire procedure seemed a little odd to me, so with curiosity taking hold I asked Peterson if there was any specific reasoning to the practice."

"This was one of the reasons I thought it best that I drive us to your new property. That bend and dip in the road has caused so many accidents over the years that the locals have come to refer to it as the 'Widow-Maker', if you can believe such a thing; gallows-humour, if you ask me."

"If it is that dangerous, why haven't the local council intervened?"

"They've tried various forms of signage, and convex mirrors on posts, but each attempt has eventually proved to be fruitless. The problem is, you see, that this road is a cut-through which leads onto the next town, so for tradesmen it is an essential link."

"We continued driving for a few minutes, and once again we came upon another tunnel of trees up ahead. This time however, as we entered the natural covering, Peterson indicated right and we turned between two large oaks, which led us on to what appeared to be a dirt track. Eventually we came to a clearing, and that was when I first saw Denby Manor looming on the horizon.

"As we drew closer to the property I found myself to be somewhat awestruck by the sheer vastness of it. The manor certainly appeared larger in the flesh than it had on the scale drawing Peterson had provided me with. Up ahead I could see a man and a woman standing in front of a pair large iron gates which, I surmised, acted as the entrance to the inner enclosure of the manor house.

"Doubtless recognising Peterson's car the man raised his arm in acknowledgement and began to fiddle with the main gate, which he then opened to allow us access."

"That's the Jarrows, who I told you about. They will be giving you the guided tour, and as I explained earlier Jarrow will escort you back into town to collect your car when you're ready."

"Peterson drove in and parked his car on the gravel drive, directly in front of the house. I hopped out of the car first, such was my excitement, and stood with my hands on my hips gazing up at my inheritance. I remember wishing more than ever that Jenifer could be with me so that we could explore the inside together. But I quelled any guilt I may have felt by reassuring myself that her not being able to join me was due to no fault of mine. Even so, I would still have loved to have her there with me.

"We waited on the drive until the Jarrow's caught up to us. Mrs Jarrow walked slightly ahead of her husband. She was a tall, thin, almost gaunt-looking woman, and the almost severe expression on her face made me wonder if she had ever worn a smile before in her life. Her husband, too, was tall and thin, and unlike his ramrod straight wife he walked with a slight stoop. His face was ruddy and somewhat raw, which I put down to a combination of someone who worked outside a lot of the time and who enjoyed a drop too much of the local brew.

"When Peterson introduced them to me, I held out my hand to the couple. Jarrow doffed his flat cap as we shook and his wife almost had to stop herself from curtsying, which I found extremely odd. Naturally I did not know how my distant relative had treated them during their time in his employ, but I was certainly not comfortable with them treating me like the laird of the manor.

"Once the introductions were complete, Peterson assured me that he would remain at my service and to contact him if I had any queries or problems, after which he said his goodbyes and drove away, leaving me in the sturdy hands of the Jarrows. Leading the way Jarrow opened the main door with a key from a bunch he had clasped in his hand. The heavy wooden door creaked open on rusty hinges, automatically making me feel as if I was stepping back in time to the Dickensian age.

"Surprisingly, upon first impression the inside of the manor house was in no way as ramshackle as Peterson had led me to believe. Judging from some of his descriptions during our meetings I had come to believe that the building was held together with chewing gum and string. But as I gazed into the large entry hall, my mind could not help but conjure up pictures of masked balls and parties of yesteryear.

"The floor was made of solid wood, and it had a dull glaze left from when it had last been polished. There were six doors leading off from the hallway, and a huge sweeping staircase with an ornate, carved, wooden bannister.

"Would you like Jarrow to show you around sir, or would you prefer to see everything on your own?"

"It was Mrs Jarrow who had asked the question, which brought me out of my reverie. I thanked her and agreed that under the circumstances I would prefer a guided tour. The downstairs housed the dining room, complete with a twelve-seater banqueting table and matching chairs. There was the front parlour, and back parlour, which from the looks of it had been transformed into a music room. I noticed a harpsichord, or possibly a spinate, housed in the far corner, with several chairs set out around it as if expecting an eager audience to take their places.

"There was a library, although sadly most of the shelves appeared to have been stripped of their tomes. Also, a main reception room, and a door at the far end of the hallway which led down to the kitchen and scullery. The main rooms all had huge fireplaces and, I was glad to see, sturdy radiators. On the walls hung gas burners held in brass brackets, with glass mantles covering them. Fortunately, there were also electric lights in each room which Jarrow flicked on and off to demonstrate that they were in working order.

"The kitchen and scullery were both extremely cold and uninviting. There was a large wooden table which dominated the centre of the kitchen, and a beautiful, if a trifle unloved, judging by the state of it, range cooker, which took up half of one side of the room. On the other side stood an enormous dresser, which again took up half the wall. It was stacked with all manner of china and crockery, and the drawers, I presumed, held the cutlery and cooking utensils. It was plain from the outset that my late relative had not been much of a fan of cooking, as the kitchen in any large house was always, as far as I was concerned, meant to be the very heart of the house but this one appeared sadly neglected.

"We went through to the scullery which contained the larders and meat stores. There was a wooden door at the back with a large frosted glass pane at the top, and Jarrow opened it with another of the keys from his bunch. Just outside the door stood an old outhouse, which for a moment, I feared, I was going to be informed was the toilet."

"That be the old generator room."

"I think I managed to hide the relief on my face from my tour guide when he made that announcement. Jarrow took me out to the rickety wooden building and showed me the electric generator, and more importantly how to start it up should it suddenly stop working. One corner of the building was full, almost to the ceiling, with wooden logs, precariously balanced on top of each other to form a makeshift pyramid. Next to the wood-pile were several rusty metal cans. I asked Jarrow about them, and he explained that they contained paraffin for the lanterns."

"The late master kept a lantern in almost every room in case the genie fizzed out during the night. I always made sure that they were filled up, just in case."

"I pointed to the generator, and asked Jarrow if that was what powered the radiators throughout the house as well. But he shook his head slowly and gestured for me to follow him back into the house. Once we were back in the kitchen, he took me over to what appeared to be a larder just behind the main door. He opened it to reveal what seemed to be a large boiler."

"This used to be what powered the radiators, but the master had a quarrel with the gas company years ago about the cost of his bills so in the end he refused to pay them and they cut him off. It might be possible to start it up again, but you'd have to speak to the gas people. I'm ok with the electric genie, but I don't ever mess with gas."

"I asked Jarrow how my relative had kept the house warm enough to live in during the winter, and he informed me that for the most part Mrs Jarrow would always make sure that each fireplace was stacked with wood, and ready to light. But apparently, even then, my benefactor tended to stick to using the ones in the dining room, front parlour and his bedroom only.

"When we went upstairs, we came across Mrs Jarrow busily making up a bed for me in one of the eight double bedrooms the property boasted. She looked almost apologetic when she explained that she felt that I would be uncomfortable sleeping in my relative's room, so she had taken the liberty of choosing a room which faced the north of the property so that the morning sun would not shine in and wake me up.

"All the bedrooms seemed about the same in size, although only five of them housed beds. The rest were filled with an assortment of paraphernalia, including trunks, suitcases, rolled-up carpets and pieces of old furniture, most of which appeared to have been dumped in situ without any real thought to space or configuration. There were even a couple of oil paintings in one of the rooms. Portraits mainly, although there was one of the manor in better days. I wondered if any of the portraits were of relatives of mine, and decided to take a closer look when I had more time.

"There were two bathrooms, one at either end of the hall, and a separate water closet which, according to Jarrow, he had plumbed in himself. The top floor housed the attic, which was accessed by a built-in wooden staircase. The structure spread virtually across the entire length of the roof, and had been portioned off into several smaller rooms which I surmised had probably once acted as bedrooms for the staff. Tucked away in a corner I noticed another couple of battered and worn old trunks. It seemed to me an odd place to have shifted them to, especially as there was ample room in several of the bedrooms below, but I surmised that at the time there had been a sound reason for it.

"Once my guided tour was complete, I thanked the Jarrows for their time, and asked Jarrow if he was ready to drop me back into town so that I could collect my car. As I mentioned this the couple exchanged an odd glance, and although no actual words were spoken I had the distinct impression that their eyes were having a conversation of the type that only those who had been married a good many years could. Finally, they broke their psychic connection, and Jarrow turned to me with a concerned expression on his face."

"Will you be coming back here this evening then, sir?"

"I was a little taken-aback by his question, as I had been under the impression that Peterson had already explained the situation to him. I explained to the pair of them that once I had collected my car, that it was indeed my intention to return to the manor for the night. At my mention of this Mrs Jarrow took in a sudden, and quite audible, gasp, which, upon realising that I had heard, she belatedly tried to muffle behind her hand. I could sense the discomfort between the two of them, and felt sure that they both wanted to say something to me but, for whatever reason, neither wished to speak out of turn. Therefore, I asked them outright if there was anything on their minds."

"Well, you see sir, Mr Jarrow and I was just wondering if perhaps you might be more comfortable staying in town. The old manor suited the old master, but as you can see, it is not the most comfortable of places to stay, and since his death, my husband and I have increased our shifts at the pub to bring in some extra money so I won't even have time to prepare you an evening meal."

"I assured them both that I completely understood their reaction, and thanked them for their concern. But I assured them that I could be quite self-sufficient when the need arose, and I intended to treat the occasion a bit like an adventure. This announcement afforded me another example of their unspoken communication, as yet another strange glance passed between them. By this time, I was beginning to feel slightly irritated with the pair of them, as it was obvious to me that they had something more to say on the subject, but neither was willing to give voice to their concerns. Even so I kept my temper in check as I really did not want to upset either of them, and decided that their mannerism was merely a result of them being country folk who had been brought up to lead a different style of life from those of us in London.

"Having realised that my mind was made up and that I could not be swayed otherwise, Mrs Jarrow insisted on making sure that the fires were made ready in the front parlour as well as my bedroom, and that all the lanterns in the house were properly filled just in case of a power failure. I thanked her for taking care of me, and followed Jarrow to his car.

"I was bemused, although not at all surprised, when Jarrow repeated the performance Peterson had treated me to when we reached the sharp turn he had referred to as the 'Widow- Maker'. Jarrow was not much of a conversationalist, so I spent the journey trying to familiarise myself with the route for my journey back later that afternoon.

"Once we had parked up near my car, Jarrow very kindly offered to wait and allow me to follow him back to the manor. But I assured him that I was reasonably confident of the route by now, and that I intended to spend some time in the town before returning. Eventually, although somewhat reluctantly, I suspected, he agreed to leave. Then just as I was attempting to climb out of his car, he reached over the seat and grabbed my elbow."

"Sorry sir, but I almost forgot to say; if for any reason you decide you do not wish to stay at the manor, you would be more than welcome to stay with the missus and me. We have a spare room, and she is a fantastic cook, the wife."

"Looking at him over my shoulder, I could not help but think that there was a look of trepidation, or possibly even fear, in his eyes as he spoke. I remember thinking at the time that Jarrow appeared to be almost fearful about letting me go. It left me with a very uneasy feeling for the rest of the afternoon, but even so, I thanked him once more for his kind offer and asked him to extend my appreciation to his good lady, but I was resolute that I would be spending the night at the manor."

## SEVEN

"I spent the latter part of the afternoon wandering around the town at a leisurely pace. The afternoon sun was extremely powerful for the time of year, and it made me feel as if it were still summer. The town had a very olde-worldly feel to it, and I was pleasantly surprised by the number of smiles and nods of acknowledgment I received whilst walking around.

"I dropped into a local supermarket to stock up on provisions. It occurred to me that I had not seen a fridge in the kitchen back at the manner, although the room itself was probably cold enough to keep items like milk and cheese fresh for days. As I made my way back to my car I passed by a telephone box, and it was then that I realised that beside a fridge, I had not seen a telephone back at the manor either.

"I glanced at my watch and saw that it was already after five. I wondered if Jenifer had arrived home yet. If she was, then all well and good, but if she was not, then I realised that I would have to hang around town for a little longer so that I could call her. I did not relish the thought of driving back to the manor, and then coming back out again later.

"I loaded up the car with my provisions, and walked back to the box. I set out the change I had received from my shopping on the directory holder, and sorted it into individual piles to make it easier for me to slot them in the phone. I dialled the number and waited. By the time the phone had reached its tenth ring I was about to replace the receiver when it was snatched up at the other end, and a very breathless Jenifer answered.

"It turned out that she had just arrived home from work, and she was standing outside the door, fumbling in her handbag for her key, when she heard the phone ring. It was so good to hear her voice and I listened intently as she spoke about the photoshoot, and how well things seemed to be going. Her father had given her the exciting news that the company who had hired them were so impressed with the way they worked that there was talk of further opportunities in the pipeline. Jenifer also told me that she hoped this present job would be finished in time for her to travel down to meet me and see our new property before I had to set back for London.

"She asked me about the manor, and I went into detail about my guided tour and the Jarrows' apparent reluctance to leave me alone there overnight. Jenifer was obviously intrigued, but just like me, she found it odd that the couple had not given any reason as to why they felt it necessary to recommend alternative accommodation for me when the manor was just sitting there, unoccupied.

"It seemed like only a matter of minutes before I was down to my last coin. As I slipped it into the slot I informed Jenifer, so that she would not be upset if we were suddenly cut off after the next time the pips went. I could tell from the sound of my wife's voice that she was beginning to grow upset. I was both touched and reassured that she was feeling the strain of our time apart as much as I was. It almost made me want to jump into my car and drive straight back to London, to surprise her. But as usual I allowed my common sense to guide me, as I knew that such a journey would be a terrible waste of time not to mention petrol.

"Finally, we both heard the pips go, and we rushed as many 'goodbyes' and 'I love you' sentiments as we could before we were cut off. I stood there for a moment in the box, holding the buzzing handset against my chest, until I noticed that there was a lady waiting outside to use the phone. I replaced the set into the cradle and held open the door after I moved out, so that the lady could move in.

"To my credit, I managed to negotiate my way back to the manor without taking a single wrong turning. By the time I reached the 'Widow-Maker' it was already dark, and I was driving with my headlights on. I stopped in the same spot that Peterson had, and pumped my horn twice. I listened out for any response, but all was quiet. As I put the car back into gear and moved off a van came skidding around the corner, heading directly for me. The driver, seemingly oblivious to the local custom, saw me at the last moment and slammed on his brakes. In that split second, I just managed to pull over far enough to avoid a collision and watched the van skid across the road, holding my breath in anticipation that it was about to plunge over the steep incline, and end up mangled at the bottom amongst the trees.

"Fortunately, by some miracle, the driver managed to regain his control of the vehicle and it skirted the verge before skidding back to the road. The driver did not even stop, but seemed to continue down the route which I had just come along without so much as a care. I, on the other hand, sat there for a couple of minutes willing my heartbeat to return back to normal. Now I understood why Peterson made such an effort to demonstrate to me earlier the importance of the extra caution necessary when passing the area. I was, in truth, extremely grateful to him at that moment.

"When I reached the manor, I suddenly realised that Jarrow had not left me his bunch of keys before departing. I stood outside the main door with my shopping bags in my arms, and pondered what my best course of action would to be. I knew that the couple lived close by, but naturally I had no way of knowing in which direction. Added to that, judging by what Mrs Jarrow had said earlier, they were probably both at work by now anyway.

"On the off chance I walked up the stone steps and pushed the front door. To my relief it opened inwards on its creaky hinges, and I breathed a huge sigh of relief. Once inside I noticed on the nearest hall table that Jarrow had left his bunch for me, presumably realising when he came back to collect his wife that he still had them on him. There was also a hand-written note from Mrs Jarrow, informing me that she had made up the fires in all of the rooms and that they were ready to be lit. She also added that each lantern in the house was full, and that the wicks had all been checked, and that those which had burned down had been replaced just in case. I reached above the hall table and tried the light switch. To my relief, the first set of lights above the hall burst into life.

"I made my way through the house, turning on lights where I thought necessary, and started the fire in the main parlour as that was where I had decided to spend my evening. Now that the sun had set the house was freezing, and the immediate warmth from the hearth was a most welcome arrival. I stood there for a while and allowed the heat to sink into my body. Once I had warmed up sufficiently I took my groceries into the kitchen and put them away in one of the cupboards. Before I set myself down for the evening I went upstairs to the bedroom Mrs Jarrow had recommended for me, and lit the fire there also. I placed the metal guard over the front, and slotted the catches into place, before going back downstairs.

"I made myself a simple dinner of ham and cheese sandwiches, with a garnish made from cheese and onion flavoured potato crisps. I had treated myself to a bottle of wine from the off licence, and managed to find where the wine glasses were stored in the pantry. I set myself down in front of the roaring fire to enjoy my repast. Having finished my sandwich, I savoured the deep berry flavours from my wine, as I watched the flames lick hungrily at the wooden logs and dance about in the grate for my amusement.

"With my belly full and the comforting warmth from the fire, I could feel the wine starting to take hold. My eyes began to feel heavy, and fortunately I managed to place my glass on a table before I drifted off to sleep.

"When I next opened my eyes the fire in front of me was almost at an end, with the last few remaining logs just about keeping the flames alive. I rose from my chair and stretched out my tired limbs, rubbing the sleep from my eyes as I released a massive yawn of contentment.

"I decided to take myself up to bed, as I was not fit for much else. I glanced at my watch and saw that it was almost eleven o'clock, which meant that I had been asleep for over two hours already. The armchair I had dozed in was so comfortable that part of me contemplated just adding a few more logs to the fire and spending the rest of the night in the same place. But, on reflection, it dawned on me that an entire night spent hunched up in an armchair - even one as comfortable as this was - would probably result in my waking up with stiff joints and a twisted neck. Therefore, I decided that my original course of action would turn out to be the most fruitful.

"As I made sure that the front door was secured I realised that I had left my luggage in the car, and even though it was only parked at the foot of the stairs, the thought of going out into the freezing cold night caused me to shiver involuntarily. I stood there for a moment, considering my options. In the end I decided that one night without pyjamas would not be the end of the world, so I turned and began to make my way upstairs to prepare for bed.

"I was almost at the top of the stairs when the lights went out. The shock of being plunged into darkness caught me unawares, and I almost tripped over the next step before regaining my balance. I waited for a moment to try and accustom my eyes to the pitch dark. I could hear the loud ticking of the grandfather clock at the top of the stairs, and that at least gave me some idea of how far away I was from the landing.

"I cautiously made my way to the top, wishing that I had had the foresight to bring a lantern with me. But to be fair, how was I to know that the generator would suddenly decide to pack up at that very moment? I managed to make it to my bedroom without incident, and once there I quickly undressed and climbed under the covers. Sleep claimed me within a few minutes.

"I was woken by the sound of a persistent banging, which permeated my sleep. It was almost as if someone was desperate to either gain entry, or to escape from somewhere they were being held prisoner. I opened my eyes and squinted and blinked to try and bring myself back from the land of dreams. With the curtains drawn I could barely make out any of the unfamiliar shapes and shadows which pervaded the darkness.

"I sat up in bed for a moment and listened intently for a repeat of the noise which had caused me to stir. But there was nothing other than the relentless ticking from the grandfather clock on the landing. I waited for what seemed at the time to be an age, but I could not hear anything else. The house appeared to be quite still. The thought of stumbling about in the dark did not appeal, so I decided that the noise which had caused me to wake had only been part of a dream, the contents of which I could not remember at that moment.

"I was just about to lie back down and continue my rest when a sudden urge came about, and I decided that I would not be able to fall back to sleep without using the water closet first. Reluctantly I threw back the covers and welcomed in a shaft of freezing air, which caused my whole body to shiver involuntarily. I decided not to bother fumbling with a lantern, as I knew that the toilet was only a few feet away along the corridor.

"Having relieved myself I made my way back to bed and to the relative warmth of my covers. The minute my head hit the pillow, I heard it again. This time there could be no doubt. It was not part of a dream, or a trick of the night. I could hear the banging in the distance as surely as I could hear the clock outside. In the darkness I tried to decipher from where the banging emanated, and it did not take long for me to conclude that it was coming from somewhere downstairs. I threw back the covers once more and shuffled my way to the mantlepiece to grab the lantern. Once I had managed to light the fuse and replace the glass cover I located my clothes and dressed hurriedly, and grabbed my keys before I made my way out on the landing and over to the top of the staircase.

"The banging was intermittent, but still no less urgent, so I crept down the stairs one at a time, keeping my balance by holding onto the side bannister. As I reached the bottom of the staircase it became apparent that the banging was not coming from behind the front door, but rather from somewhere at the back of the house. I lifted the lantern so that I could check the time on my wristwatch; it was three fifteen. A thousand and one thoughts raced through my mind as to just who it might be hammering on my door at this ungodly hour of the morning. The only person that came to mind was possibly Jarrow, but what on earth would possess the man to think that whatever he wanted could not wait until a reasonable hour?

"At the sound of the next bout of hammering I suddenly began to feel extremely vulnerable, and my reserve - such as it was - started to wane. I immediately began to swing the lantern around me, hoping that I might be able to spot some sort of weapon in the arc of its light. Alas, there was nothing to hand which would suffice as a makeshift club. The banging grew more fervent, and I realised that there was nothing else for it but to find out what was going on. I considered leaving through the front door and circling the house so that I could surprise my early-morning visitor, and perhaps as a result gain the upper ground. But I reasoned that the noise the front door made on its rusty hinges whenever it was opened or closed would be more than enough to alert the caller anyway. So, instead, I decided to make my way through the kitchen and locate the source of the hammering before deciding what action to take.

"As I entered the kitchen, the frantic banging sounded once more. It was now obvious to me that the sound was coming from the door in the scullery which led out to the generator shed. How I wished at that moment that there was some way of magically causing all the lights in the house to come on simultaneously! If nothing else, it would have given me some much-needed assurance.

"I slowly made my way into the scullery. I was now able to see the back door for the first time. I lowered my lantern to allow me the best possible view through the glass, but to my surprise there were no shadows of anyone standing outside reflected in the frosted pane. I held my breath and waited. The moon must have been at the side of the house, but there was still enough light to illuminate the figure of someone had they been standing outside the door.

"It occurred to me that my unwanted visitor may have made their way around to the front of the house, as they had received no response from the back. For a moment I considered retracing my steps and making my way back to the front door, so that I could stand guard and fling the door open upon the first knock; thereby possibly surprising my visitor. But in that same split second there came another ferocious pounding on the scullery door, hard enough this time to rattle the wood in its frame.

"Overwhelmed, and seriously short on courage I am not afraid to admit, I took a deep breath and screamed out, demanding to know who was outside. I stood there in the semi-darkness, shivering as I waited for a reply, but none came. I called out again, this time insisting that I would not open the door unless whoever was outside identified themselves. Although there was still no evidence of a shadow from behind the door, to my astonishment I heard a tiny voice carried on the wind outside."

"Please, help me!"

"There was a fierce wind blowing outside, and the cry was barely audible above the sound of it. The voice was female, and from what I could ascertain she sounded both desperate and terrified in equal measure. I lifted my lantern and examined the bunch of keys in my hand, trying to identify the correct one for the scullery door. It took me three attempts before I found the one that fit the lock.

"From outside I could hear the pitiful voice calling to me once more, and in my desperation to assist her I kept trying to turn the key the wrong way. Finally, I made it to my senses and I heard the bolt slot open inside the chamber. I grabbed the handle and, twisting it, wrenched the door open.

"Framed in the doorway stood a beautiful young woman, no more than nineteen or twenty at a guess, wearing a floral-print dress. She had long black hair cascading over her shoulders, and the most piercing green eyes I had ever seen. Although I only had a moment to take in her face I could not help but notice that her eyes held a faraway gaze in them, which seemed to convey a sadness which was the result of having experienced a great deal of suffering during her young life.

"I stood there for a second, transfixed by her beauty, as she looked at me in a way that made me feel as if she were capable of seeing right through me. But no sooner did she have me captivated and frozen to the spot, like a frightened rabbit caught in the headlights of an oncoming vehicle, she suddenly turned to her left and pointed off into the darkness."

"They're trying to take my baby, please help me, don't let them take him!"

"The suddenness of her plea shattered my trance-like state, and brought me down to earth with a bump. I rushed out past her, my heart racing, and turned towards the direction she had indicated. I had no idea what I was about to face, or who I might be confronting, but at that moment it did not matter. This poor girl had come to me for help, miles from anywhere, and if I did not assist her in every way that I could I knew that I would never forgive myself for it.

"However, all I faced once I was outside were the shadows the moonlight cast across the vacant land of my property. I stood there for a moment, my lantern still by my side, trying to focus my gaze through the darkness for any sign of movement. But there was no sign of any assailant, nor was there any sound of footsteps crunching on the gravel drive, trying to make good their escape.

"I peered into the darkness for a little while longer, just to make sure that we were not being watched by someone crouching in the undergrowth, and once I was confident that all was clear I turned back to reassure the girl that she was safe now.

But she was nowhere to be seen!

I quickly turned back around, and as I did so I felt as if something as cold as ice had passed through me. I turned back, but I could still see no sign of the girl. It dawned on me that she must have run into the scullery whilst I was looking for her pursuers. I moved to the open doorway and lifted my lantern to peer inside. There was no sign of her. I called out to reassure her that I meant her no harm, but still there was no response. Either she had made her way deep inside the house so that she could not hear me, or more than likely she was within earshot but still too afraid to show herself.

"I slowly re-entered the scullery and announced in a loud, but gentle, voice, that I was about to close and lock the door behind me. Once I had done so, I stood there once more behind the door and announced to the young girl that she was perfectly safe and that I did not mean her any harm. As my announcement receive no response I carefully made my way through the scullery and back into the kitchen, checking each nook and corner with my lantern as I did so in anticipation of finding the poor girl crouched in a corner, in fear of her life. But, by the time that I had made my way back out into the main hallway, there was still no sign of her.

"I stood there for a moment, confident that my voice would reach most corners of the house, and called out to her once more, assuring her again that she was in no danger and that I only wanted to help her. Yet again, there was no response. I resigned myself to the fact that the girl was obviously so terrified that I would have to make a complete search of the house in order to locate her.

"It suddenly occurred to me that I knew nothing whatsoever about my uninvited guest, other than the fact that she had turned up at my back door in the middle of the night seeking refuge. For all I knew she might have been an escapee from some local hospital for the criminally insane, and could this very moment be waiting for me behind some darkened corner of the house with a huge carving knife she had found in the kitchen or even had concealed about her when she first arrived.

"I shook such thoughts from my mind, and decided that I needed to rationalise my imagination before I ended up jumping at my own shadow. I searched each room downstairs carefully and thoroughly, listening out all the while for the sound of footsteps creeping from one room to another.

"Once I was satisfied that the downstairs was clear, I made my way back up to the rooms on the first floor. I began a systematic search of every room, checking in cupboards and even under the beds, but it was to no avail. Having checked the bathrooms and the toilet I made my way up to the attic, surmising that there was nowhere else inside the house for the girl to be hiding.

"I called out yet again - as I had done sporadically throughout my search - as I made my way up the wooden flight to the top of the house. I shone my lantern all around, moving as close as necessary to each darkened corner to make sure that it was empty, before moving on to the next partition. By the time I had reached the last portioned off area of the attic and discovered that the girl was nowhere to be seen, I began to wonder if in fact she had never entered the house in the first place. Such was my concentration in seeking out her alleged pursuer that it was distinctly plausible that she could have crept back around the back of the house and turned the corner before I had turned back to find her missing. In which case I had just wasted the best part of an hour searching the house for nothing!

"Just then, I heard someone singing. It was a woman's voice, high and pitch perfect, and the sweetness of the melody had me held in a trance for a moment as if all I wanted to do was stand there and listen."

Jonathan looked up at the band, and nodded, as if in answer to a silent question which he somehow knew that they wanted to ask.

"Yes, it was the song you played at the end of your set this evening. It is a song that I will never be able to forget."

The old man looked up as if trying to read something from an invisible prompt card or blackboard. Then he began to sing, his voice higher than those around him imagined it might sound.

> As the waters run deep, so my soul yearns to soar.
> On the wings of an eagle, I'll wait nevermore.
> In the arms of my true love, I will pause for my time.
> So, hold me forever, until you are mine.
>
> Cry for me my lover, 'til the seas have run dry.
> Never seek answers, and never ask why.
> The path I am destined is not paved with gold,
> But the warmth of your love, keeps out the cold.
>
> So, sleep sound my baby till morning sunrise.
> See the beauty around you, through your baby-blue eyes.
> Know that I love you, and I'll keep you from harm,
> Until you are safe in the warmth of my arms.

There was a ripple of applause for his effort, and Jonathan acknowledged his audience with a smile. He took another sip of his beer to clear his throat before he continued with his story.

"Although I was in a tiny room and could see clearly that there was no one else in there with me, the voice sounded as if was all around me so the singer had to be nearby. I held my lantern out in front of me and walked back through the attic, re-checking every corner of each partition. The voice appeared to be everywhere, all around me, no matter where I went. But as for the singer, there was still no sign.

"I made my way back down to the landing, and as if on cue the flame from my lantern began to flicker. I lifted it up so that I could see the wick, and using the lever at the side, I adjusted it so that it was fully exposed. This afforded me a tad more illumination than before, and the flickering lessoned somewhat. As I stood poised on the landing, the singing sounded as if it was now coming from downstairs. The sweet voice echoed throughout the house, but definitely sounded to me at that moment as if it was coming from one of the downstairs rooms. But how could this be? I had already searched the downstairs thoroughly, without success.

Somewhat annoyed, I began to descend the stairs once again. But by the time I had reached half-way, the singing seemed to have changed direction and was now above me. I stood there unable to fathom what was going on. How could that girl have stayed hidden from me when I had searched the entire house from top to bottom? On top of which, if it had been her intention to remain hidden, why had she started singing if not to draw my attention?

As abruptly as the singing had started, it suddenly stopped!

All was silent for a split second, and then came an ear-piercing scream which permeated the air and cut straight through me like a razor-sharp knife.

"With the lantern in one hand I could not block the sound out by clasping my hands to my ears, so I had to endure it until it eventually stopped. I stood there, on the stairs, my mind a jumble of mostly irrational thoughts. If the girl was in the house, why had I not been able to find her? Likewise, if she was not, then where did the singing, and that horrendous scream, come from?

There was nothing else for it; I decided that I must search the entire house again. I carried my lantern into the front parlour, and located a second lantern there. I lit it, and swapped it for my original one, which was now starting to flicker once more. I made my way back out into the scullery, and began my new search with verve and determination. Sleep was now a distant memory; I was fully wide awake and felt that if I had tried to lie down at that moment, I would have remained awake for hours to come.

"I searched the entire house from the bottom up. As I moved from room to room I could almost hear the earlier scream reverberating in my ears, and I was convinced that at any moment it would come again.

"This time my examination of the house took a little longer than before, as instead of merely swinging my lantern to try and see into all corners of the rooms I now made a point of actually walking over every part of each one, ensuring that I tried every cupboard, even those I knew would be far too small to hide a body.

"I could hear my heart starting to drum in my ears as I went about my investigation. This time I was sure that if that girl was in the house that I would find her, no matter what. But, yet again my efforts were in vain, and she was nowhere to be found.

"Eventually, I gave up my search and carried myself back up to bed. This time I kept the lantern burning on the night stand by my bed. The glow of its light offered me some much-needed comfort as I lay there gazing up at the ceiling.

"Just as I began to drift off, I could hear the sound of the girl singing her song once more. But this time I forced myself to keep my eyes closed, and finally I fell back to sleep."

# EIGHT

"Understandably, I spent the rest of the night in an extremely fitful state. When I did dream, my dreams were interspersed with visions of my early-morning visitor. Except this time my subconscious had somehow managed to twist and obscure her angelic features, so that now when she appeared to me, instead of being the beautiful young girl I had met all so briefly, she resembled some kind of hideous hag. Her mouth was now full of broken and crooked teeth which were stretched taut in a rictus grin. Her skin, so pure and perfect when we had met, now looked completely gaunt and seemed to have the texture of rough sandpaper, although it was bleached a sickly shade of pale off-white. Even her fingers no longer looked like those of a beautiful woman, and now resembled long, talon-like claws instead.

"But worst of all was the expression in her eyes, which conveyed none of the simple, sad emotion from our first meeting; but instead reflected a sinister, almost malevolent spirit, which bore straight through to my very soul.

"As she reached out in my dreams, I knew that it was not because she was in need of comfort or protection but more because she was intent on wrapping those scraggly fingers around my throat, and squeezing the life out of me, and, as with all such nightmares, I felt completely powerless to defend myself or even make good some form of escape. Like a babe in arms I was completely without offence, lying there at the mercy of this harridan as she drew ever closer, ready to seal my fate.

"Worse still was yet to come. Once I had resigned myself to whatever the creature had in store for me, my wife would appear, gazing at me in her usual loving way, holding out her arms as if to embrace me and keep me safe. For a moment my fears would melt away like wax in a fire, and the old hag would be all but forgotten. But just as I relaxed and began to lose myself in the prospect of feeling Jenifer's tender embrace, the old hag would reappear. This time she was hovering behind my beautiful wife, her attention drawn to her new target.

"In my dream I would call out, scream and gesticulate, frantically, trying to warn my beloved of the impending threat behind her. But it was all to no avail. For whatever reason, Jenifer could not see my desperate attempt to alert her. Instead she continued making her way towards me, her arms still extended, that same sweet, loving smile on her face. As she drew closer to me, Jenifer's body at times appeared to almost obscure the malevolent form behind her. But I knew that she was still there, drifting ever closer to my beautiful wife, her evil intent now focused on her instead of on me.

"I tried to scream out to the hag demanding that she leave my wife alone, and when that did not work I began to plead with her to turn her anger back towards me, telling her that I would not put up a fight, and that she could do her worst to me, so long as she undertook to leave my lovely wife alone. But all she would do in response was grin at me with those misshapen fangs, with a sinister sneer of wickedness and malice etched into her face.

"Mercifully I was roused from my nightmare by the sound of hammering coming from downstairs. I sat up in bed with a start, the remnants of my horrific dream still lingering in my mind. The sheets on the bed, like me, were bathed in sweat, and I wiped my forehead to prevent it trickling into my eyes.

"I remember sitting there for a moment, unsure as to whether or not the hammering noise was part of my dream, or a reality sent to save me from my night terrors. I waited, just to be sure. Then I heard the sound once more. For a second I feared that it might be the girl returning.

Banging on the scullery door for all she was worth, ready to lead me another merry dance. But this time the sound was more akin to metal striking metal, rather than a fist beating against wood. Also, it sounded far less urgent than what I had heard in the early hours.

"The daylight which illuminated my room from behind the curtains gave me the courage I so desperately needed to investigate further. If the scenario turned out to be a repeat of last night's, then at least I was reassured by the maxim that everything always appeared more settled in the morning. I swung myself out of bed and dressed, hurriedly, before grabbing my keys from the table by my bed and making my way downstairs.

"When I was halfway down the flight, I realised that some of the downstairs lights had come back on. I suspected that Mr Jarrow had paid a visit to the generator room that morning, and was instantly grateful for his intervention.

"The knocking came again. This time I was close enough to realise that it was coming from outside the front door, and I remembered that there was a brass knocker in the shape of a lion or a wolf, or some such animal, which I had noticed on the door when Peterson first brought me to the manor.

"I unlocked the door and swung it open to find Mrs Jarrow standing outside in a thick woolly overcoat and scarf, carrying a wicker basket over one arm with a chequered cloth covering its contents. When she saw me, I am not sure if she noticed the look of absolute relief on my face at seeing her standing there, because her expression was more akin to embarrassment than anything else."

"I am sorry to have disturbed you, sir, but I did try knocking earlier, but I suppose you were still asleep, so I thought I would leave it for a while and come back."

"I looked at my watch, it was already after eleven. Obviously, I had slept for longer than I realised, after all."

"I invited her inside, out of the cold morning air, and asked her where her husband was. She informed me that he was gathering some more logs to add to those already in the shed, and that she had come over to cook me breakfast as she used to do for my late relative."

"Both me and Jarrow have been paid up until the end of the month, so we want to make sure that we earn our keep and we weren't sure what duties you might want us to carry out while you're here."

"I had to admit that the sound of a cooked breakfast sounded like just what the doctor ordered, so I thanked her for her kind attention to my needs and left her to go to the kitchen while I went outside to collect my suitcases from my car so that I could change.

"I drew myself a bath; the water was slightly more tepid than I would have preferred, but I put that down to the generator only having been running for a short while having been off overnight. All the same I enjoyed what comfort it offered, and laid all my clothes out before choosing something to wear, and then placed the rest of my things in the wardrobe and chest of drawers in my room.

"Mrs Jarrow certainly knew the way to a man's heart. The breakfast she had prepared for me barely managed to fit on the plate, and I had to struggle with the last few mouthfuls because I did not want to appear ungrateful.

"When she came back in to clear my plates, I asked her if she fancied joining me for a cup of coffee. I could tell from her reaction that my offer had caused her a certain amount of discomfort. I realised that, for whatever reason, Mrs Jarrow believed in keeping a distinct line drawn between employers and employees, and, under the circumstances, she obviously saw me as her employee for the time. So, I explained that I wanted to ask her about my benefactor and the house. Once I mentioned that she seemed to relax somewhat, and almost manged a smile as she went back down into the kitchen to fetch our drinks.

"At that time, I was not sure whether or not it was prudent to mention my night-time visitor. I already had several theories whirling around my mind concerning the young girl. I thought perhaps that she may have been my benefactor's mistress, and that her turning up in the middle of the night had been their arrangement. Or perhaps she might also be a relative, one who thought that she was entitled to my inheritance, and with that she came over specifically with the purpose to remonstrate with me about the unfairness of the situation.

"I must confess that in the cold light of day it did not occur to me that she might be a ghost. It was not that I did not believe in such phenomena; it was more the fact that I did not think that such occurrences would manifest themselves to someone like me. In my mind ghosts were restricted to visions in white, with clanking chains, drifting around the battlements of old castles and the like. I had a colleague at the bank whose uncle had been a yeoman at the tower of London, and he had apparently seen the ghost of Anne Boleyn on several occasions wandering around the grounds with her head held beneath her arm. That also seemed quite fitting to me, and I had no reason to doubt such an apparition. But my visitor had seemed so real, and not at all as scary - my dream aside - as I believed ghosts were meant to be."

Jonathan paused, and sighed.

"It seems rather an odd thing to say out loud, now that I come to think of it. Anyway, at the time I was more interested in learning what I could about the house and my relative than worrying about some poor girl wandering around the estate in the early hours. That said, once Mrs Jarrow returned with our coffee, during the course of our conversation I did enquire if she knew of any visitors that my relative may have received from time to time."

"Visitors, no, no-one comes to mind I'm afraid. If you'll forgive me for saying so sir, your cousin was a bit of a queer old bird, begging your pardon. He was very set in his habits, and never strayed from them, not to my knowledge."

"I suggested that he must have lived a very lonely existence if he never ventured out of the manor, or invited anyone back."

"Oh, he made a point of visiting the pub in the village not far from here most days for his lunch. My husband often saw him in there, but even then, he would generally nod to him in acknowledgment, and my husband said he never felt comfortable going over to sit with him because he did not feel his company was sought. But as I say, he was a little set in his ways, like many old folks are, and I'd say he just preferred his own company."

"I asked her if, to her knowledge, he had ever been married, and Mrs Jarrow admitted that the subject had never come up in conversation and that she would not have felt comfortable prying into his past like that. But she confirmed that she had never seen any evidence of a woman ever having lived in the house, not so much as an old photograph."

"There are some old paintings upstairs in one of the bedrooms, and now I come to think of it one of them is of a young lady. I remember seeing it when I was dusting them. I wasn't prying or anything, you understand, your late cousin was very particular about the way certain things were done. So, I just happened to notice this particular painting."

"I thanked the housekeeper for her candour, and again for the wonderful breakfast she had prepared for me. She then asked if it was all right with me if she continued with her general housekeeping duties; sweeping away the ashes from the fires and replacing the wood and kindling, clearing away in the kitchen and making sure that the cupboards were properly stocked, cleaning the bathroom, and making my bed.

"I assured her that so long as she was happy to continue with her chores, I would be very appreciative. I mentioned to her about the state of my bedclothes after my nightmare, although I did not go into any detail about the content of my ordeal. Mrs Jarrow replied that she would strip my bed and wash everything at her house and bring it back tomorrow. In the meantime, she informed me, she had aired several sets of bedclothes in anticipation of my arrival, as Peterson had not been specific with her or her husband as to how many people would be staying. Therefore, re-making the bed would not be a problem.

Just then there was a knock at the scullery door. For a second I was transported back to the early hours of the night and my unwelcomed visitor. I felt an involuntary shudder course through my body, as if someone had just walked over my grave. I was extremely glad at that moment for Mrs Jarrow's company, as well as for the daylight just outside the window."

"That'll be Mr Jarrow come for his mid-morning cuppa, if you will excuse me, sir?"

"I could not convey to Mrs Jarrow how comforting her words sounded to me at that moment, for fear of me coming across as a little unhinged. I could feel myself visibly relaxing at the mention of her husband's arrival. Such an everyday, normal occurrence seemed to me to be a million miles away from my last experience of hearing a knock at that particular door. I left her to go and see to her husband, and made my way back upstairs to complete my morning ablutions.

"I returned back downstairs, having chosen what over clothes to wear out for the day. I intended going back into town to speak to Peterson once more. It dawned on me that as my benefactor's solicitor he might be the only other person who would possibly be aware of anyone else who might have some claim on my inheritance, be they another relative or not. By this point I had convinced myself that, the young girl's disappearing act apart, there was nothing spectral about her and that my initial suspicion that she had merely ducked around the back of the building whilst my attention was focused on her supposed pursuer was by far the most obvious answer.

"I went into the scullery, where Jarrow was enjoying his mid-morning tea accompanied by a large slice of fruit cake. He stood up, scraping his chair back upon seeing me, so I signalled for him to be seated. I must say that I was finding the way the couple were treating me quite uncomfortable, in respect of the fact that they insisted on acting as if they were my servants. Naturally I realised that to all intents and purposes I was their landlord and, I suppose, employer, of sorts. But it made me feel very uneasy to be treated as someone else's superior, especially by people who were older than me, as I had always been brought up to respect my elders.

"Jarrow was obviously uncomfortable with the prospect of having his mid-morning break in front of me, so I encouraged him to continue. His wife opened a large round tin which had been sitting on the table, and offered me slice of the same cake. I respectfully declined as I was so full after her magnificent breakfast, but I made a point of commentating on how delicious it looked as I suspected that it was home-baked.

"I mentioned that I was about to drive into town and Jarrow immediately jumped up once more and offered to go for me, to save me the drive. I thanked him for his kind offer, but explained that I needed to see Peterson concerning some paperwork I needed to sign. I thought it best on the spur of the moment to embellish the truth, as I did not want to seem ungrateful for Jarrow's kind offer.

"As there was no way of phoning ahead I anticipated a frosty reception from Peterson's secretary, as I did not have an appointment. So I resigned myself to the possibility that, upon arrival, I may well have to make one if the solicitor was already in conference. Given the choice I would rather not have to spend any more time in his waiting room under the disapproving gaze of his secretary than was absolutely necessary.

"By the time I set off from the manor it was already early afternoon, and the autumn sun was at its apex; bringing with it much-appreciated warmth. As I neared the steep bank of the Widow-Maker I adhered to the procedure I had been taught, and this time there was no incident to speak of. I made fairly good time, and even managed to find a parking space a short distance from Peterson's office.

"As luck would have it his secretary was nowhere to be seen when I entered through the main door. I could hear the sound of Peterson's voice coming from his office, so I walked over and stood just outside the door while he finished his phone call. I knocked as he replaced the receiver on its cradle. Peterson stood up and welcomed me in as he had done previously."

"Come in please, Mr Ward, how are you getting on at the manor? Are the Jarrows looking after you?"

"I was happy to confirm that the couple were indeed catering for my every need, and, once we had the pleasantries out of the way, I came straight to the point of asking him if he knew of any other family members, or anyone at all, for that matter, who might think that they had some claim to my inheritance. I could tell immediately from the puzzled expression on his face that my question had thrown him."

"I'm not sure that I understand you, Mr Ward, has someone said something to you?"

"I had already decided that I did not wish to mention my visitor to the solicitor; at least not for the time being. So, I made a casual remark that as I had never met my distant cousin, I was unaware of any residual relatives or close acquaintances who might be about to spring out of the proverbial woodwork to make a claim on the manor. I was not altogether convinced that Peterson believed my explanation, but even so he assured me that as far as he was concerned no such individual existed.

"Yet again he took the opportunity to press home the fact that he had an interested party who was willing to pay me a good price for the manor and the acreage it came with. But I explained to him once more that I was not willing to make any firm decisions without consulting my wife first.

"When I left Peterson's office I took myself down the high street and found an ironmonger, from which I purchased a good stout torch and some replacement batteries in anticipation of the generator back at the manor failing me again. I walked around the town for a while, enjoying the unusually warm weather. Along the main road I discovered several restaurants which I imagined that Jenifer might want to visit when she came down. The thought of her reading the menus from outside and excitedly deciding what she was going to try made me miss her even more, and I wished that it was time for me to call her already.

"I decided to pass the time by enjoying a leisurely pint in one of the local pubs. I found one which was a little off the beaten track, but not so far away that I could not still hear the passing traffic from the main road. The bar was particularly small, and would have appeared far too claustrophobic for a London crowd. But somehow, in this rural setting, it seemed to fit quite snuggly.

"I noticed that they served the same local brew I had chanced upon at the hotel on my first night, so I ordered a pint of that and picked up a free copy of the local paper from the pile on a table near the door. I sat myself at a corner table right by a window, so that I could gaze out at the passers-by while I enjoyed my drink.

"As small as it was, the pub still offered hot food for lunch and dinner. But I barely glanced at the menu as I was still full of Mrs Jarrow's breakfast. I flicked through the paper only half-reading a couple of articles as I sipped my ale. The view out of the window, I decided, was far more interesting. The pub backed onto what appeared to be a medieval church and, from where I was sitting, it was possible to see the incredibly beautiful structure in all its glory. The sun was just starting its decline, and the sunlight was reflecting against the stained-glass windows.

"It was at that moment that I remembered Peterson mentioning that my late benefactor was buried in the graveyard of a local church, and I wondered if I was looking at the exact one now. It occurred to me that I should at least pay my respects at his grave. After all, even though we had never met, he still bequeathed all his worldly goods to me. But in the waning daylight I did not wish to appear like some ogre with a morbid curiosity, shuffling around the tombstones with my torch trying to locate the correct grave.

"I decided that I would try and make a point of coming into town earlier one day, to allow me the chance to visit his grave properly.

"Having finished my pint, I took my empty glass back up to the bar, and complimented the landlord on the quality of his ale. He informed me that it was a local favourite; so much so that he sold it bottled for take-away, so I could not resist purchasing several bottles to take back with me.

"I still had some time to spare before calling Jenifer, so I re-visited the shop where I had bought my provisions the day before and purchased some more supplies for dinner. Whilst there I noticed that they had a transistor radio for sale so I decided to treat myself, as the thought of listening to some tranquil music during dinner seemed extremely inviting.

"I took my purchases back to my car, and locked them away. As the late afternoon drew in I began to wonder if I should expect another late night - or more precisely early morning - wake-up call from my unwanted visitor. It may have just been coincidence, as the wind had started to pick up as I made my way back to my car. But I have often wondered whether or not the sudden chill that ran through my body at the time was as a result of the encroaching darkness and subsequent drop in temperature, or was it because unconsciously the mere prospect of returning to the manor alone, and in the dark, had suddenly taken a toll on my resolve?"

# NINE

"Hearing my wife's voice on the phone was the ideal cure for my present melancholia. I let her chat away about all the contacts she was making from her latest shoot, and how much fun she was having designing some of the layouts. Apparently, as the article they were shooting for was aimed at the younger generation, her father had stepped back and allowed Jenifer to take charge and he was acting more like her assistant, which also tickled her.

"She sounded so bubbly and full of life that I did not have the heart to bring her down by voicing my concerns regarding my visitor. Instead I told her about how well I was being looked after by the Jarrows, and that I had decided that it might be appropriate to find my late cousin's grave so that I could pay my respects. Jenifer agreed that it would be the proper thing to do, and reiterated how much she wished that she could be with me. I knew how much she was aching to see the manor and if anything, I was missing her even more than she was me. But now there was a part of me which housed concern regarding the young girl, and the prospect of her returning.

"It had already occurred to me that perhaps she was someone suffering from some type of mental disorder, and although she never did me any harm, I did not want to put Jenifer in any kind of danger, regardless of how remote it might be.

"Whilst we were on the phone I made a mental note that should the young girl appear again this evening, I was going to confront her about her and try to ascertain exactly what she wanted. If it did turn out that she was in any way unhinged, then I fully intended to report her to the police the following morning and to let them intercede in whatever way they saw fit.

"That said, there was still a part of me that could not believe that she honestly meant me any harm. I remembered her beautiful eyes, and the look of sheer terror reflected in them. The way that she had pleaded for my help and the urgency in her voice had convinced me of the genuineness of her predicament. Until she had disappeared! Which again, I determined had probably just been a case of her running away whilst my back was turned.

"But then if that were the case, where did that singing come from? Not to mention that awful scream?"

"Hello, are you still there?"

"The sound of Jenifer's voice brought me back around from my reverie. She had obviously realised from my lack of response to her speaking that I was no longer paying attention. I apologised, profusely, and she laughed at my grovelling attempt at asking for forgiveness. I made the excuse that the sunset over the small town was so captivating that for a second I had lost myself in it. It was only a small white lie, and I did not feel overly guilty for telling it. After all, I could not tell Jenifer the truth!

"As my change dwindled we said our goodbyes, and Jenifer promised me that the minute the shoot was finished she would be on the first train down. I made a mental note to locate the train station, so that I could be there to meet her when she arrived.

"I set off back for the manor, and arrived there in good time without incident. I could understand why the locals had concerns regarding that abrupt, foliage-covered, steep turning, especially after my near miss with that van. But I did think that the given name for it was a little exaggerated, and wondered if there had in fact ever been any fatalities as a result of any accident taking place.

"I parked up outside, as usual, and unloaded my latest purchases and carried them inside. Once more there was note from Mrs Jarrow waiting for me on the hall table. This one informed me that she had made some soup for the couples' supper, and that she had left me a bowl full on top of the stove ready to be heated. She had also set up fresh logs in all the fires which I had used the previous evening, and made up my bed with fresh sheets and pillowcases. Her husband had also checked the generator and she wrote that she hoped that it would remain working for me throughout the night. I was not sure how much my late relative had paid the couple, but they certainly earned their keep as far as I was concerned.

"I switched on some of the lights, and they came on straight away. I heaved a small sigh of relief that, at least for a while, I would not have to rely on my new torch alone to see my way around. I took my groceries and ale into the kitchen and uncovered the saucepan of soup Mrs Jarrow had left for me. I inhaled deeply, and my senses were struck by the aromas of tomato, garlic and basil. Immediately, my stomach began to gurgle. By chance I had purchased some crusty bread rolls in town, the perfect complement to soup. I was really looking forward to my supper now!

"First, I decided to go upstairs and light the fire in my bedroom. As promised my bed had been re-made with fresh, clean sheets, and I gathered from the faint odour of cherry blossoms in the air that Mrs Jarrow had seen fit to spray some air freshener; doubtless to combat the sour smell of my sweaty sheets from the previous evening.

"Once I had the fire roaring, I pulled back my top sheets and blankets to allow the warmth from the fire to penetrate my bed. I wondered if my benefactor had owned any form of hot water bottle, or perhaps an old-fashioned bed warmer, and made a note to myself to have a look when I went back downstairs.

"As I was about to descend the stairs I remembered Mrs Jarrow's recollection from that morning of there being a portrait of a young girl in amongst those stacked up against the wall in one of the other bedrooms. I made my way along the corridor until I located the room in question, and went in to investigate.

"Typically, the light in this particular room was not working, and as I had no idea where, or if, there were any spare bulbs in the house, I went back downstairs to retrieve my torch. Once I returned to the bedroom I laid my torch on the bed so that the beam could illuminate as much of the room as possible, and I carefully began to remove the paintings and place them individually around the room so that I could get a better view of each one.

"There were about fifteen or so, and although I am no expert I believe that they were oil rather than water-based productions. There were a couple of the manor, created from different angles. Several were of horses and a couple of those had carriages in them also, with grooms standing smartly to attention in the foreground. There were a couple of portraits but they were all of men; some single, others in groups of various sizes. But alas, there was not even one with the girl in it. In fact there were no females in any of them whatsoever, which I must admit I did find a trifle odd. Especially as Mrs Jarrow had seemed so sure that she had seen one amongst them!

"I noticed at the far end of the room there was an empty frame leaning up against the window, and I wondered if perhaps at some time that might have contained the portrait Mrs Jarrow had spoken of. If so, the chances were that it must have been damaged or destroyed in some way, which would explain its absence from the rest.

"Somewhat disappointed I turned to leave the room, when in another corner I noticed a medium-sized rather splendid ornate wooden frame, leaning against the wall. I picked it up and turned it over, only to find that it was a mirror. I checked the glass for any sign of cracks, but there were none. So, I turned it back over to see if the fixings at the back were still in place, which they were.

"I decided to take it downstairs with me, as I seemed to remember thinking the previous evening that there was a rather obvious blank patch above the fireplace. The mirror fitted perfectly, in fact, and as I inspected the space above the fireplace more closely it appeared as if something of the exact size as the mirror had once hung there. Once it was in situ, I stood back to admire it. I decided that it was a perfect complement to the rest of the room.

"Before attending to my dinner, I spent the next ten minutes or so searching, in vain as it turned out, for some form of bed warmer. Eventually I gave up, as my hunger was beginning to get the better of me.

Therefore, I took myself back down to the kitchen to fetch my supper. Once down there, a sudden inner sensation drove me to check that Mrs Jarrow had remembered to lock the scullery door. Reason and sanity argued against my action, as there was no plausible reason to suspect that someone who had been locking that same door, night after night, for more years than I could count, would suddenly forget. But, alas, reason and sanity did not make their argument forcibly enough.

"Naturally, when I tried the handle, the door was secure. Feeling a little foolish, as well as guilty for questioning the housekeeper's attention to duty, I took out my keys and opened the door; just to prove to myself that it was safe to do so. I must admit that as I pulled the door open I half-expected to see the young lady standing outside on the threshold, but to my delight the doorstep was clear.

"I crossed the threshold and stayed outside there for a few moments, breathing in the late evening air and gazing out over the darkened countryside. The moon was just beginning to appear in the night sky, although this evening it was frequently lost behind scudding clouds. I took in several deep breaths and listen out for the sound of the night creatures. Curiously though, I could not hear any. Not so much as a bird, a bat, an owl or even a barking dog off into the distance. In fact, the only sound I could hear was that of the wind rustling the branches of the surrounding trees.

"After a while I went back into the kitchen and prepared my food. I carried my soup upstairs and sat once more in the large armchair which I had fallen asleep in the previous evening. The soup was delicious, and I made a mental note to thank Mrs Jarrow the next day.

I took my empty bowl down to the kitchen, and made myself a cheese and ham sandwich using some of the crusty bread rolls I had purchased earlier in town. I carried them back upstairs, along with a couple of bottles of the ale I had purchased, and settled back down in front of the fire.

"I managed to tune my new transistor radio into a local station which was playing a live classical concert and settled down with my ale and sandwich in front of the fire. By the end of my second bottle of ale, I could feel my eyes growing heavy with sleep. But I decided that as the fire was still blazing, I would give it a little while longer before carrying myself upstairs. I closed my eyes to concentrate on the concert - the music from which blended perfectly with the occasional crackle from the logs on the fire - and within minutes I drifted off.

"I woke with a start. I had heard something, but I could not be sure what it was or even if it was just a part of a dream. I stayed there, slumped in the comfort of the armchair, as I tried to distinguish any sounds drifting through the air. The station I had been listening to had obviously gone off the air for the night, so I leaned down and switched off the low humming which was coming from the front of the speaker.

"The fire was almost out, although a few flames still licked at what was left of the logs. As I might have expected the overhead lights had gone out once more, and it was then that I remembered that I had left my torch upstairs. I was grateful for the faint illumination afforded to me by the remaining flames. Something was better than nothing as I made my way up to bed.

"Rubbing the sleep from my eyes, I placed my hands on the arms of the chair and forced myself up. There, reflected in the mirror which I had recently placed above the fire, was the young girl!

"It took a few seconds for my poor, weary, still half-asleep brain to register what my eyes were witnessing; and even then, I did not want to believe it. I spun around on the spot so fast that I almost lost my balance and went over. As I looked up, the girl was gone! I slowly turned to look back into the mirror, fearing for a moment that she somehow had the power to hold her reflection in the glass without physically being in front of it. But, when I turned, all I could see was my own startled expression gazing back at me.

"I slumped back down in the armchair with my head in my hands. I just could not seem to get my brain to function properly. I had seen the girl's reflection - I was in no doubt of that. But then at the same time, how could I have done when she was not there? I considered that it might just be a case of my imagination working overtime. Perhaps a combination of being in that strange house, the incident from the previous night, the fact that I missed my wife so desperately, and, although I hated to admit it, perhaps I had misjudged the strength of the local brew.

"Added to everything else, since last night I had had the girl on my mind for most of the day. Therefore, it was not beyond the realms of possibility that my subconscious had continued to imagine her while I was asleep. But I had not been asleep when I saw her - I was wide awake! Or was I? Perhaps I had been caught in that netherworld between sleep and wakefulness when I genuinely believed that I had seen her reflection.

"Just then I heard a loud banging coming from the direction of the scullery! It had to be her, I just knew that it had to be her!

"I stood up on legs made of jelly and stumbled around the armchair to make my way out into the hallway. My heart was beating so fast that I believed that I could feel it vibrating in my ears. I considered running upstairs to grab my torch, which by far would have been the most sensible thing to do. But at that moment something inside me was compelling me to answer the door instead.

"A sudden thought struck me. Had I even locked the scullery door after I had been outside that evening? Was there in fact nothing stopping whomever was out there from coming inside? I dropped my hand down by my side and felt the bunch of keys safely enclosed in the fabric of my pocket. I must have locked it, surely. But how ironic was the fact that I had only opened it in the first place was to check that it had been locked by the housekeeper, only for me to be the one to subsequently leave it open!

"The banging came again. This time it was much more forceful, with the same kind of urgency behind it as last night. Instinctively, I turned and began to make my way slowly towards the kitchen. The fact that I did not have so much as a candle with me to light my way was not completely lost on me. But something inside me was driving me forward. It was almost as if I had to answer the door, no matter what.

"I felt my way around the kitchen table and entered the scullery. Just like before I could not ascertain any kind of shadow behind the frosted glass of the back door, and for a moment my heart leaped at the possibility that no-one was there. That momentary feeling of elation was extremely short lived when the hammering returned, once more causing the door to rattle in its frame.

"This time, I did not bother to call out. Instead, once I managed to unlock the door I just grabbed the handle and wrenched it open.

"There she was again, standing outside my door. Still dressed in that same floral-print dress with her beautiful hair shimmering in the moonlight, and her piercing green eyes pleading to me for help. I screamed at her, demanding to know what she wanted from me. But then I regretted my action almost immediately. I realised that now I was confronted by her in the flesh I did not have the heart to be rude or abrupt with her. She seemed so vulnerable, so scared, so in need of protection. For a second I considered stepping over the threshold and sweeping her up in my arms to reassure her that I would take care of her. But instead I stayed fixed to the spot, waiting.

"As before, she turned to her left and pointed out into the darkness. I knew what was coming next, and so it was."

"They are trying to take my baby. Please don't let them get him."

"The same words delivered in that same pleading tone which had melted my heart upon first hearing her utter them the night before. Once again, I stepped outside and pointed my eyes in the direction to which she had pointed. Only this time, I made sure that I could still see her in my peripheral vision. I was not about to be led the same merry dance by her that I had been the previous night. Yet again, there was no one coming for her from any direction that I could make out. I turned back to face her, relieved that at least she was still there and had not managed to somehow slip away without me realising.

"From this distance, she appeared even more afraid. Her angelic face held an expression of sheer terror, even though there was no reason for it that I could ascertain at that moment. I looked her squarely in the eyes. In the dim light of the moon her eyes almost seemed to have the power to see right through me. It was almost as if she were capable of focusing on what was taking place behind me, without actually acknowledging that I was standing there.

"I asked her directly who it was that she was running from, and pointed out as calmly as I could that there was no one chasing her. But she just kept her gaze fixed straight ahead. A pleading little girl look that I could not help but allow to tug at my heart. I was about to ask her if she wanted to come in, when from behind me I could suddenly hear the sound of music being played on the harpsichord in the music room."

# TEN

"I instinctively turned around to face the direction from which the music was coming. The melody was very familiar to me, although at first, I could not place it for sure. But as I concentrated a little more, it came to me. It was the same song that I had heard the previous night.

"I spun around to confront the young woman, but she was gone!

"I looked around frantically, trying to see where she might have disappeared to. At least this time I knew that there was no way that she could have slipped into the house, as I had been blocking the doorway. Yet again there was no sign of her, and this time I was in no mood to go venturing outside. I decided that whatever game she might be playing, I was not going to become part of it - not tonight.

"I slammed the door and turned the key back in the lock to ensure that it was secure. I walked out of the scullery and made my way to the kitchen door. I stood there for a moment, listening to that sweet melody as it drifted through the house. The playing was flawless; I do not know how else to describe it. It was almost as if the musician was barely touching the keys and was a true master of their craft.

"After a moment I crept along the hallway towards the music room, straining to adjust my eyes in the darkness. The glimmer of light which had come from the fire in the front parlour was all gone, which was not surprising considering the final few logs were already on their way out when I had left the room. As I reached the door of the music room I reached out my hand to grab hold of the handle; and then I froze. The girl outside was one thing. She was real and alive, I had seen her twice now, but how could there be anyone else in the house without me knowing it? Who could possibly be playing on the other side of the wooden door?

"I pressed my ear against the wood. I am not sure what I was listening for; perhaps a familiar and comforting voice. Somehow Jarrow or his wife had maybe let themselves I while I was tending to the scullery door, because this was the time of year when one of them tuned the harpsichord for my dead relative. But I knew in my heart that I was merely grabbing for insane straws. Whoever or whatever it was behind that door, I had to confront them and demand to know what was going on.

"I stood poised, ready to make good my attack. The sound of the music seemed to penetrate the door in such a way that it filtered through the house as if it were being played in every room simultaneously. Slowly I turned the handle, careful not to make a sound and warn my intruder. It occurred to me that I should have some weapon to hand, but it was too late now as releasing the handle might cause the latch to squeak and give the game away.

"I flung the door open. In that instant the music stopped, leaving the last note hanging in the air as if it were somehow reluctant to expire. I ran over to the harpsichord, but I could already tell before I reached it that there was no-one sitting on the stool. What's more when I looked I could see that the lid that protected the keys was down, so nobody could have been playing the instrument. Yet I had been listening to the music for several minutes by then. So where had it come from?

"Just then, the singing began. That same beautiful voice which I had heard the previous night took over from where the music had left off. Once again, it seemed to permeate the house, and echoed all around me. I truly felt as if I was losing my mind. I listened for a moment, entranced as I had been by the playing, for even though I had not heard the song before last night it was almost as if I had known it my entire life. It captured me, body and soul, and when I closed my eyes I was lost in a reverie which gave me the feeling of drifting along a tunnel leading to who knew where.

"A sudden crash from upstairs brought me back to my senses. I ran from the room out into the hallway. When I reached the bottom of the stairs I gazed up, but it was too dark to be able to make out any form in the shadows. I stood there for a moment trying to focus on the grandfather clock at the top of the stairs, but it was too dark even for that. Suddenly I realised that the singing had stopped, and now the only sound I could hear was the faint ticking from that same clock.

"Slowly, I began to climb the stairs. I considered that with everything else that had happened, there was still a chance that the crash I had heard from above might have been the result of some innocent happening. Perhaps something had been teetering on a shelf without me noticing, and it just so happened that at that moment it decided to fall. I comforted myself with such thoughts as I made my way up.

"Once at the top, I decided to retrieve my torch before undertaking an investigation. I found it where I had left it and switched it on. The strong beam that emanated from it gave me an instant feeling of comfort, almost as if I was no longer alone. I shone my torch around the room, and sure enough, when the beam hit the far wall, I noticed that some of the pictures I had been looking at earlier had toppled over.

"I heaved a huge sigh of relief. That at least I could rationalise as something that could happen without outside intervention. I decided to leave the fallen paintings where they were for now. At least on the floor they could not topple over again and scare the life out of me. My heartbeat began to settle once more. I had no way of explaining the harpsichord seeming to play by itself, but I recalled that I had seen pianos which were designed to do just that so I decided that for now, that was as good an explanation as any.

"I turned to leave the room, and saw the girl standing directly behind me. The shock of seeing her took me immediately by surprise. I stumbled backwards and tripped over a foot stool or some such thing, and went flying backwards. The torch flew from my grasp and I heard it hit something behind me as I fell, instantly going out. Fortunately, I managed to land flat on my back, and although the wind was knocked out of me I was otherwise unhurt.

"I lay still for a moment, trying to regain my breath. I kept my eyes fixed straight ahead of me where the girl had been standing. But, even from such a short distance, in the darkness I could see nothing of her. Once I regained my breath, I edged backwards along the floor to retrieve my torch. I was afraid to take my eyes away from the spot where I had seen her standing a moment before, just in case I missed a movement in the shadows which would signify her leaving.

"I managed to find my torch and flicked the switch on it back and forth, but alas, no light came forth. I felt along the glass front and to my dismay I could feel that the glass had cracked, although it was still holding in place. I kept the switch in its 'on' position and rapped it against the palm of my hand a few times, which was a trick I had once witnessed my father trying. When the beam came back on I was elated.

"I aimed the light at the space where the girl had been standing, but she was nowhere to be seen. I was sure that I had not heard her run out onto the landing. But then neither had I heard her creep up behind me in the room, so that by itself did not substantiate a great deal.

"Now, for the first time, I truly began to believe that I might have a ghost! The thought alone sent a flood of icy cold down my spine. It would certainly explain how the girl seemed capable of appearing and disappearing at will. Not to mention the singing and the music, but why would a ghost be haunting me? I had never dabbled in the occult, or attempted to invite spirits from the other side to cross over via a Ouija board. In fact, the nearest that I had ever come to such hocus pocus was my experience with the gypsy in Brighton.

"It was true that many people believed that old houses were famous hunting grounds for all manner of spooks and spectres, but surely not my house. Not while I was out there alone, miles away from anywhere and in virtual darkness, surrounded by nothing but forest and stars and nothingness! I admonished myself immediately for losing my grip on reality. Granted the entire situation was somewhat unusual, and I was not even bothered about finding a rational explanation for everything which had occurred. But I would not allow myself to fall apart and start drifting into the realms of fantasy and the supernatural.

"I decided that with the lateness of the hour, bed was where I needed to be. But I must admit that with everything else that had taken place that night, I felt that I deserved a nightcap to help me back to sleep. I used my torch to guide my way back downstairs. A large glass of wine would suffice, and at that moment, the thought of this comforted me enough that I could feel my while body start to relax once more.

"As I reached the bottom of the stairs, I heard the banging once more on the scullery door. I could not believe it; tonight, I was to be treated to a second visit, no doubt. I tried to steel myself for whatever lay ahead. I knew that I would have to answer the door, or else no doubt the banging would simply continue to grow in velocity until I submitted and gave in.

Just as I was about to make my way back to the scullery, the singing began again!

"The doleful tune filled the house once more, this time in direct contrast to whoever, or whatever, was hammering at the back door. From the corner of my eye I thought that I could see something moving at the top of the stairs. I raised my torch and there, standing at the top of the stairs, was the young girl! My torch held her for a moment in a halo of dim light. Even from this distance I could still make out that same pleading, yearning expression on her face that she had treated me to each time I had opened the back door to her. Her eyes, although so young, appeared as if they had experienced far more suffering than was natural for her years.

"Her head was tilted slightly to one side as if she too were listening to the singing. Even though I was convinced that the singing came from her, I could tell in the torchlight that her lips were not moving. I gripped the side of the bannister tightly with one hand, as if to try to steady myself. My mind was by now a complete jumble of thoughts and ideas, and I was finding it impossible to come to terms with what was happening. Either she was a ghost, or spirit of some sort, or else, more logically, she had merely been hiding upstairs waiting for the right moment to show herself.

"The singing appeared to be increasing in volume, as if someone had turned up a stereo. I focused my concentration on the girl, although in the background I could still hear someone hammering on the back door. As I watched, the girl slowly began to lift her arms until they were outstretched towards me. It was as if she were inviting me to hold her in a tender embrace. Then I noticed that she was beginning to descend the stairs. She was not actually walking though; it was more as if she were drifting down. I let the light from my torch drop slightly to see if I could see her feet, but there appeared to be nothing under the long hem of her dress as it dragged over the stairs on her descent.

"I raised my light once more. The girl never once seemed to take her eyes from me; she drifted down at a slow, steady pace, barely perceptible to the naked eye. I gripped the bannister harder, fighting for my resolve to keep me upright. I wanted to call out to her, ask her what she wanted from me, convince her that I meant her no harm, but at that moment I had no voice. It felt as if I was glued to the spot, unable even to move my legs let alone make my escape.

"I looked up into her sweet, innocent face as she came ever nearer. I had nothing to fear from this young girl. She was the one in need of help, in need of comfort and support. Yet then why was it that my legs felt as if they were ready to buckle underneath me? Then I saw it; as she came ever closer, I noticed that the expression in her eyes was changing. The change was subtle, but nonetheless it was still there. That look of yearning and longing was metamorphosing into one of fear!

"She appeared to be staring at me as if I was somehow the orchestrator of her plight. Within seconds that look of fear in her eyes had turned abruptly into one of pure hatred, and as she neared me she dropped her arms to her sides and let out a terrible scream which seemed to shake the very foundations of the house. To my horror at that moment my torch went out, and in the darkness, I could sense more than see, that the girl was coming ever closer towards me. I do not remember losing consciousness, but presumably I must have, because that is all I can remember.

"Once more I was roused from my unconscious state by the sound of someone banging on the door. When I opened my eyes, I saw from the daylight filtering in through the hall windows that it was morning. I realised that I must have been out all night, and when I lifted my head off the hard stone floor I immediately felt a lump at the back which was incredibly tender to the touch. I rose to my feet too quickly, and straight away I felt a little giddy so I grabbed onto the bannister for support. The movement reminded me of the previous night when I had first needed the solid wooden beam for assistance, and suddenly I had a flash-back of all I had witnessed before I passed out.

"As always, in the cold light of day everything felt normal once again. I looked up the wide staircase and could see nothing out of the ordinary. But I surmised at that moment that even if the same spectral vision appeared that I would not be in the least bit phased by it. The daylight belonged to the here and now, which put me back in command.

"I opened the front door to be greeted by the sombre Mrs Jarrow standing on the doorstep, her basket in hand. When she saw me, it was obvious that my dishevelled appearance caused her some alarm. However, being as she was the very epitome of the perfect servant, she did not voice her disapproval, but merely instead greeted me in her familiar way, and waited for me to stand aside to allow her in."

"Good morning, sir, will you be wanting a strong coffee before I make your breakfast? Jarrow is outside seeing to the generator. I see it let you down again during the night."

"I thanked her for her offer. A strong coffee would certainly hit the spot. I followed her into the kitchen and slumped down at the table while she prepared my brew. After my coffee, I dragged myself upstairs so that I could bathe while Mrs Jarrow prepared my breakfast. I still felt guilty that the poor woman felt that she had to treat me as if I was her new master, but at that moment I did not have the fortitude to turn down another of her delicious breakfasts.

"After my bath, which seemed even more tepid than the previous morning's, I dressed and came back down just as Mrs Jarrow was about to call up to tell me that my meal was ready. I remembered to thank her for the marvellous soup she had left for my dinner, and as usual she received my praise without cracking a smile. While I ate she busied herself around the house, re-making up the fires, dusting and cleaning without a word.

"With each mouthful I began to feel more human again. The back of my head still felt very tender, but I was relieved to feel that the lump seemed to have shrunk slightly. Mrs Jarrow kept the coffee coming, at my request, and I had finished three more cups by the time I ate my last forkful of bacon and eggs. When Mrs Jarrow came to collect my plates, I thanked her for yet another amazing breakfast, and as she turned to go back to the kitchen I remembered the portraits that I had rummaged through the previous evening. I mentioned to her that I could not find any with a woman in them, but that I had found one which seemed to have its picture missing."

"That's very odd, sir, I know that I saw it clear as day. Perhaps the master dropped it or spilt something on it."

"I agreed that that would explain its disappearance, and asked her if she remembered what the girl in the painting had looked like. She stood there beside me for a moment, holding my empty plates in her hand while she pondered my question."

"I seem to recall thinking at the time that she was a young girl, maybe early twenties or late teens. She was wearing what I would class as maybe a late Victorian-style dress, oh and she had lovely long black hair which framed her face and came down over her shoulders."

"It sounded like too much of a coincidence to me. The girl that Mrs Jarrow was describing had to be my late-night visitor, which in turn would mean without a doubt that it was a spirit I had encountered and not a living being. The trouble was, without a picture I had no specific form of reference to quantify my suspicion.

"I thanked her once more, and she turned and left the room. The fact that I could not find the picture Mrs Jarrow had described was bothering me more than perhaps I should have allowed it to. After all, I knew what I had witnessed; my own eyes did not lie to me. So, regardless of whether my visitor was real in the flesh or not, was completely beside the point in one respect at least.

"But of course, if she were a ghost, a spirit from the past, then what did she want with me? That was a different matter altogether. Whoever she was, or might have been, she could certainly have no issues with me. After all, we had never met. Well, not person to person, as such. So, in that case, she must have some connection to the manor. The question was, what connection? It dawned on me that with my late cousin gone, and the Jarrows, and Peterson for that matter, none-the-wiser, any chance of my finding out about her story were all but gone.

"Then, there was a knock at the front door!"

## ELEVEN

"Before I had a chance to rise and answer the door, I could hear the sound of Mrs Jarrow running up the steps from the kitchen which led to the hall. I decided that it was best to allow her the responsibility of playing the part of housekeeper-cum-cook-cum-maid, as it was already quite apparent to me that she was intent on ensuring that she earned the money my late distant cousin had already paid her.

"I stayed seated at the table and could hear the distant sound of muffled voices outside. After a few moments Mrs Jarrow re-emerged in the doorway to announce that a Mr Jefferies had arrived, and wished to speak with me. Naturally I had no idea who this stranger was, but as Mrs Jarrow made no more of her announcement I decided to not to ask any questions, and asked her to show him in for me.

"I stood up and greeted my new guest as he entered the room. He was a tall, slender individual whom I estimated must be in his late sixties or early seventies. He was smartly dressed in a tailored hacking jacket, dark green trousers, and brown brogues. We shook hands and I offered him a chair, which he gratefully accepted. I noticed that Mrs Jarrow was still loitering in the doorway, and when I acknowledged her presence she asked if I wished to have some more coffee served. I forwarded her offer to Jefferies but he declined, and as I had already consumed four cups that morning, so did I.

"Once we were alone, Jefferies introduced himself formally."

"I am sorry to burst in on you unannounced Mr Ward, but the truth is that I have been speaking to a mutual friend of ours, Mr Peterson, the solicitor. I believe that he has already mentioned me to you; I am the annoying individual who keeps badgering him about the possibility of purchasing this house and the grounds."

"I assured him that Peterson had mentioned him to me, but that as I had made clear to the solicitor, I had no intention of making a decision before consulting with Jenifer. Jeffries claimed that Peterson had conveyed my feelings and that he completely understood my feelings. He emphasised that he had no intention of pestering or harassing me to make a decision, and that he merely thought that, under the circumstances, it might be in both our interests to be formally introduced. He went on to explain that he had inherited his farm and land from his father, who had in turn inherited it from his, and so on, as far back as town records documented.

"He further explained that, when he inherited his property, the family holding had always been modest, though comfortable, but that he had always fancied himself as a business man, which was why he had set about acquiring all the property in the area which took his fancy. It now appeared that my manor was the last piece in his empirical puzzle."

"I won't try and spin you a yarn, Mr Ward, but if you decide to call in an expert I am sure that they will tell you that this manor needs a great deal of structural work to make it habitable. Your land was also sadly neglected by your late cousin and, I believe, his father before him, so that too is in need of attention. Over the years I made your cousin several generous offers, but alas, he chose to decline them all. I even offered to pay for a structural surveyor to come in and supply him with a comprehensive report, but he would have none of it - he was indeed very set in his ways. Now, I realise that you don't know me from Adam, so naturally I don't expect you to take my word for it solely, but I can assure you that there are no hidden gold mines or oil wells beneath this land, and that my interest is purely personal."

"He was right of course, I did not know him whatsoever, but as he spoke I had the sense that he was a man of honour and trust, and although I would not be so foolish as to let the property and land go, if it came to it, without seeking the advice of an expert first, I also felt that such an expert's findings would tally with what Jefferies was telling me. Furthermore, Peterson had already vouched for the man, which I believed that his ethics would not allow if there were anything underhand about my visitor.

"I gave him my promise that if I did decide to sell that I would allow him first refusal, which from the look on his face appeared to be more than enough to satisfy him. He thanked me for allowing him to intrude on my time, and I assured him that the pleasure was all mine. As he stood to leave a thought struck me, and I asked him if he would mind indulging me for a moment. He re-took his seat, smiling, but with a quizzical expression across his eyes.

"I was initially hesitant in deciding how best to begin this part of our conversation, and took a moment to consider where to start. I did not feel at all comfortable merely blurting out my suspicions regarding my late-night visitor, but by the same token as Jefferies and his family had lived in the vicinity for so long, there might be a chance that he could shed some much-needed light on my predicament. In the end I decided to start by asking Jefferies what he knew of my late cousin, in pretence that I was interested in the kind of man he was."

"Well Mr Ward, I cannot honestly say that I knew him that well. He tended to keep himself to himself a lot of the time. In all the years I've been here, I could probably count the amount of times that I saw him in town on the fingers of one hand. Although, as I mentioned earlier, I did come to the manor on occasion to see if he had reconsidered my offer to buy, and to his credit, he never once refused to see me. Although naturally our conversations always ended the same way - with an emphatic 'no sale' from the old fellow."

"I asked Jefferies if he was aware of anyone else, other than the Jarrows, who might have visited my benefactor from time to time. But I could tell instantly from my visitor's puzzled look that he was thrown by my question. In fairness to the man he had already mentioned at length that he hardly ever saw my late cousin, so I could hardly be surprised by his curious stare when I had virtually asked him the same question, albeit in a roundabout way.

"My little ruse had obviously failed, dismally. So before Jefferies had a chance to think of a reply I cut back in, apologising for the vagueness of my enquiries, and assuring him that I had no ulterior motive in asking such questions, which of course, I did. So I decided to make one more stab at it, and this time I undertook not to make such a ham-fisted job of it. Therefore, I changed my approach and informed Jeffries that, because of my lack of contact with this side of my family, I wondered if he, Jefferies, due to the fact that he had lived in the area all his life, had any knowledge of who might have lived in the manor when he himself was a boy."

"Well, now that you come to mention it, I do remember when I was a very young lad, hearing my parents discussing something once about 'those up at the manor' as they put it. I remember that we had a horrendous storm that night, with winds stronger than I had ever seen, or have seen since. We had trees uprooted and all sorts. Anyway, I recall that it was the thunder that woke me up, and although I knew that I would probably expect a hiding if I was caught venturing downstairs after bedtime, my curiosity got the better of me.

"Due to the storm my father had to stay awake to tend to the livestock, just in case any of them broke free, and on this occasion my mother must have stayed up to keep him company because it was their voices that I could hear from downstairs when I stuck my head out of my bedroom door. When I edged out a little further I could see the shadows from the open fire blazing in the parlour, so I tip-toed out onto the landing and made my way across to the stairs so that I could hear what they were talking about.

"It was fortunate for me that my parents had opened a bottle of whiskey to keep them company, because one thing was for sure; when they drank, their voices increased in volume, and with the storm raging outside, under normal circumstances, it would have been very difficult to hear what they were saying from my vantage point. I remember that the lock on our front door was faulty, which my father was forever promising my mother he would see to, and sure enough at one point the wind grew so strong that it blew in our door, and sent it crashing against the stone wall. Fortunately for my father, the hinges at least held, for I could hear my mother berating him as he went over to secure it again.

"Once the drama had passed my father slumped back into his chair, and then I heard him say to my mother something about that being the worst storm he had seen since the night that girl up at the manor was killed."

Jonathan shifted on his chair, as if to make himself more comfortable, before he spoke again.

"At the sound of this I leaned forward, desperate not to miss any detail. By the sound of Jefferies' story there was a good chance that I might finally find out something about my unwelcome visitor. I remained silent so that he could continue."

"I remember my mother agreeing with him. She took another drink from her glass and nodded her head before saying that she remembered seeing the young woman, swimming in the lake in the summer, and how pretty she was, and how fond she always appeared to be of the young girl who was visiting at the time. My mother also reminisced that when she would walk through the field she would often hear the young woman singing to herself, and my mother remarked on what a lovely voice she had, and how sad her song was.

"Typically, as I moved to make myself more comfortable, and one of the loose floorboards creaked under my weight, so I stole back into my room before either of my parents caught me."

"I had to press the point home so when I realised that Jefferies appeared to be finished with his story, I enquired as to whether he recalled the subject of the young woman ever being raised again. He pondered my question for a moment before answering."

"Oddly enough, now I come to think of it, the subject did come up again a few years later. I remember my father saying that the young woman who was killed was the wife of someone staying at the manor, but he died, not sure how, and a little while later she was run over by a carriage during the storm. No one knew what she was doing out on the road in the middle of the night, especially in such inclement weather, but for whatever reason the fact she was there was not disputed, and then she was knocked over. The accident occurred not far from here, by that awkward bend in the road where the land suddenly dips and veers down the steep embankment."

"The Widow-Maker, I ventured."

"Oh, I see you've heard of it then? Well you know what we locals are like in our rural settings, we do like to hold on to our old stories, and quirky little names like that tend to stick."

"I asked Jefferies if he knew when the accident took place but he was a little vague, and said that he believed that it was sometime around the turn of the century. Then I remembered him saying that his mother had seen the young woman swimming in the lake with a little girl, and enquired further if she might have mentioned who the little girl was. But this time he could offer no assistance. What he did remember, however, was that shortly after the young woman was killed, my late cousin's father also died, and there was gossip around the town that there was something odd about his demise. But again, Jefferies could offer no further information on the subject."

"I could see that Jefferies was still lost in thought as he stared into space, so I left him to ponder on the off chance that he would remember something else of use. I was glad that I did, because a few seconds later he remembered something else which might prove pertinent."

"I am sure that I am right in saying that your late cousin married too, sometime after his father passed away, but that his wife also died in her sleep just a few short months after they returned from honeymoon. And again, there was gossip about the way she died, but I never heard anything specific."

"My guest held up his hands as if to emphasise that he could be of no further assistance. I thanked him for his time, and assured him that he had indeed been a great deal of help to me. I was almost on the point of confiding in him the real reason behind my inquisitiveness, but I stopped myself. Jefferies seemed like a salt of the earth, but nonetheless, he was a virtual stranger to me, and I was far from ready to tell him about my visitations.

"The most positive information I had gleaned from him was that I now had some idea of who my visitor had once been. The fact that his mother had mentioned the girl singing in the fields was a direct clue as far as I was concerned. It would have been helpful to know more, and indeed, to find out who the little girl the woman had been swimming with was, but at least now I was better informed than I had been before his visit.

"As I was escorting Jefferies to the front door, having assured him once more that I would contact him should Jenifer and I decide to sell, he suddenly turned and snapped his fingers as if a thought had struck him from out of the blue."

"You know what you could do Mr Ward, as you're down here already - our local library has a stash of books written about our fair town, and I am sure that anything of note which occurred would be in one of them at the very least. Furthermore, now that I come to mention it, the librarian is about a hundred, and has worked there certainly since I was at school, so I am sure that she would know something of the manor's history or at least be able to point you in the right direction."

"Although Jefferies spoke with a certain amount of humour in his voice, he had made a very valid point, and one, if I am honest, I would not have considered had he not mentioned it. But the more I thought about it, the more sense it made. Where better than the local library to learn about local history? Although my knowledge of my distant family was somewhat poor, to say the least, the mere fact that they had owned the manor house and the land surrounding it must surely mean that once upon a time they must have been prominent members of the town, so it followed that their provenance must be documented.

"Having closed the front door after Jefferies, I turned to see Mrs Jarrow standing at the far end of the hallway, looking in my direction. I walked over to her and asked if anything was the matter, and she inhaled a deep breath before she spoke."

"Please forgive me if I'm speaking out of turn, sir, you know that is not usually my way, but I could not help but overhear part of your conversation with the gentleman when I was dusting earlier. Forgive me for asking, but have you been troubled since coming to the manor?"

"It was the oddest experience, but as she spoke to me I could not help but feel as if somehow, she already knew the answer. I certainly had not mentioned anything about my late-night visitations to anyone, so it was not as if she could have overheard me in conversation. So I wondered if perhaps my late cousin had also been the recipient of these unwanted disturbances, and perhaps he had mentioned them to her. If that were the case then it was quite understandable that Mrs Jarrow, feeling beholden to look after me during my stay, which she evidently was, might have picked up on the fact that when I had answered the door to her on the last two mornings it was obvious that I had suffered from a broken night's sleep.

"I do not know why but at that moment I was about to take her into my confidence, but then at the last second I changed my mind. She would doubtless have been an excellent listener, and I had no doubt whatsoever that she was completely trustworthy, and that if I specified to her that I did not want my confidentiality breached she would have probably taken my confession to the grave. Yet something still made me hesitate long enough to decide not to reveal my distress to her.

"So, when I shook my head and tried to act as if I had no idea what she might be alluding to, Mrs Jarrow politely apologised for having spoken out of turn and swiftly turned and went back to her chores. At that moment a part of me did feel guilty that I had not been honest with her, and, as I said, I was almost positive that somehow, she knew the truth anyway, regardless of my denial. I remember standing there for a good while arguing with myself on whether or not I should take her into my confidence. After all, having served my late relative for so many years there may well have been all kinds of relevant information that she was privy to, which she would be only too willing to share with me if I would ask for her candour.

"In the end I decided that, for the moment, I would keep my nightly disturbances to myself. I only hoped that Mrs Jarrow would not take umbrage at my decision. She and her husband were obviously good, honest, hard-working people, who deserved to be told the truth. But my indecisiveness convinced me that I was not yet ready to divulge it.

"I went back up to my bedroom and collected my jacket for my daily foray into town. I could not help but notice when I came back down and went into the kitchen to thank Mrs Jarrow again for her wonderful breakfast, that she acknowledged my thanks without turning to look at me. Something which she had never done before. By this point Jarrow had joined his wife for his tea, and I could tell from his uncomfortable demeanour that he too noticed the shift in his wife's deference towards me.

"I suppose that I could not blame her, so I pretended not to notice anything untoward myself and wished them both a pleasant day before leaving."

## TWELVE

"It was another beautiful autumn day, with the sun already at the height of its summit. I stood there in the fresh air and inhaled deeply before climbing into my car. I remember that I had a very positive outlook on my venture ahead. Jefferies had certainly planted a seed in my mind that brought with it great potential. I wound down my window to enjoy the cool rush of fresh country air as I drove into town.

"As I approached the Widow-Maker, I pondered how incredulous it now appeared to me that the local convention of treating that somewhat treacherous blind bend in the road to town was actually as a result of something that had occurred all those years ago, which actually involved members - all be they distant - of my family. I wondered how long after that terrible incident it was before the locals gave the area its present nickname. This was something which I hoped I might find out, along with some far more urgent and pertinent details, from the library.

"I managed to park close to where I had the day before, which was only a five-minute walk to the library. As soon as I reached the building I ran up the stone steps and almost crashed into the solid wooden doors which blocked the entrance. I pushed each door again in turn, but they were obviously locked. I turned to my right, and there on the notice-board in broad lettering was the library's opening times. I was completely crestfallen when I read the notice that the library was closed on Thursdays and Sundays. Of all the rotten luck.

"I just stood there for a moment, staring at the wooden barricade which separated me from, potentially, learning about my heritage, and the house I had now inherited. Feeling totally dejected I turned around and began to descend the steps back to street level, when I noticed an old lady standing on the pavement, staring up in my direction. At first I thought that she too must have been wishing to enter the library, not realising that it was closed.

"In spite of my disappointment I managed to conjure up a reasonable smile for the sake of politeness, one which she did not reciprocate. Instead, she continued to look directly at me with a look of some distain on her face. As I reached the last step I moved to one side to avoid bumping into her, and was just about to turn away when she called out to me and asked me in a very stern, almost disparaging, tone, why I was attempting to gain entry to the library when it was obviously closed.

"I smiled, in spite of the severity of her manner, and explained that I was a trifle over enthusiastic in my venture and that I had not seen the notice until it was too late. My attempt at justification did not seem to have any effect on her stony expression, and she replied in an equally curt manner that the library had always been closed on Thursdays, and she enquired as to why I might have supposed that this Thursday would be any different.

"Although I could feel my frustration starting to creep up on me I took a deep breath and tried to keep my voice as calm as possible, mainly out of respect for the lady's age. I introduced myself and enlightened her further to the fact that I was not from the town, and so, until that moment, had no idea of the opening times of the building. Furthermore, I stressed that my reason for being so enthusiastic in my attempt to gain entry was because I had inherited a property in the area, and was desperately trying to find out some information about the manor house, and hopefully, something about my distant ancestors who had lived there.

"At the sound of my mentioning the manor, the old lady suddenly appeared to prick up her ears. She asked me if I was referring to Denby Manor, and when I confirmed that I was, she suddenly seemed to grow more receptive to me. She informed me that she was a Miss Wilsby, the senior librarian, and that she could confirm that the library did indeed have in store a couple of books relating the great houses which were dotted around the county.

"I wondered if this new-found benevolence in her attitude towards me might stretch to her affording me entrance to her hallowed building under the circumstances, and, to be fair to her, she was almost apologetic at having to refuse my request. She explained that on Thursdays she was a volunteer for the local hospital, and spent the day visiting those too infirm to make it out themselves - which was where she was off to when she saw me attempting to gain entry to her library.

"I told her that I fully understood, and hoped that she would accept my apology for asking in the first place. However, I purposely did not try to hide the disappointment in my face, and, although it did not incite her to a change of heart, she did however offer me another option."

"I am sorry that I cannot be of any immediate assistance to you, Mr Ward. However, the library opens tomorrow morning at nine o'clock, but if you like, I am willing to meet you here at eight, so that I can assist you and give you my undivided attention for the first hour at least. How would that be?"

"I could tell from her tone that this offer was a one-off compromise, which she obviously did not make a habit of offering. Therefore, I decided that it was not worth pushing my luck any further, and accepted her kind offer with due gratitude. As we parted company I had a distinct feeling that the old librarian was watching me leave, and, sure enough, when I caught sight of her in the reflection of a nearby shop, she was indeed still standing where I had left her and looking in my direction.

"I put her attitude down to her age and the fact that small-town communities often bred such individuals, each with their own curious caprices. One thing was for sure; Jeffries' description of the librarian was spot on. I doubted her to be a century, but I would not have been at all surprised to discover that she was in her eighties. The fact that she was still working at the library I also put down to my small-town theory.

"As deflated as I was at not being able to visit the library that afternoon, I decided to make the best of my time so I visited the old churchyard which I had seen from the pub window the previous afternoon. As I approached the entrance to the quaint-looking church I noticed that there was a black hearse just pulling into the driveway, followed by several smaller black cars, each containing several mourners.

"I did not wish to appear disrespectful, so I waited back until the procession entered the church for the service. Once the doors had been closed, I made my way to the graveyard and started to read the inscriptions of the headstones. Most of them, judging by the dates etched into the stones, were from the previous century, although I did find several from around the time of the two world wars. Judging by the size of the available space left, I wondered how it was decided who would be buried there. Briers Market was by no means a large town, but by the look of things the deceased would be hard pushed to be able to guarantee their resting place in those grounds.

"As I turned a corner by the main church building I saw a gravedigger standing by an open plot, smoothing down some loose soil while doubtless waiting for the service to end so that he could complete his duty. He was a ruddy-faced individual of about fifty years of age. He was dressed in a thick check-coloured shirt which was tucked firmly inside his trousers which had thick red braces holding them up. The bottom of his trousers, I noticed, were tucked into his sturdy hiking boots, and he had a pipe lodged firmly in the corner of his mouth.

"I could tell that he had seen me so I waved a greeting, which he responded to, so I decided it might be worth asking him if he knew if my late cousin was buried there. As I approached him he stopped patting down the loose earth around the grave he had dug, and leaned on his shovel. I opened with some small talk about the weather, and how I bet he was glad that it was not raining today. He shrugged his response and grunted, removing his pipe from his mouth before replying to me. Apparently, he informed me, there was no consideration given to him and his co-workers when it came to funerals. Regardless of the weather they were still expected to do their job, without complaint, and often they did not even receive a gratuity from the organisers for their effort.

"I found it easy to sympathise with him. As I worked in a comfortable bank, indoors, naturally, I had often listened to the rain hammering down outside my branch and thanked my stars that I did not have to work outdoors in such inclement weather. I had the distinct impression that the old gravedigger appreciated my understanding, and he began to talk quite amicably for a couple of minutes, informing me about past experiences he had had there over the years. I had the distinct impression that the old boy did not often have anyone to share his stories with, so I listened and did my best to appear engrossed.

"Eventually, I managed to find a suitable gap in the conversation in which to introduce my enquiry. When I mentioned the name of my distant cousin the old man looked straight at me in a quizzical, almost unnerving, way. For a moment he did not reply, and simply removed his flat cap with one hand, and whilst still holding it, used the same hand to scratch his head. Next, he glanced at his wristwatch, and then towards the locked doors of the church before replacing his hat, and digging his shovel back into the ground."

"Come with me, lad."

"Before I had a chance to respond, he was off and walking towards the far end of the graveyard. I followed behind, hoping that he had heard my request, and was not just taking me on a merry jaunt as he believed me to be someone who appreciated a good tale about funerals. But then, as we walked, he began to talk, although without turning to face me."

"That were funny business that, with your cousin, an' all. There were plenty of talk about here concernin' how he died. People often listen to gossip an' start getting' all fired up for nothin', but I ain't one of them. Been around too long to get spooked by nonsense."

"I waited until he had finished speaking before I asked him to elucidate on the gossip he had heard concerning my cousin's demise. He did not answer right away, but waited until we had reached our destination in a small alcove behind a jutting wall."

"I heard that when 'e was found, your cousin's face was a mask of sheer terror, like 'e'd been scared to death. White as a sheet 'e was. Me mate what works at the funeral 'ome told me they couldn't get 'is eyes to stay closed. They 'ad to sew 'em shut in the end."

"He glanced back at me to see how I was taking the news, and doubtless he could tell immediately from my expression that I was none too enamoured by his tale. Even so he turned back to the plot in front of him, and pointed down."

"'ere's where we put 'im. 'e's with his own kind, now."

"Just at that moment, we both heard the sound of the main doors from the church opening. I watched the old gravedigger shuffle away as the congregation began to pour out of the church, led by the four stout pallbearers holding the coffin squarely on their broad shoulders. I saw him take up his position about twenty feet away from the open grave, doubtless so that he would not intrude on the mourners as they gathered around for the lowering of the coffin.

"I felt that I was far away enough from the grave site so as not to be seen as being discourteous if I stayed and examined the grave stones that the gravedigger had led me to. There were four in total, all clustered together in a relatively small plot, tucked away in one corner.

"The least unsoiled of the headstones, upon inspection, bore the name of my recently departed distant cousin, 'Spalding Reginald Hunt'. The inscription below his name was in what I presumed to be Latin, and unfortunately, as I had no Latin whatsoever, I could not make out what it said. Adjacent to the headstone was one which bore the name of 'Spencer Jethro Hunt, which again had some Latin verse beneath the name, and according to the inscription above he had passed away at the tender age of twenty-four.

"The stone on the other side of my late cousins belonged to a Phyllida Rosemary Hunt Nee Cotton, and from the English etchings it appeared that she was my late cousin's wife, who also died tragically young at the age of twenty-three. The final headstone stood behind the others and was by far the biggest and most ostentatious. It almost appeared as if it had been designed to allow the occupant of the grave to bare down over the others resting there, as if it were in some position of authority. For a moment it reminded me of my manager back at the bank, who clerks often complained had an annoying habit of appearing behind them and hovering over their shoulders while he inspected their work.

The last stone bore the name of one Artemis Cedric Hunt, and judging by the age at which he died, I presumed that he must have been my late cousin's father. I stood there for a moment, glancing from one headstone to the next. In the background I could hear the priest repeating the rites of burial and turned my head for a moment, just as the pallbearers were preparing to lower the coffin into its final resting place.

"I found myself making the sign of the cross, feeling that a simple act of respect was quite fitting at that moment. I turned back to the graves of my kin, and a thought suddenly struck me. Could my nightly visitor be my late cousin's wife, Phyllida Rosemary Hunt? I quickly rooted through my pockets until I found a pen and a piece of paper on which I could write down her name and dates of birth and death. It occurred to me that these details might come in handy the following morning when I was with Miss Wilsby in the library.

"I am not entirely sure if it was as a result of my being in the graveyard, or the fact that I had just witnessed another poor soul being laid to rest, but at that moment it dawned on me that the graves before me would probably never see another visitor after I left, and the thought brought on a profound sadness which I could not easily shake. I remembered passing a florist just outside the main gates of the church on my way in, so I walked along the side wall of the graveyard keeping as closely as I could to the railings so as not to disturb the mourners as they passed on their condolences before moving back to their cars.

"I purchased a bright bunch of mixed-coloured flowers and waited outside the gates as the cars carrying the attendees began to exit. I took the flowers back to the family plot and laid them in front of the lady's grave, as it seemed the most appropriate. I even found myself speaking to her out loud, asking her if she was indeed my late-night visitor, and telling her that whatever was troubling her I hoped that she would soon be able to find peace. I bowed my head and said a little prayer for the souls of all four of the deceased before me, and when I was finished, I turned back to see the old gravedigger heaving great shovelfuls of dirt into the hole where the coffin had just been placed. Naturally I did not want to disturb him during his labours, but there were still a couple of questions I wished to ask him before I left.

"The sun was starting to wane in the western sky, and I estimated that we would have little more than an hour's light for him to finish his task which was another reason that I felt loathed to disturb him. But, to my surprise, when he noticed that I was gazing in his direction, he stopped working and resumed his position of leaning against his shovel, almost as if he was waiting for me to approach him.

"Not wishing to allow the moment to pass, I strode over to him and apologised for stopping his work, but I assured him that I would only take a few moments of his time. As it was he seemed almost glad of an excuse to take a break. As I said he was not a young man, and the exertion of his task had left him dripping with perspiration and sucking in great gasps of air. As I neared the side of the grave I could not help myself, so I peered over and was shocked to discover that he had already filled the chasm half way up.

"I am sorry to be a nuisance', I explained, apologetically, 'but I was wondering about what you said about my late cousin looking terrified when he was found. I appreciate that you do not like to listen to gossip, but are you aware of any rumours circulating around the town about why he might have died with such a disturbing expression on his face?' The gravedigger removed his cap once more and wiped away the sweat from his forehead with the back of his hand. He looked at me as if he was contemplating how much to trust me with what he knew. Fortunately for me, he decided in my favour."

"You know the Jarrows I suspect; they kept 'ouse for your cousin. Well it was them that found him that morning, and don't get me wrong, they don't gossip neither, they're good folk, but I sometimes go for a drink in the pub where they work, and one-night Jarrow were sharing a couple of pints, an' 'e tells me about the mornin' they found him. I remember the look on Jarrow's face when 'e was describin' the state of your relative, with 'is skin pale white as milk, and 'is eyes open wide, starin' straight at yer, though without seein' owt, naturally."

"I did not know why I had not considered this before myself; of course, it made perfect sense that the Jarrows would have discovered my late cousin's body, and after the way Mrs Jarrow had spoken to me that morning, it was obvious to me now that if anyone in town knew anything pertinent that might explain my unwanted visitor, it would be them. After all they had worked for my cousin for years, and although I was quite sure from their demeanour that he probably spoke to them as servants and nothing more, there was still a possibility that he had confided in them one night when perhaps he had had a drop too much of port.

"I turned back to the old gravedigger who was waiting patiently beside me, and asked him if he was aware of any reason why my relative may have died with such a terrible expression on his face. At this I could tell that the man was still apprehensive to divulge too much, and I knew that our time was short as he could not afford to waste too much time with me with the light starting to fade. Growing desperate I shoved my hand in my pocket and pulled out all the change I had received from the florist; there was easily enough there to pay for three pints of beer, so I held out my hand with the money clenched in it towards him. He was obviously a man of some pride, and at first, he shook his head as if to refuse my offer. But I kept my hand out and insisted that I was merely being grateful for his kind assistance. Eventually he acquiesced, and quickly shoved the money into his trouser pocket without taking the time to check how much was there. I did wonder if perhaps he was afraid that the priest might see him take it, and, for whatever reason, he was not allowed to accept gratuities."

"You've gotta understand there are a lot of old woman in this town 'ho like nothin' better than to make up stories for the sake of it. Years ago, they would've bin 'anged as witches. Any'ow, some of say that there wus some kind o' curse on your cousin. An' old gypsy curse which had bin placed on the family from years back, an' that your cousin had lived with it for years, before he finally died."

"The old man looked about him as if he was suddenly afraid that our conversation might be overheard. Once he was assured that we were quite alone, he continued."

"Some of 'em say that it was the curse that done fer your cousin's wife, and his father before 'im. All I do know fer a fact is that no one other than the Jarrows were ever willin' to go there on a regular basis an' keep 'ouse fer the old man. Even some of our local tradesmen, big blokes an' all, not the type to be afraid of nothin', refused to go there fer work. The Jarrows often 'ad to arrange for out-of-towners to come in when somethin' needed doin' which Jarrow couldn't do iself."

"I took the opportunity to enquire further as to whether the old man had heard what form this alleged curse took. The old man shrugged his shoulders in a 'matter-of fact' manner and averted his gaze from me, as if to demonstrate that he had told me all he knew, and I was certainly grateful for his candour. But something told me that he did in fact know more and was possibly afraid of being ridiculed if he let on as to what it was. I decided on one more assault, then if he refused to divulge any more I would gracefully retire.

"I waited for a moment for him to turn back in my direction and attempted my most disarming smile. My neighbour, Mr Jefferies, I began, I'm sure that you must know him, he spoke to me only this morning concerning the same subject oddly enough. He seemed to think that the curse might have something to do with a young woman who used to live up at the manor. Apparently, she was killed over by that treacherous embankment not far from my house, which locals have named the Widow-Maker."

"The mention of Jefferies' name appeared to stir up courage in the old gravedigger. I surmised that it was because he felt that if a prominent member of the community like Jefferies was willing to talk about the matter, then nobody could accuse him of gossiping. I waited a moment, hoping that the pregnant pause would entice him to continue with what he obviously knew. Finally, my patience paid off."

"Well, it sounds as if Mr Jefferies 'as 'eard the same stories as me, so no one can't blame me for talkin' out of turn if a great man like 'im is willing to speak. Now again, what I'm tellin' yer I can't prove, so yer either believe it or not. Me personally, I'll have no truck with such things, but that's for me, you can make up yer own mind without my help. We all grew up 'earing about the young lass what got killed at the Widow-Maker, not that she's bin the only one over the years, but folks around 'ere say she might be the first. Well rumour 'as it she was some sort of gypsy, an' before she died, she put a curse on your cousin an' his father, an' since then, according to local gossip, her spirit haunted the old man, an' that's what finally killed 'im."

"I tried not to react too overtly at the sound of his words, but naturally I knew that what he was telling me was true. It made perfect sense that my unwanted visitor was merely a restless spirit continuing to visit the same location she always had done. Whatever the reason for her initial foray back into the land of the living, I would have hoped that now my distant cousin - who it appeared may have had something to do with her premature demise - had passed on himself, she might feel that she no longer had a reason to pay her nightly visits.

"I had heard it said that ghosts were often the spirits of the dead who, for whatever reason, did not feel ready to pass over. I wondered if the next time she came to me I might be able to convince her that her task was now complete, and that I had never done her any harm, nor wished any on her, so she no longer had a reason to keep reappearing. If that was all it would take to convince her to rest in peace, then I was more than willing to give it a go.

"Just to clarify the point I asked the old man if he knew anything about my cousin's late wife, whose grave was in amongst the others. From what he had already told me I presumed that she was not the gypsy girl whom he had mentioned, so presumably she was also not my spirit."

"Well, I can't say for sure as you can well understand, but folks do say that the gypsy girl's curse did for everyone livin' at the manor, your cousin, 'is wife and 'is old man. But as I say, there's no way of me provin' none of it."

"I could see the exhaustion etched into his features, and I was increasingly aware of the shadows across the graveyard growing longer by the second as well as the fact that he still had a fair amount of shovelling to do before his task was complete. But the fact that he had not mentioned the name on the last headstone did make me curious. I asked him if Spencer Jethro Hunt was also a victim of the gypsy's curse, and again he shrugged his shoulders in his matter-of-fact manner before relaying what little he knew."

"No one knows for sure, least no one is saying, but I seem to remember being told that 'e died afore the young gypsy lass, but as to whether it were a result of 'er curse, I can't say."

"I shook the old man's hand in gratitude. The information which he had given me was well worth the handful of shillings I had parted with. What's more, he did not come across as someone who would just embellish a story for the sake of someone to talk to. So, even if what he had told me turned out to have only a slight ring of truth to it, I still felt as if my time with him had been well spent."

## THIRTEEN

"I walked out of the churchyard and began to stroll along the high street. The wind was starting to pick up and some of the dead leaves from the church whipped up behind me, almost as if they were reaching out, willing me not to leave. I buttoned my coat to keep the warmth in and thought long and hard about what the old gravedigger had told me. It seemed somewhat implausible to me that merely a week ago I had such a negative opinion concerning fortune tellers and spirits and the like, and yet here I was, having experienced first-hand such ethereal phenomena, discussing the plausibility of gypsy curses with a complete stranger in the middle of a graveyard, no less. It many ways, the experience had been a humbling one. As someone who had discounted such events outright, I had certainly been brought down to earth with an almighty bump.

"I walked back past the library and wished that it was already the following morning. After what the old man had told me, Mrs Wilsby's assertion that there were papers and books housed in her inner sanctum which may allow me to piece the whole story together gave me a fresh enthusiasm to glean all I could before Jenifer came down. I had already made my mind up that I did not want my wife to spend so much as one single night in that house. Although she was a very level-headed person who would not shy away from whatever was happening at the manor, for my own peace of mind I would not feel safe with her in the place after dark, even if I was there with her.

"I checked the time on my watch. My heart lifted when I realised that Jenifer should be home from work. I made my way back to my usual stop-off for groceries and provisions and made a few random purchases so that I would have change for the phone box. Jenifer answered on the second ring. After all this talk of death, curses, ghosts and spirits, the sound of her sweet voice was like a river of calmness being poured all over me. Within seconds I had pushed to the back of my mind any thoughts about my unwanted visitor, and listened happily as she regaled me with the exciting tale of how well her shoot was going and the fact that they would definitely be able to wrap it all up by the following evening.

"I made a mental note right then to check the availability at the hotel I had stayed in on my first night in town. It was just as a failsafe, should Jenifer decide to travel down on the Saturday to see the manor - which I felt sure that she would. That way, if it grew too late for us to reasonably drive home, then at least we would have some where to stay for the night. In my mind I could almost imagine the argument that I would have with her about the feasibility of us spending the night at the manor, and, knowing how easy it was for her to wrap me around her little finger, I decided that I might have to play up the fact that Jefferies and Peterson had warned me that the foundations were not safe or something equally as likely. Even then, I knew that I must prepare myself for an argument.

"Yet again, we spoke until my money ran out, and when I finally replaced the handset on its cradle I felt a deep sorrow emanating from the pit of my stomach, reaching up through my heart and right into my mouth, to the extent that I could almost taste the misery. I was really missing Jenifer, and I knew that she felt the same. I decided at that moment that this was to be the last time we would ever spend so much time apart, regardless of the circumstances.

"On my way home I stopped off at the Wild Boar to check the availability of rooms for the following night, and was happy to discover that, being out of season, we were literally spoilt for choice. I made a provisional booking and decided to stay for a pint of ale to help fortify myself before the night ahead. My bravado from earlier when I had promised myself that I would challenge my late-night caller, if she came again, was beginning to ebb away, and I decided that some Dutch courage was just what the doctor ordered.

"By the time I left the hotel the wind had really begun to stir up with a vengeance, and there were even a few spots of rain starting to hit my windshield as I slid into my seat. I took my time driving back, partly because en route the rain really started to pelt it down, but also because the strength of the ale on an empty stomach began to make me feel a little woozy.

"I managed to make it back to the manor in one piece, taking extra care when I approached the steep bend of the Widow-Maker, due to the driving rain and wind. I heaved a huge sigh of relief as I pulled up outside the house and spent a few moments in the car gathering up my purchases before making a dash for the front door.

"Once inside, as expected there was a note from Mrs Jarrow informing me that she had baked a pie for their dinner, and that she had left me a slice in the oven. I hoped that any unintended slight she might have felt that morning due to my unwillingness to divulge the events of the previous two evenings was now passed and forgotten. While I thought of it I scribbled a quick note to her for the morning, as I knew that by the time she arrived I would already be at the library. I mentioned that I would miss her splendid breakfast very much, but that I had an important appointment to keep for which I could not be late.

"I switched on the lights in the main parlour and lit the pre-built fire. I took much comfort in the light and warmth from the flames and remained in the room for a time to absorb as much heat into my body as possible. Until that moment I had not realised just how cold I was from the night air and the rain.

"Having warmed myself sufficiently I went down to the kitchen to see what delights the good Mrs Jarrow had left for my dinner. I certainly was not disappointed. Not only had she left me a huge slice of steak and kidney pie, but she had also left me a helping of assorted vegetables to accompany it. I presumed that she and her husband must have dropped it off on their way to work that evening because the meal was still quite warm, and although I was tempted to heat it up I was so hungry that I just carried it up to the parlour and wolfed it down in front of the fire.

"I buttered a crusty roll which I had bought in town that afternoon, and used it to mop up the meaty gravy the meal had been swimming in. I probably ate too quickly but I was famished, and each morsel tasted like heaven on my tongue. Once I was finished, I took the dishes downstairs and uncorked a bottle of wine. I took the bottle and a glass back upstairs and settled back in front of the fire.

"By my second glass that evening I was struck by a sudden urge to work. It was true that having been in the house for three days now I had only made the smallest effort to sort through my late cousin's effects, and with the weekend almost upon me I decided that I would make a start that evening, and hopefully continue the following afternoon, after I had seen the librarian. I almost regretted having opened the wine prematurely as it, no doubt along with my earlier pint, was starting to make me feel drowsy.

"I decided to save the rest of a bottle as a treat for after my labour was complete, and took myself upstairs and splashed some cold water on my face to help wake me up. I went into the room adjacent to mine and opened the first trunk in the corner of the room. I appeared to be full of men's clothes. They were all neatly folded and apparently placed into the trunk with great care. I began taking them out one at a time. They were all made of good quality material, although they did appear to be rather old fashioned in their style. Some of them even appeared as if they might have been more suited to a gentleman from the turn of the century.

"There were several long coats and waistcoats amongst the selection, but definitely not of a style from recent times. I had the distinct impression that the clothes must all have been tailored, rather than just purchased off the peg at a local Burtons or John Collier. At the bottom of the first trunk, underneath the last item of clothing, I found a large leather pouch, bound together with straps. I undid the straps and found inside several papers and documents which seemed to be legal in nature.

"I scanned through the papers, but even those which were not in Latin I could barely decipher as they were written in a hand which was incredibly hard to make-out. The paper used for the most part had all succumbed to decay, and several of the papers almost crumbled in my hands when I tried to unfold them. I decided that it might be best to leave those for Peterson to go through, and I hoped that I had not destroyed anything pertinent in my haste.

"Once I had all the papers back in their holder, I secured the straps and began to replace the clothes as neatly as I had found them, back inside the trunk. The second trunk in the room, I discovered, was also full of men's clothes, roughly from the same period as those of the first one, and again, all neatly folded and placed inside with care. Once more I carefully took out each garment, one at a time, hoping that I might find something more interesting at the bottom. But this time, alas, there was nothing to pique my curiosity, so I replaced them once more and closed the lid.

"I moved from room to room in the same fashion, and each time I was disappointed to find that all the trunks contained were men's clothes of the same ilk as my original finds. Feeling somewhat deflated, I made my way up to the attic rooms where I seemed to remember seeing another trunk tucked away in a corner, on my first inspection of the house. When I found it, I was surprised to discover that it was locked. I tried to prise open the clasp at the front, but it refused to give to brute strength alone.

"I was intrigued by the fact that this particular trunk had been locked, when all the others were not. So, I went back downstairs to retrieve my keys to the house, hoping to find the correct one amongst the others on the bunch. Before taking them upstairs I went to the kitchen and found a stout knife, which I hoped might do the trick should I be unable to locate the key. I went back upstairs and began trying all the keys which looked as if they might fit the lock, and when none of them did I proceeded to use the knife.

"It took far more effort than I would have believed necessary, but eventually I managed to pop the lock and the catch came free. I lifted the lid and was immediately disappointed to discover more clothes, although these were quite obviously for a woman. I stared down at them, more than a little frustrated by the fact that someone had thought such a prize fit to be locked away.

"The one thing which did strike me as being a little odd was that whereas all the men's clothing in the other trunks had been neatly folded and placed in order, these appeared to have been merely chucked in in any old way, almost as if whoever was packing them cared little, or not at all, for the garments or their owner. As before I decided that it might be worth investigating the trunk, so I began removing each piece of clothing, taking the time to fold them before laying them next to me, as it seemed almost disrespectful not to. They were mainly dresses, again rather old-fashioned in style, though I must admit to not being much of an expert. There were also a couple of patterned shawls and scarves mixed in with everything else. As I reached the bottom of this trunk I saw what I believed was another packet of papers, loosely bound with ribbon.

"I took out the bundle, and upon touching it I realised it was not made of paper but some form of good-quality parchment, and I released the retaining bow before spreading it out on the floor. As I looked down at it, my heart turned cold. Staring up at me from the floor was the face of my nightly visitor.

"I scuttled back across the floor, as if by some magic she had the ability to reach out of the painting and grab hold of me. As I let go the parchment began to re-roll itself, having doubtless been in that position for some time. I waited from across the room for a moment, feeling completely unnerved by the unexpected experience. I waited until I could catch my breath, before moving back over to what was now an innocent-looking parchment tube lying on the floor.

"I steeled myself before unravelling it again. At least this time I knew what to expect, but even so the thought of staring into those eyes still gave me the shivers. This time, once it was unrolled, I placed the corners at the top under the trunk and used my bunch of keys to steady the bottom so that I could look at the painting in all its glory.

"Now that I had had a chance to calm myself down, I had to admit that the painting was beautifully done and the artist, whose name I could not make out at the bottom, clearly had a marvellous eye. The girl was standing in a meadow, surrounded by flowers, with white fluffy clouds drifting above her. Oddly enough she speared to be wearing the same floral-print dress I had seen her in, and her lovely, long, dark hair flowed down around her shoulders. She had a single yellow flower placed behind one ear, and her head was tilted ever so slightly to one side; almost as if she was trying to hear something in the distance.

"She was, without question, an incredibly attractive girl, and if it had not been for her unwanted visits to me I would have thought no more about her other than that. But the closer I stared at the painting, the more that I could tell, even from here, that her eyes seemed to carry a look of melancholy which was in complete contrast to the rest of her face.

"I stared at her painting for some considerable time before finally deciding to place it back in its trunk. Only this time I made sure that all the clothes went in first, so as not to crush the painting under their weight like they had before.

"I took myself back down to the main parlour with an odd, almost heavy feeling in my heart. Whoever that girl had been, gypsy or not, she had evidently cast a spell over me, to the extent that I believed that I could actually feel her pain, whatever the cause. I was now more convinced than ever that if she appeared to me later, as per her usual habit, that I would prostrate myself before her and assure her that I knew she was troubled, and doubtless had good reason to be, and then I would plead with her to allow her spirit to rest.

"I knew that my intentions were not completely selfless. Although I certainly did want the poor girl's spirit to find peace there was also the matter of her frequent spectral appearances, which naturally it was in my interest to help put a stop to. I sincerely hoped that my visit to the library the following morning would help to fill in some of the gaps regarding the story behind my sad visitor.

"The thought of morning suddenly reminded me that I needed to ensure that I would not be late, otherwise the formidable Miss Wilsby would doubtless refuse to assist me in my task. I was grateful to her for offering me the opportunity to visit the library before opening time, and I wondered if it was an offer which she had ever extended before. Although our first meeting had been somewhat brief, she certainly did not come across as the kind of person who was willing to break the rules very often.

"With all this in mind I went back up to my bedroom and lit the fire, so that the room would be more inviting when I retired. I had no intention of having a late night, although if my visitor decided to call then there would doubtless be a break in my sleep. I rummaged through my suitcase and found my old alarm clock at the bottom. I was relieved that I had remembered to pack it, and I set it for six-thirty the following morning. This would at least give me time for a bath and a cup of coffee before setting off.

"I went back downstairs and added some more wood to the dwindling fire. I tuned in my transistor to give myself some background music, and I turned off the main light in the front parlour to allow the flames to create the right atmosphere. I left one of the lights in the hallway on, just for some added comfort, and their light did not intrude on the yellow glow of my fire.

"I poured myself another glass of wine and sat back in the armchair in front of the fire to relax. I was not tired enough for sleep just yet, so I decided to give myself an hour or so of listening to music before heading back upstairs. As I sat there sipping my wine, I ran over the conversations I had had earlier that day with Jefferies and the old gravedigger. I had learned so much from the pair of them, but still I had huge gaps in the story. I considered making a list of potential questions that I could ask the librarian in the morning. Not that I expected her to be too forthcoming with her personal reflections! She did not come across as the sort of person who would give much credence to rumour and gossip. But perhaps if I had something more specific in mind, it might encourage her to add some weight to whatever we could find available amongst the library's archives.

"I had already made up my mind that I was going to enquire about the young gypsy girl, who was killed by the steep bank known as the Widow-Maker. Such a death was bound to have been recorded, and hopefully she would be able to uncover some record of it. Which in turn, I hoped, might lead to us discovering more about her and her relevance to the manor. From there, it was not inconceivable that we would eventually find a record of the reports of the deaths of the rest of my distant relatives who had lived there. This might explain if there was indeed any truth to the gravedigger's speculation that the young gypsy girl was somehow responsible for their deaths.

"I sat back in my chair and drained my glass, with every intention of rising and seeking out paper and a pen with which to start making a list of my thought processes. But before I managed to drag myself from the comforting warmth of my position, I drifted off to sleep."

## FOURTEEN

"Once more I was woken by the sound of hammering penetrating my slumber. I sat up with a start, convinced at first that it was only a dream. The fire was still burning, although the flames were barely visible. The radio station which I had been listening to was still on the air, but the programme had changed and in my half-asleep state I found the new music quite irritating, so I reached over and switched it off. I could see over my shoulder that the hall light was still burning, so at least the generator had not given up on me.

"I leaned forward with my elbows resting on my knees and rubbed the sleep from my eyes. I strained to see my watch in the dim light afforded me by the last of the burning embers and saw that it was a little after eleven o'clock. I waited in my chair, convinced that at any moment I would hear the banging again. It was far too much of a coincidence for it just to have been a dream, I decided, and any moment now I could expect another battering on the scullery door.

"When it eventually came, as I knew it would, the knocking sounded different in some way; closer, and not as urgent as it had been before. As I rose from my chair it occurred to me that the noise was actually coming from the front door, and not from the back of the house. At first, I was not sure if this was something I should rejoice at or not. As I stood there in the hallway I pondered the likelihood of my nightly visitor deciding to use the front of the house, and compared to the other option =that on this occasion I had a late-night visitor of a more natural kind.

"I made my way to the front door and pressed my ear against the wood. I could hear the sound of the rain pelting against the side of the house, but nothing else, so I decided to call out and demand that whoever was outside identify themselves."

"It's me sir, Jarrow, and my wife."

"I unlocked the door and sure enough, there stood the couple, soaking wet from the rain. I invited them both in, as it seemed to me that regardless for the reason behind their visit at such an hour, I could not very well leave them standing out on such a vicious night at the mercy of the elements. In truth, though I did not wish to admit it to myself at the time, I was really very glad of the company.

"Once they were inside I closed the door. I noticed that the wind had picked up quite considerably since I had arrived home, and now it felt as if it were blowing a full-scale gale. I invited the couple to remove their coats and to join me in the front parlour where at least there was still some warmth emanating from the fire. They both accepted my offer, and as we entered the parlour the moment Jarrow saw the dying embers he went straight over and replenished the wood and stirred up the kindling.

"I offered them both a glass of wine, but they politely refused. I offered Mrs Jarrow the option of taking my chair as it was the closest in proximity to the fire, but she declined and sat across from me on one of the hard-backed chairs at the table. Before I could offer him my chair, Jarrow moved over to his wife and stood behind her, almost making it appear as if, for some reason, he felt the need to protect her.

"I was certainly intrigued by the unusualness of their sudden appearance at my door, and as they had both refused a drink, I presumed that this was not a social call. I noticed that Mrs Jarrow was clutching in her hand a large leather bag, which seemed much sturdier than the usual handbag she always brought. In the dim light I could still see that she was holding onto it with such verve that the whites of her knuckles were showing. Jarrow, for his part, had placed one of his hands on his wife's shoulder, and he appeared to be squeezing it gently.

"It was obvious to me that the couple were extremely anxious about being there, so I tried to put them at their ease by thanking Mrs Jarrow for the splendid dinner she had left for me, which almost raised a smile from her. There followed a moment's silence as I waited for one of the couple to make an announcement as to why they were there, but as it became apparent that neither of them wished to offer such an explanation, I came straight out and asked them myself, making sure that I did not imply that their visit was anything but welcome."

"Well you see, sir, it's like this. My wife here is a very sensitive soul, and she has always felt that there was something queer about this house. She brought it up once with the master, but he shushed her away and told her not to be so daft, so she never broached the point with him again. But the fact of the matter is, sir, my wife feels very strongly that there is some kind of presence here which, in the absence of your late cousin, has attached itself to you, and to be honest she has started growing very concerned for you and your safety. So much so that she hasn't been able to think of anything else all day, and all evening at work she's been badgering me to come and see you, so, here we are."

"I listened carefully to what Jarrow was saying. It was obvious that his wife had not been fooled by my denial that morning. It was actually quite touching that they had felt so protective towards me that they felt that this twilight visit was necessary. What was also quite apparent from their shared mannerisms was the fact that they both felt quite nervous about being there and advancing their theory to me. I imagined that after my repudiation, Mrs Jarrow especially must have felt that I, just like my late cousin, did not wish to discuss the matter, and that I would probably not appreciate the pair of them sticking their noses in my affairs.

"But as it was, nothing could have been further from the truth. The fact was that I had been lying to myself by thinking that I could not divulge what had been happening to me over the past few nights to anyone else, because I myself could not accept it, was nonsense. The real truth was, now that I was finally willing to admit it to myself, that I was too ashamed and possibly even paranoid to mention it, for fear that I would be ridiculed or, at the very least, thought to be bonkers.

"I had even persuaded myself that I would not discuss the goings on at the manor with Jenifer, and we did not keep any secrets from each other. But if I could not even tell my wife, how was I to discuss the situation with two relative strangers? What I could not deny to myself, however, was the immense relief that washed over me at the sound of Jarrow's explanation that he and his wife already knew, or at the very least suspected, what was going on.

"I could feel myself physically shaking at the prospect of finally sharing my burden. I offered the couple some wine, which they politely refused once more, but I knew that I needed something so I poured myself a half-glass and knocked it back. The alcohol eased its way down my throat, warming me from the inside. I looked back up at the couple and noticed a pensive expression on Mrs Jarrow's face, which made me feel guilty for keeping them both in suspense.

"In that instant I made up my mind that I was going to tell them everything, in the hope that they might be able to shed some more light on my predicament. My hands were still shaking, so I replaced my glass on the floor to avoid an unnecessary accident. I cleared my throat, and tried my best to steady my nerves before speaking. It was hard to know where to begin, so I decided to come right out and start at the beginning with my first night in Denby Manor.

"As I relayed my tale, I was struck by the lack of response from either of the Jarrows. It was almost as if I was revealing the latest mortgage rates to them, rather than baring my soul. Neither seemed at all shocked by anything I said, and although I did not specify that I now believed the young girl to be a ghost, my inferences were clear enough for them to comprehend.

"Once I had finished my tale the pair of them looked at each other, and exchanged another of those unspoken acknowledgements they seemed to share. After which, it was Jarrow who spoke up once more."

"You see sir, my wife and I, well, we share a gift, so to speak. We don't make a show of it, in fact, very people we know are aware of it. We're not the kind of folk who like to draw attention to ourselves. You might say, we treat our special ability as more of an inconvenience than anything else, because the truth of the matter is, we've got it whether we want it or not."

"I was naturally curious to discover what this 'gift' was that Jarrow spoke about, and to my shame for a moment I began to believe that they were about to try and flimflam me with some well-rehearsed confidence trick. Whether or not they caught the suspicion in my eyes I do not know, but Mrs Jarrow decided that she needed to take over from her husband's explanation and move swiftly to the point."

"What Jarrow means is sir, there are times, when we put our mind to it, that my husband and I can contact those who have passed over. Especially if it happens to be a troubled soul who has not found peace, just yet, and as Jarrow explained, I have been feeling the presence of this soul who is bothering you, growing stronger with each passing day, since you arrived."

"Listening to the way Mrs Jarrow was almost imploring me allow them to take action on my behalf, I began to feel more confident that they were indeed in earnest. I must admit I was grateful for their proposed intervention on my behalf, and the more I considered the possibility of giving them my blessing, the less of a weight I felt my burden to be. However, as the sceptic in me was still questioning the efficacy of what they were proposing, I asked, tentatively, what it was exactly that they intended to do to assist me in my plight.

"Still with an air of caution, tinged with nervousness, Mrs Jarrow leaned forward in her chair, as if someone else was in the room besides us and might hear her proposal, and spoke just above a whisper."

"If you are in agreement, sir, Jarrow and I would like to conduct a séance, here, tonight, in this room."

"Her words were obviously well chosen, and carefully delivered. I was not sure exactly what I had expected her to say in response to my enquiry, but now that her words hung, awkwardly, in the air, the full realisation of their offer began to hit home. Naturally I had never actually partaken in a live séance before, and to be honest, had I not been in the position I was in at that moment, especially with Jenifer's arrival pending, I would probably have never considered the prospect. But the fact remained that my situation was anything but normal, and there was no way that I could close my eyes and pretend that it was.

"Given all that I still found myself having to ponder Mrs Jarrow's offer, carefully, before making my decision. I kept trying to fathom would others might do in my position. Jennifer, my sister, my parents. But, try as I might, I could not gauge how anyone else I knew might react to my situation. So, after a while, I conceded to the Jarrows' kind offer of assistance.

"I waited patiently while the couple set about removing their paraphernalia from the large bag Mrs Jarrow had brought in with her. The pair of them worked in silence, each skilled in their own adept part. Mrs Jarrow removed a large black cloth form her bag, and together they both covered the table with it. Next, Jarrow took out three silver candleholders, and placed them around the table to form an arc. Mrs Jarrow followed her husband and slotted a dark red candle in each holder, forcing each one down to ensure that it was properly planted. Once she was satisfied that it would hold fast, she lit the wick.

"Jarrow, meanwhile, removed a large cardboard frame from his wife's bag, and unfolded it before setting it on the table, within the semi-circle created by the candles. Next he took out a small red velvet cloth bag, and from it he removed what appeared to be a small glass without a stem. He polished the glass vigorously with the cloth bag he had just removed it from, and held it up so that he might study his handiwork in the light from the candles. He nodded, almost unperceptively, before placing it upside down in the middle of the board.

"Once they were finished, they both surveyed their handiwork before turning to each other to allow another silent signal of approval to pass between them. Mrs Jarrow took her seat, and Jarrow ushered me to take the seat to his wife's left while he turned out all the lights, leaving only the candle flame and fireplace to afford us illumination. He then took the seat to his wife's right, so that now we were all in position with a candle between each of us."

"One thing sir, if you will forgive my rudeness, I must insist that no matter what happens, you do not try and bring my wife around from her trance."

"I nodded my understanding, and looked down to make a quick study of the Ouija board. I had never seen such an instrument before, and other than the letters of the alphabet, and numbers, I could not make out what any of the other symbols might mean. I sat there for a moment while Mrs Jarrow seemed to be meditating, with her eyes closed and her hands laying, palms down, on the board, with her fingers spread out. Mr Jarrow kept his eyes open and fixed on his wife;

I presumed awaiting her acknowledgement that she was ready to begin.

"Without warning, Mrs Jarrow's eyelids suddenly shot open. I had been looking directly at her at the time, and the unexpectedness with which she opened her eyes made me almost jump back in my seat. Now her eyes seemed to stare at me without focus. It was an incredibly eerie sensation, having her look directly at me and through me at the same time, and yet I found it almost impossible to avert my gaze.

"After a moment, she extended her right hand and placed her index finger on the top of the glass. Jarrow looked at me and indicated for me to follow suit. I added my finger to the glass and Jarrow completed the pattern with his.

"We sat there in silence for several minutes. Unbelievably, throughout this process, Mrs Jarrow kept her eyes open, without blinking, staring straight ahead. Outside I could still hear the rain bucketing down, and from somewhere in the distance came the faint rumble of thunder.

"Now that we were all situated around the Ouija board, waiting for what I presumed was Mrs Jarrow's gift to take hold, I was beginning to wish that I had never agreed to this arrangement. Even though I was desperate to try and find out more about my unwelcome visitor, at that moment I was seriously thinking that dabbling with the occult was not really the best way to go about it.

"The problem now of course was how could I possible say that I had changed my mind after the Jarrows had gone through so much trouble? Bearing in mind they had only come over in the first place because Mrs Jarrow was afraid for my safety, not to mention sanity. I knew that I had let things go too far to pause before the end.

"At that moment Mrs Jarrow let forth an almighty gasp, as if she had been holding her breath for some time, and her head lolled backwards so that she was now looking up at the ceiling. I looked at Jarrow for some indication of what we should do but he sat quite still, calmly watching his wife's performance, without reaction. A low, almost guttural sound, began to emanate from the woman's mouth, and this continued for a good five minutes before she slowly lowered her head back down until her chin was resting on her chest.

"Once again, I glanced quickly over towards Jarrow, deciding to take my cue from him. But he was merely watching his wife without any obvious look of concern on his face. At that moment, as if it had been rehearsed in advance, there was an almighty rumble of thunder directly outside, which sounded as if it were about to break in through the window. At that precise moment, Mrs Jarrow began to speak."

"Are you there, child? Do not be afraid, we do not mean you any harm."

"We waited, but there was no response to her invitation. After a moment, Mrs Jarrow tried again."

"Will you come and speak to us? We only want to help you to find peace."

"Miraculously the glass beneath our fingers began to tremble, and move under its own steam. I watched in amazement as it began its voyage across the board. The glass stopped over the word 'No'. As Mrs Jarrow could not see the board with her head still bowed, Jarrow repeated the word for her benefit. We waited for the glass to move on, but it stayed put. Mrs Jarrow continued with her entreaty."

"Why will you not speak to us child? We may be able to help you."

"Once more I felt a slight trembling through the glass as it started to move once more. This time it began to spell out a word, letter by letter. Jarrow read out each letter in turn as the glass moved, and then repeated the word."

"A…F…R…A…I…D…Afraid!"

"You have nothing to fear from us, my child."

"Again, the glass moved."

"B…A…D…M…E…N…Bad men!"

"There are no bad men here anymore; please tell us why you were afraid of them?"

"T…H…E…Y…W…A…N…T…M…Y…B…A…B…Y…They want my baby!"

"No one here wants to take your baby away from you. Please tell us your name."

"For a couple of moments, the glass stayed still. In the end Mrs Jarrow repeated her question, keeping her voice calm and her tone gentle."

"Please tell us your name, my child, we mean you no harm."

"The glass began to move once more, but it appeared to do so more slowly than before. It was almost as if the 'guider' was unsure whether or not to divulge the requested information."

"A…M…Y…Amy."

"Amy, who is trying to take your baby?"

"B…A…D…M…E…N…Bad men!"

"Who are these bad men, Amy? There's no one here now."

"Once more the glass stayed still, although I for one could definitely feel a slight vibration under my finger as if it were about to move at any second. In the end, Mrs Jarrow decided to try and again to coax the information out."

"Please tell us who these bad men are, Amy? We only want to help you to find peace."

"The glass shifted again."

"F…A…T…H…E…R…A…N…D…B…R…O…T…H…E…R…Father and brother."

"I looked over to Jarrow, and we exchanged a concerned glance. Mrs Jarrow kept her head down throughout, so there was no way of acknowledging the expression on her face."

"Do you mean your father and brother, my child?"

"No…No."

"Whose then?"

"S…P…E…N…C…E…R…Spencer."

"The name immediately rang a bell with me. I remembered from my afternoon in the graveyard that one of the headstones in the family plot had belonged to a Spencer Jethro Hunt. Therefore, it followed that if the spirit of this young girl, Amy, was talking about that Spencer's father and brother, then she was almost certainly referring to my benefactor and his father.

## FIFTEEN

"There is no Spencer here my child, nor his father, or his brother. You have nothing to fear from them now."

"I presumed that the Jarrows would not be aware of the names of my kin, unless of course they had ventured to the graveyard at some time and read the names on the gravestones. As it was, the information the spirit had given married rather well with what the gravedigger had told me, so a clearer picture was starting to form in my mind.

"I considered sharing the information with the Jarrows, but I was sure that Mrs Jarrow for one would not be able to hear me as she was lost in her trance. Either way there were still several pieces of the puzzle missing as far as I was concerned, so I decided that it was best to just sit still and see what else I could glean from this girl Amy."

"Why are you still troubled my child? Why do you still visit this place?" "R…E…T…R…I…B…U…T…I…O…N…Retribution!"

"As the glass spelled out the letters, I could feel the tingle of icy fingers running down my back. With my late cousin in his grave, and I being his next of kin, I suddenly had a horrible feeling that the spirit of the dead girl was indicating that she wanted to take her revenge out on me!

"But I was blameless, I had never done her any harm, and if she was indeed the girl I thought that she was, well then, she must have died long before I was even born, so what possible reason did she have for coming after me?

"I guessed what Mrs Jarrow's next question was going to be, and I desperately wanted to reach across the table and implore her not to ask it. But I had heard that it was extremely dangerous to try and wake someone from a trance, so instead I bit my tongue and waited with a sinking feeling in my stomach."

"Retribution from whom, my child?"

"This time the glass moved immediately, as if the answer was a foregone conclusion and needed no time for thought."

"H…I…S…K…I…N…His kin!"

"As he read the words out loud, Jarrow must have realised what the implication was because he looked straight at me with a combination of fear and pity etched on his face. Whatever it was that my ancestors had done to the poor girl, it made sense to me that the fact that her spirit was still drawn to the manor meant that she was still unable to rest in peace after all these years, presumably because one of their ancestors still owned it. Had Jefferies been present at that moment, I think I would have accepted his first offer without question and happily made my grovelling apology to Jenifer for not letting her even set foot in the place before I decided to sell up.

"My mind began to race with all manner of strange, and mainly irrational, thoughts and notions. What had happened to the poor girl's child? Had my benefactor and his father somehow been involved in its death? Had they killed it themselves, or had the deed performed by someone on their payroll? Were the poor child's remains buried somewhere on the property?

"Outside the window we could hear the rain lashing against the glass, and it appeared to be growing heavier with every passing minute. Another crash of thunder roared, much closer this time than before. It appeared as if the night itself wanted to play some part in our proceedings. I had visions of lightening striking the side of the house and shattering the glass of the room's main window, which in turn would make it possible for us three inside to hear the sounds of the night as they penetrated our enclosure. Dogs howling, maniacal screaming, horses galloping across the fields outside with terror in their eyes and in their hearts, spurring them on, faster and faster.

"I knew that I needed to get a grip on myself and to curb my imagination. But somehow, I found myself lost in the moment and my sanity appeared to have abandoned me, unleashing my senses and allowing them to run wild with abandon. These thoughts were still cascading through my brain as Mrs Jarrow continued with her own investigation."

"All those who have wronged you are gone now, there is no need for you to seek revenge on anyone on this side. Why do you not take the rest that you deserve?"

"C...A...N...N...O...T...R...E...S...T...Cannot rest!"

"Why, my child?"

"M...U...S...T...H...A...V...E...R...E...V...E...N...G...E...Must have revenge!"

"Why must you take revenge against someone who has never done you any harm?"

"For a moment the glass remained still. I found myself holding my breath in anticipation of the next reply, almost willing the glass to move to offer me some form of reassurance that I would not have to suffer further torment. After a couple of minutes with no response, Mrs Jarrow pursued the matter on my behalf."

"You have nothing to gain by taking revenge on someone who has never done you any harm. All those who hurt you have moved over."

"I could feel the glass starting to tremble once more."

"N...O...M...U...S...T...H...A...V...E...R...E...V...E...N...G...E...F...O...R...M...Y...B...A...B...Y...No, must have revenge for my baby!"

"No-one on this side hurt your baby, if your baby has passed over then why can't you go and be with..."

"Before Mrs Jarrow managed to finish her statement, the glass began to move across the board so violently that it took a real effort for the three of us to keep contact with our fingers. The letters it hovered over appeared completely random and made no actual sense. Jarrow attempted to follow them a couple of times, but each time he realised that the glass was not spelling anything conclusive he stopped and tried to start again. Finally, the glass stopped over the word 'No'; as before, Jarrow repeated the word for the benefit of his wife."

"No!"

"But why, my child? If your baby has already passed over you do not need to concern yourself with those on this side anymore."

"M…U…S…T…T…A…K…E…R…E…V…E…N…G…E…W…A…N…T…B…A…B…Y…Must take revenge, want baby!"

"Without warning, the glass sprang off the board and hurled itself straight at me. I just managed to duck out of the way at the last second, and it sped past my head before hitting the wall behind me and shattering into a million fragments. The shock of the explosion appeared to cause a simultaneous reaction in Mrs Jarrow. She lifted her head and once again looked straight at me with eyes that could not see. Her stare unsettled me to such an extent that I found myself turning to Jarrow for moral support.

"Jarrow too, it appeared, had noticed his wife's sudden change in posture, and he reached across the table to hold her hand. For a moment all was still, and the only sound seemed to come from the driving rain outside and the crackling of the wood on the fire. I sat there for a moment, totally unsure how, or if, I should act. I could see Jarrow gently squeezing his wife's hand, but there was no evidence of any reciprocation coming from her. She merely sat there, staring at me with those vacant eyes of hers.

"From outside a sudden clap of thunder caused me to almost jump out of my seat. I was sorely tempted to dart across the room and switch on the lights to bring me some much-needed comfort, but once again I realised the potentially devastating affect my action may have on Mrs Jarrow so I stayed put.

"I tried, desperately, to tear my eyes away from those of Mrs Jarrow, but it felt almost as if the woman had me trapped in some kind of malevolent spell. Then I saw her lips start to move, as she began to sing the same song I had heard whenever the spirit of the young girl appeared. As the words began to pour from her lips, I could see that Jarrow was growing increasingly concerned for his wife. I had no way of knowing what kind of sequence their séances normally followed, never having witnessed one before. But Jarrow's unease did nothing to allay my own trepidation. Mrs Jarrow continued to sing, her voice almost cracking under the strain as she attempted to reach some of the higher notes.

"Then I saw her. The young girl who had plagued my night-time hours suddenly appeared behind the housekeeper, hovering behind her as if suspended by some form of unseen wire. Her face in the dim light held that same sad expression she always wore. For a moment, I was unable to tear my eyes away from her spectral form. Like Mrs Jarrow, she too was staring directly at me, those same soft, incredibly sad eyes, pleading with me to help her. Her head was once again tilted slightly to one side, like an animal straining to identify an unfamiliar sound. Her long, dark tresses framed her face perfectly, and spread down past her neck like a robe around her shoulders.

"The young girl's impassioned stare held me, transfixed. I felt completely powerless to resist. As Mrs Jarrow continued to sing, the suspended spirit of the girl behind her started to raise her arms. At first, I thought that she intended to wrap them around the housekeeper, in some kind of eerie embrace. But instead she held them out towards me, beckoning me to come to her, and, were it not for the fact that I was frozen to my seat in fear, I probably would have. Such was the spell the young girl seemed to have cast over me, I was almost oblivious to the fact that Jarrow was starting to ever so gently bring his wife out of her trance.

"With my focus still firmly fixed on the floating form of the young girl, I could hear Jarrow's voice beside me almost begging his wife to come around from her trance-like state. The level of concern in his voice was not lost on me, and I realised that especially after his earlier warning to me, that for him to be trying to rouse his wife while she was still under must mean that he feared for her very life.

"I had to do something! I had no idea what, but I could not just sit by and let anything happen to Mrs Jarrow after she had put herself in this position only to help me. I forced some feeling back into my limbs. While Jarrow concentrated on his wife, I knew somehow that her condition would not improve without my intervention. I steeled myself by taking several deep breaths and then I shot to my feet, the speed of my action toppling back my chair.

"Amy! I screamed, keeping my eyes fixed directly on the young girl. No! In that split second, the entire house seemed to come to life around us. A huge gust of wind tore through the room, blowing out the candles and leaving us with only the faint radiance from the fire to see by. The table before us uprooted itself and tumbled to the far corner of the room, taking the Ouija board and candlesticks with it.

"From upstairs I could hear the sound of doors opening and slamming shut under their own volition. Now there was no longer a table between them, Jarrow scraped his chair along the floor until he was directly beside his wife and threw his arms around her in a protective embrace.

"In the poor visibility afforded us by the firelight, the young girl's features appeared to distort until her face, seconds ago so beautiful, now resembled that of a hag, scowling down on me as if in anticipation of attack. I stood my ground although I could feel my legs turning to jelly, making me feel as if at any moment they would collapse beneath me. I tried desperately to tear my eyes away from the hideous visage which now hovered over the poor housekeeper and her husband, but I found it impossible.

"The hag-like form began to drift towards me, its arms still held out in front of it, and the closer it came the harder it was for me to try to flee. With the apparition barely a few feet in front of me, I could see its terrible visage in every detail. Her skin, once so soft and white, was now taut and leathery, as if it had been stretched to bursting around her skull. The eyes which had beckoned and pleaded with me were now two bulbous orbs of pure, hatred-filled white, with tiny specks in the middle where the eyeballs had once been. Her hair, which had been such a lustrous black only seconds before, was now matted and tangled as if she had been pulled backwards through a hedge.

"As the hag's talon-like claws reached out to touch my face, I mercifully managed to snap my eyes shut. At that moment I heard Mrs Jarrow let out a petrifying scream, which seemed to fill the entire room. Her cry seemed to last forever, although in truth it was probably no more than a couple of seconds, but I must confess that I kept my eyes shut tight until it was over."

## SIXTEEN

"When I opened my eyes, I saw Mrs Jarrow slumped against her husband. Her shoulders were shaking up and down and I could tell that she was sobbing uncontrollably. Jarrow himself seemed only slightly better off than his wife, and I had the impression that he was only holding back his own tears, which doubtless were result of his fear for his wife's safety, because he was concentrating on comforting her.

"Mercifully, the hag was gone! The rush of wind also seemed to have dispersed, and there was no more banging from doors being opened and slammed shut upstairs. Outside the window I could still hear the rain lashing the panes, and another crash of thunder signalled that the storm was not over yet.

"I left Jarrow to comfort his distraught wife for a minute and began to right the furniture that had been upset by the unwelcome rush of wind. Now that the séance was over it seemed to me unnecessary for us to be sitting in relative darkness, so I went over and switched on the overhead lights. In the comforting glow of the bulbs I managed to locate the Jarrows' Ouija board, and folded it and placed it back on the table.

"I desperately needed another drink, but first I went over to the Jarrows and placed my hand on the gardener's shoulder. He turned to me and I could see the tears welling in his eyes. His wife was still sobbing, although she sounded as if she was starting to catch her breath in between sobs. I asked Jarrow if I could fix him and his wife a drink to help calm them down. Jarrow nodded and informed me that my benefactor used to keep a couple of bottles of cognac in a sideboard in the back parlour, and that he and his wife would appreciate a glassful.

"I located the sideboard in question and sure enough discovered three bottles of cognac, so I took one and three tumblers back into the front parlour and poured each of us a stiff measure. Mrs Jarrow had virtually stopped crying by now, and she was blowing her nose in her husband's handkerchief. I passed both glasses to Jarrow and he gently coaxed his wife into taking one.

"It may sound a little odd, considering the circumstances, but I almost laughed out loud as I watched the housekeeper grab the glass from her husband and down the contents in one go. I presumed that it was because of the shock and the trauma that she had suffered during the séance, but what made it seem even odder was that once she had downed her glass Jarrow handed over his and she finished that off too.

"I immediately offered them both a refill and Jarrow accepted gratefully, but his wife shook her head in response. While I replenished Jarrow's glass, he manoeuvred the table I had righted earlier back into position so that we had somewhere to rest our glasses. I offered my cheers and took a large swig, straining slightly as the burning liquid seared my throat. I was not a big lover of spirits, but at the time I believed that my nerves would benefit from it.

"Mrs Jarrow was now drying her eyes and wiping her nose with the hankie, and she appeared to be fully back in control of herself. But when I asked her how she was feeling her expression immediately clouded over once more, and her whole body seemed to shake as she prepared to speak."

"You must leave this house at once! There is a wronged spirit that still seeks revenge, and it will not leave until it has exacted that revenge on the owner of this house; you!"

"The venomous way in which she delivered her announcement took both Jarrow and I by surprise and he reached over to try and calm his wife down, but much to his obvious surprise she slapped his hand away and slammed both of hers on the table whilst still looking directly at me."

"Listen to me, sir, I cannot emphasise enough the importance of you leaving this house now, tonight, before it is too late. Jarrow and I have a spare room; you can stay in that if you don't fancy driving into town in this weather to find a room."

"Jarrow turned around and nodded his agreement, and the thought of leaving the manor was definitely appealing. But I was not going to be driven out of my inheritance by a ghost. It had become a matter of principle to me. Admittedly I had already decided that Jenifer was not going to spend a single night in that property, but for myself I would be staying put, no matter how many disturbances my unwelcome guest caused me during the night.

"I thanked the Jarrows, sincerely, for their kind offer, but emphasised that I was not in the least bit concerned for my welfare and explained that the girl had already visited me each night since I had been there. When I mentioned her in detail, describing her sad eyes and pitiful demeanour, the couple both looked at me with the oddest expressions on their faces. After exchanging a glance between them, Jarrow looked back at me."

"Do you mean to say that you have actually witnessed the spirit that is making these threats?"

"I confirmed that I had, and what was more so had he this very night. For I could not be one hundred percent sure if Mrs Jarrow could see the ghost hovering behind her, but there was no way that Jarrow could have missed her. But when I ventured my opinion Jarrow looked completely bemused, and denied that he had seen anything.

"I could not believe my ears. Jarrow had no reason to lie, but he had been facing his wife whilst the young girl hovered over her, right throughout his wife's rendition of the song, and what was more he was right there when she transformed into the old hag and began floating over the table towards me, just before his wife let out that ear-piercing scream which appeared to have the desired effect in exorcising the spirit from the manor."

"Sir, I can assure you that I did not see any vision during the séance here tonight."

"I could not accept his supposition, and perhaps the cognac inside me was starting to work its magic, but I ran upstairs to the trunk I had tidied earlier and carefully retrieved the painting of the girl in the floral dress from the chest and brought it straight down to the waiting couple. I unfolded it on the table and laid it out before them. The pair studied the picture for quite a while, but neither seemed to recognise the girl in the paining as the one who had, only moments before, been hovering across the table at me."

"Are you telling me that while I was under you actually saw this apparition appear before you, in this room?"

"I confirmed with Mrs Jarrow that not only had I seen her, but that she was the same girl who had visited me in the past. I just could not get my head around the fact that Jarrow himself had not seen her when she had been hovering virtually in front of him, above which she had to float right by him to get to me. Was she just invisible to anyone who was not in her line of fire? That would certainly explain how neither of my guests seemed to have noticed her.

"I let the couple study the picture for as long as they needed, while I went down to the kitchen to fetch some more wine. I offered some to my guests, but they declined. I, on the other hand, needed something more familiar to wash away the taste of that cognac. I poured myself a large glass and I think that I must have quaffed it down too quickly, because it immediately made me feel giddy. I retook my seat at the table, and looked on as the couple continued to study the portrait.

"At one point, Mrs Jarrow placed her hand on the girl in the picture, and closed her eyes. I presumed that she was attempting some psychic connection, which I must confess I thought was extremely brave of her, considering what she had already been through. As it was Jarrow obviously shared my concern, because no sooner had his wife closed her eyes to concentrate then he shot his own hand forward and placed it firmly on top of hers, gripping it with his fingers as if to prise it off the portrait. Mrs Jarrow opened her eyes at once and stared at him. From my angle I could not see the look he gave her, but it was obviously enough for her to reconsider her action and she removed her hand without question.

"The three of us sat there in silence for several minutes. I think that we were all too shocked and too exhausted to speak. I, for one, could feel my eyelids starting to battle against the onset of sleep, and considering the Jarrows had been awake since before me, worked at the manor and then completed a shift at the pub before coming over to perform the séance, I felt sure that they too must be feeling about ready to drop.

"In the end I broke the silence by thanking them for their kindness, and especially for putting my welfare ahead of their own by attempting to banish my unwanted spirit. But as the hour was fast approaching midnight, I suggested that they retire to their cottage and we would see what the morning would bring. I took the opportunity to mention to Mrs Jarrow about my early morning appointment with the librarian in town, and emphasised how much I would miss her wonderful breakfast.

"To her credit, the lovely lady offered to come around early the next morning so that I could eat properly before I left for town. But I insisted that the pair of them enjoyed what I presumed must be a rare lie-in the next day, as a small token of my gratitude, as well as in consideration for the lateness of the hour. They both thanked me, profusely, and apologised, as if such an apology were necessary, for not achieving a more positive result from the séance. I assured them once more of my undying appreciation, and emphasised that I was fully aware that they had done everything in their power to assist me.

"I could sense that they were both still somewhat reluctant to leave, and I surmised that it must have something to do with them not wanting to leave me alone. But I knew that there was no more that they could do for me, and as tired as I was feeling I did not wish to appear rude, so I pretended that I had not seen the concern in their expression and shifted my chair back and stood up so that I could escort them to the front door. With some hesitation Jarrow packed away their belongings, and they followed me out into the hallway. When we reached the main door, I turned back to wish them both a pleasant night, and was taken somewhat aback when Mrs Jarrow practically launched herself at me, and grabbed hold of my sleeve with both hands."

"Please sir, I beg you to reconsider spending the night with Jarrow and me. This house does not want you here, and I fear that the longer you stay, the more you will be placed in danger!"

"I could see by the look on Jarrow's face that he too was taken by surprise by his wife's antics, and subsequently it took him a moment to react. He moved in closer and eased his wife away from me. She turned to him with the same pleading look she had just given me, and tried to urge him to assist her in convincing me to leave with them. As insistent as she was I could tell that Jarrow was more embarrassed by his wife's behaviour than he was interested in the message she tried to convey. It struck me that the Jarrows were obviously kindred spirits, and both extremely humble in their ways, neither wishing to force an opinion or an idea on someone else, which was possibly why Jarrow felt so uncomfortable with his wife stepping out of character at that moment.

"Although I was extremely grateful for Mrs Jarrow's concern for my welfare, I could still sympathise with Jarrow's unease. I placed my hand on the housekeeper's shoulder and assured her that I would be fine, even though she still looked none-too-convinced. As he ushered his wife out of the door, I gave Jarrow a friendly pat on the back to convey both my thanks and my understanding. I could not think of anything to say at that point which would not cause the gardener more embarrassment, so I left him to take his wife home.

"I watched them as they walked slowly along the gravel drive, until they turned at the main gate and disappeared out of sight behind the treeline. I felt guilty watching them huddle against the beating rain, and wished that I had had an umbrella to hand to offer them. Or, at least, invited them to stay until the rain subsided. But at least their cottage was only a short walk away, and with the protection that the trees lining the route would afford them I presumed that they would not end up being completely soaked.

"As I closed the door, as if on cue the overhead lights went out, plunging me in virtually total darkness. I let out a long sigh, cursing the bad timing. My initial thought was to just leave things as they were. After all I was just about to retire for the night, and I hoped that with all the alcohol I had consumed that I might be able to sleep through until the morning. Naturally, there was no guarantee that I would not receive another unwanted visitation during the twilight hours. But by the same token I was reasonably confident that having visited the manor during the séance, that the girl, Amy, might leave me alone, at least for the rest of the night.

"Then it dawned on me that, with my planned early start in the morning, if the generator stayed off all night there might not be any hot water in the morning for my bath, and I was adamant that I wanted to create a good impression with Miss Wilsby. After all I really needed her help with sifting through the library's archives to try to uncover some more information about my house and family, and even more importantly about this young girl, Amy.

"I ran upstairs to fetch my torch from my bedroom, and before I ventured outside I pulled on my overcoat which I had left hanging in the hallway. Turning up my collar I opened the front door once again, and checked my trouser pocket for the housekeys before venturing out into the rain. I stayed as close to the manor as possible as I made my way around the side of the house, shining my torch on the floor ahead of me, thereby minimising any chance of my tripping over. It only dawned on me when I had reached the halfway mark that it would have been far more sensible for me to exit via the scullery, rather than the front door. That would have saved me at least three-quarters of my journey around the manor, as the generator shed was only a short walk from the back of the house. But it was too late to bother with retracing my steps, so I continued on my way.

"Once I entered the shed, I dusted off my coat and used the beam from my torch to locate the starter switch for the generator. My first two attempts resulted in the machinery just coughing and spluttering without actually coming to life, and I remembered Jarrow explaining to me the first time he demonstrated the system for starting it up that it did not always take on the first couple of tries. Sure enough, on my fourth attempt the generator spluttered back to life.

"I locked the shed door behind me as I left. From this side of the house it was impossible to tell if the lights in the hallway had come back on, and again I kicked myself for not leaving via the scullery. That way I could have switched on the light in there before coming out, so that now I would be sure that the generator was working properly without having to trudge back around the manor. I shone my torch over the back of the house, and momentarily froze with terror when I saw the familiar silhouette of Amy staring down at me from one of the upstairs windows!

"I stayed put for a while, shielded from the rain by the overhanging ledge above the shed door. Amy did not move! In the sadly inadequate beam afforded me by my torch, it was impossible to see anything other than the faint outline of her form behind the window. But I knew that she was staring straight down at me, although it was impossible to see from where I was standing what kind of expression she had on her face. Even so, after the night's activities I fancied it was not a look of compassion or forgiveness.

"The rain was veering towards becoming torrential, and I could feel my overcoat growing heavier as the water absorbed into the material. So, in the end I left Amy to her lonely vigil, and made my way back around the manor to the front. Once inside I shook off my coat, and raced up the stairs to the room which housed the window from which I had just seen Amy peering down at me. But when I reached it, there was no sign of her!

"I walked over to the large pane and looked out, just to satisfy my curiosity that I was in fact in the right room. When I looked out and saw the generator shed below, I was in no doubt that I was standing exactly where she had been moments before. As I stood there, I felt a sudden cold shiver run through my body. In truth I could not be certain if it was as a result of my having just come in from outside, or from something more eerie and sinister. The feeling reminded me of the saying people often repeat about having someone walk over their grave. I shook off the sensation and went back downstairs to ensure that I had locked the front door, and to switch off the lights.

"When I finally climbed into bed, I was so exhausted from the day's events that I fell asleep the second my head hit the pillow."

## SEVENTEEN

"Amy did not allow me to sleep at all well that night. Each time I closed my eyes, no sooner would I drop off then I would be woken by the sound of doors slamming all around the house, or else she would sing her mournful little song right in my ear, but naturally when I opened my eyes she would not be there. When I did manage to catch forty winks she would invade my dreams, appearing as she had earlier that evening; not as the sweet, gentle, pretty, young girl, but instead as the evil hag-like creature, reaching out towards me as if she wished to rip my heart clean out of my chest.

"After being woken for the umpteenth time during the night, I turned onto my side and covered my exposed ear with a pillow in an effort to block out the sound of her constant racket. But, alas, it was to no avail. I could feel my eyes burning due to the lack of sleep. My entire body cried out for rest, but she refused to let up. At one point, out of desperation I sat up in bed and called to her, demanding to know what she wanted from me. But her only response was to send another gush of wind through the house, which, yet again, caused several of the inner doors to slam shut.

"At one point I heard the familiar sound of hammering on the scullery door. Try as I might to ignore it the endless pounding continued, growing progressively louder with each strike, until finally I gave up and threw back the covers to make my way downstairs. As I descended the stairs I caught myself shouting to Amy, informing her that I was not in the least bit impressed with her performance that night and that I refused to feel guilty, or take any responsibility, for any distress my distant relatives may have caused her.

"Once again, as I reached the scullery I could see Amy's lone figure in shadow, just outside the door. My patience had grown incredibly thin by that point, and once I had unlocked the door I wrenched it open to confront her. By now my entire body was aching from lack of sleep, and my temper was well and truly frayed. When I saw her standing on the doorstep, for the first time I was not taken in by her pitiful expression. Before she had a chance to beg for my help in her usual manner, I shouted at her; insisting that she tell me what I had to do to be rid of her once and for all. Instead of replying, she just opened her mouth and screamed. In an instant her cry appeared to be coming at me from all directions. The entire house appeared to vibrate from the severity of her pitch, and I was forced to shove my fingers in my ears and close my eyes.

"I backed away from the open door, cradling my head in my hands. The noise of Amy's screaming was so intense that I actually believed that my head might explode. There seemed to be no way of escaping the deafening row, but instinctively I continued to back away from the door. As I was not concentrating on where I was going I lost track of how many steps I had taken until it was too late. I caught my heel on the corner of the large table, and before I could help myself I had pitched backwards, and then everything went black.

"The next thing I remember was waking up from my concussed state, still splayed on the hard stone floor, with the scullery door flapping back and forth in the wind. I eased myself back to a standing position, using the same table that had been the cause of my downfall to prop myself up. I stood there for a moment just to check that I was still in one piece. I could tell from the dull ache across my shoulders that they must have borne the brunt of my fall.

"In the dim, shadowy light that the night sky afforded me I managed to locate my torch, but to my horror, when I depressed the button it did not come on. Sighing to myself I checked the glass covering the top, and discovered to my amazement that it was still intact. Next I undid the front cap and removed the large battery, so that I could get access to the contact spring to make sure that it had not bent or broken because of my fall. It appeared to be holding fast, so I slipped the battery back into its casing and re-fitted the lid. Holding my breath I tried the switch once again, and to my amazement it spluttered back to life.

"I staggered to the doorway and stood there for a while, letting the wind envelop me. The sharp coldness of the rushing air helped to bring me back around, and I stayed there until the driving rain became too intense for comfort. I stood back just far enough to allow myself to shut the door. Once it was bolted I leaned against it for support, and contemplated taking myself back up to bed. A quick glance at my watch told me that it was almost three o'clock, so it appeared that I must have been unconscious for at least an hour.

"I took heart in the fact that the house seemed to have settled down. There were no more banging doors to be heard, and once again I prayed that Amy had finished pestering me for the night. If that were the case I still had a chance of three or so hours sleep before my alarm would go off, which was more than I had enjoyed so far that night. I considered making myself a glass of hot milk to help me sleep, but decided that my time would be better spent just trying to fall asleep as soon as possible.

"I made my way out into the kitchen and from there to the hallway, using my torch to guide my way. I had been in too much of a hurry to vent my frustration at Amy to bother turning on any lights on my down to the scullery. I kept the torch beam directed at the floor in front of me as I manoeuvred my way across the hall and towards the bottom of the staircase. I held onto the bannister for support as I began to climb the stairs. By now my entire upper body had started throbbing, doubtless because of my fall. I was fairly sure that I had not packed any kind of painkiller in my luggage, so I knew that I would just have to make the best of it.

"Halfway up the staircase, I suddenly heard a creak on the landing above me. I lifted my torch, and in the hollow beam I saw Amy hovering in front of me at the top of the staircase. The shock of suddenly seeing her apparition before me caused me to drop my torch once more as I swung around to grasp the bannister with both hands to steady myself.

This time I could hear my poor torch bounce and bump its way down the solid wooden staircase, and I was in no two minds that it was gone for good when I heard it shatter on the hall floor below.

"As I watched Amy from the corner of my eye, she appeared to be drifting towards me. Through the dim, shadowy gloom, I could just make out her face. Those sweet, gentle features, that beseeching look she always wore, pleading with me for help. I discovered, at that moment, that I could not move my legs. It was almost as if she had cast a spell over me, forcing me to remain captive until she was close enough to inflict whatever torment she had in mind for me. I held onto the bannister post for dear life. My legs began to give way beneath my weight, and I felt myself crumple into a heap on the staircase.

"Eventually, I had to turn my face away from the approaching apparition. I closed my eyes and squeezed them shut in the vain hope that if I could not see her, then she would not be able to come near me. I knew that I was only fooling myself, but without any means of escape, I think that my brain was merely offering me false hope, which it had deemed better than no hope at all.

"With my eyes tightly shut, Amy obviously decided that she would assail my ears instead. She began to sing her song, so loudly that I felt as if my eardrums would burst. I released my grip on the bannister and shoved a finger in each ear to try and block out the sound. But the effort was futile. Her singing pervaded my defences, making it seem as if she was actually inside my head.

"I could feel myself growing dizzy once more. It reminded me of that feeling you often had as a child when, against your parent's command, you would spin around really fast and then abruptly stop, and the world around you would suddenly feel as if it was about to collapse in on you.

"I felt myself crouching down as low as I could on the stairs, almost as if I was attempting to turn myself into a human ball. The din inside my head was still raging, and I could almost feel Amy's presence within reaching distance. I had nowhere to go! My legs would not support my weight if I tried to stand up and flee. My only alternative now was to let my body roll down the stairs and hope that by the time I reached the bottom, Amy's spell over me would be vanquished, allowing me to make good my escape.

"But I knew that I was only fooling myself. I was frozen rigid to the spot, just like the proverbial sitting duck, merely waiting for the hunter to come and finish me off. At that moment I believe I would have actually welcomed the end, so that I could finally be put out of my misery. But Amy was toying with me, purposely prolonging my torment to enhance my suffering. She was not about to kill me. Instead, she wanted to drag out her little game to give it maximum effect.

"When I could finally take no more, I let out an almighty scream borne of anguish and despair. Somehow my cry appeared to shatter the spell, and within seconds Amy had stopped singing in my head, and I recaptured the feeling in my legs once more. I paused a moment before I dared open my eyes. For although I could no longer hear her, I was still afraid that her apparition might be hovering over me, just waiting to pounce the second I opened my eyes.

"When I finally conjured up the courage to look, I was relieved to discover that Amy was nowhere to be seen. I picked myself up and stood there for a moment longer, trying to focus my vision in the darkness which surrounded me. I knew that there would be no purpose served in trying to retrieve my torch, for I had heard it smash on the hardwood floor when it slipped from my grasp.

"For a moment I considered returning to the front parlour, re-lighting the fire for warmth, and turning on all the overhead lights downstairs for comfort, before spending what was left of the night curled up in the armchair. However, by that point I felt convinced, although not for the first time that night, that Amy had already thrown her entire arsenal at me, and that now, finally, she would leave me alone. With that in mind I crawled back up the stairs to bed, and again I fell asleep within seconds of my head hitting the pillow.

"Yet again, Amy refused to let me sleep in peace as she invaded my dreams; both as herself, and as the hag-Amy with that maniacal look on her face, as she drifted ever closer towards me. In one of my dreams I was actually married to Amy, and we were about to have a child. Our life was as idyllic as anyone could hope for, and we were both hopelessly in love. But, as she presented me with our new born child, I gazed up and was horrified by the sight of Jenifer coming at me through some ethereal mist. Her face, contorted into a mask of horror. Her beautiful blond hair, once so soft and golden, was now matted with what appeared to be dried blood. Her slender, well-manicured fingers were now deformed into talon-like claws, just like the hag-Amy, with long, cracked, blackened fingernails reaching out to pluck our child away from me, and carry it away to her lair to face its doom.

"I sat up in bed with a jolt, and as soon as I realised that it was nothing more than a hideous dream, I looked around the room and noticed the daylight outside my window. I grabbed my alarm clock and saw to my horror that it was seven forty-five. My alarm had either malfunctioned, or else I had slept through it. Either way, I had only fifteen minutes to reach the library. Otherwise I was sure that the good Miss Wilsby would withdraw her kind offer, unreservedly.

"There was no time for me to complete my morning ablutions, and, although I had, yet again, woken up in sheets drenched in my perspiration, I only had time to spray some deodorant under my arms and splash on some Old Spice before getting dressed.

"I ran out to my car with my overcoat under my arm, and immediately shivered as the early morning cold permeated my layers. There was a thick covering of frost on the lawn, and, to make matters worse, it had also taken hold on my windscreens. I spent several valuable minutes scraping the excess ice off the windows until I was satisfied that they were clear enough to see out of. Once behind the wheel, I turned the key in the ignition and the engine, at first, refused to turn over. I checked to make sure that the choke lever was fully extended, and then tried again.

"It took four attempts before the engine caught, so I sat there for a moment and revved the accelerator to make sure that the car would not cut out on me as I moved off. Finally I set off down the driveway towards the main gate. The first time I had to brake, the tyres slid underneath me, and I knew that I was going to have to take it easy, regardless of how late it made me. I reasoned that there was no point in rushing and risking an accident on the icy roads, and hoped that the old librarian would show some compassion under the circumstances.

"As I reached the Widow-Maker bend I slowed right down and honked my horn, but there was no response. Even so, I took the turning in second gear with my left foot hovering over the clutch, just in case I had to slam on the brakes. Fortunately, the way was clear, and I carried on as fast as I dared into town.

"As I approached the high street, I glanced at my watch and was disheartened to see that it was already a quarter past eight. Although I had in fact made reasonably good time, especially taking the road conditions into account, I still was not convinced that Miss Wilsby would appreciate my effort. As the library came into view I expected to see the stern figure of the librarian waiting for me with a look of utter distain on her face. But she was nowhere to be seen. For one horrible moment, I actually thought that when I had not arrived by the dot of eight that she had taken herself back home, or to a café for breakfast.

"I parked up outside the library and climbed out of my car. I stood there on the pavement for a moment, gazing up and down the street in the vain hope that the librarian herself might be late, and that she would be the one offering an apology. But after a while it became apparent that either she was not coming back, or indeed she was already inside the library.

"I walked up the steps of the large red-brick building and peered in through the glass pane in one of the doors. There was no sign of any movement from within, although from outside, my angle of reference did not allow me full disclosure, due to the inner doors which housed frosted glass as their upper panes. There was, however, a faint glimmer of light coming from behind them, which encouraged me to think that someone was inside. I stood there for a while, hoping that I might see a shadow of movement from inside. But, after a while with no such evidence, I decided to knock.

"Within a couple of seconds, the willowy frame of the librarian came into view. As she strode, purposefully, towards the door, I could tell immediately from the expression she wore that she was no best pleased with my tardiness, and I immediately prepared myself for a stern admonishment. Miss Wilsby did not disappoint!"

"Good morning Mr Ward, I had expected you almost twenty minutes ago."

"She glanced at the watch which hung from a chain attached to her outfit, as if to emphasise her displeasure."

"I am not accustomed to opening the library earlier than advertised, and on those rare occasions when I do concede to such a request, the very least I expect is for the individual who requested such a trespass to be punctual."

"She hit me with a stern glare, which I presumed she had practised over the years to use on those who returned their library books late. I apologised as profusely as I was able and tried to explain that my alarm clock had let me down, but I could tell from the way she stared at me that she was willing to accept no such defence. For one terrible moment as she stood there, blocking my way in, I was afraid that she was going to insist that I return at the scheduled opening time. But after an extremely tense moment she relented, and stood back to allow me to enter.

"Having locked the main door behind us, the librarian walked ahead of me, without instructing me to follow, through the inner doors, and into the main library. Her inner sanctum was exactly as I expected a small-town library to appear. The walls on three sides were crammed from top to bottom with dark-wooden shelving, each one heaving to the brim with books of various sizes, from extremely weighty tomes to more moderate paperbacks.

"Once inside Miss Wilsby made straight for a large wooden table in one corner, upon which, as I drew nearer, I could see housed three, large, hard-covered volumes. The first was entitled, 'How We Used to Live', the second, The Growth of Industry', and the third, 'Our Town'. I stood by the table adjacent to the librarian and waited for her to say something. Finally, she pointed to each work in turn as she offered a brief summary for my edification."

"These were the only editions which I could think of that might offer you any assistance with your enquiry, Mr Ward. This first one describes life during the Victorian era, and how life began to improve for those who lived in small communities such as ours, with regard to everything from working conditions to sanitation. The second deals primarily with the history of factories and shops, and it goes into some depth concerning which imports and exports helped to shape our current industry. The third actually names our fair town. But alas, it is a very small piece which concentrates on our dairy production at the turn of the century."

"Once she had finished her introductions she turned to look at me and waited in silence, presumably for my acknowledgement and appreciation for her efforts. But the truth was that I was sorely disappointed with the meagre offering laid before me. I knew that what I desperately sought would not be contained in the general information which those three volumes doubtless offered.

"I thanked her for her time and made a point to emphasise how much I appreciated her efforts, and the fact that she had gone to the trouble of opening the doors for me before the official time. But I was, understandably, unable to hide my frustration at the meagre fruits of her labours. Miss Wilsby quickly picked up on my melancholia."

"Is there something wrong, Mr Ward? If you don't mind me saying so you seem a little indifferent with my selection."

"I turned to the old lady with as much cheer as I could muster. I explained to her, once again, that although I was immensely grateful for all her hard work, the fact remained that I was hoping, after our conversation outside the previous day, that she might be able to find something more specific concerning the manor, and my ancestors. The librarian considered my proposal for a moment."

"I am afraid that I am unaware of any books written specifically about your ancestors, or the manor, Mr Ward. If such a tome existed, I am sure that we would house a copy here as this is the only library in town."

"I nodded slowly in agreement and offered to assist her in replacing the three large texts back on their allotted shelves. I could tell that the old librarian was somewhat miffed at my lack of enthusiasm for her efforts, but I felt that I had made my apologies quite adequately, and the fact was that she had not managed to find anything even remotely helpful with regards to my quest.

"Following her instructions, I replaced the three volumes back in their allotted homes. In my mind, I was attempting to fathom where else I could turn for information. Perhaps it was because I had put so much faith in the librarian that now, as a result of her fruitless search, I was feeling so dejected. The truth was that having gleaned so much over the past couple of days thanks to my neighbour Jefferies, the old gravedigger, and the Jarrows with their séance, I felt as if I was on the verge of learning the truth about what happened to my spirit - visitor all those years ago, and perhaps as a result, the reason her ghost insisted on haunting the manor, and more to the point, me.

"Once I had placed the weighty tomes back on their respective shelves I thanked Miss Wilsby for the last time, and turned to leave. The librarian followed me out, as she would have to unlock the main door to allow me to exit. I waited with a heavy heart for her to turn the key in the lock, feeling that as I left the building, I was also leaving my last chance to connect with the past and solve my dilemma. It was at that moment, just before she opened the door for me, that she spoke again. Her words were tinged with frustration and irritation, which she did not bother trying to hide."

## EIGHTEEN

"I am sorry, Mr Ward, that you feel your journey was a waste of time. Perhaps if you had been more specific in your request, I might have been able to assist you further in your endeavour."

"She held the door open for me to leave. As I was about to cross the threshold I stopped myself, and stared back at her. Her words had given me the merest jot of anticipation that the old woman might still be a valuable ally. My problem was that I did not feel comfortable revealing to her the events of the past few nights, and certainly, I had no desire to break the trust put in me by the Jarrows in revealing their assistance the previous evening. But, on the other hand, if I did not intend to let her into my confidence, how on earth could I expect her to be able to help me?

"We both stood there in silence, whilst I battled with myself as to whether or not to reveal all to Miss Wilsby. She could doubtless tell from my hesitation that I had more to reveal, and whether or not it was as a result of her curiosity or her sheer willingness to still afford me her help I do not know, but to her credit, she too stood there in silence allowing me to make up my mind in my own good time.

"Finally, I decided that a moment's candour could not possibly do any harm. After all, I did not have to go into every detail here and now to find out if the librarian could offer me any more help. I took a deep breath and turned back to her. Instead of mentioning last evening's events, or the hauntings, I explained to Miss Wilsby that I had learned of an incident which had apparently occurred near the Manor approximately seventy years earlier, and that what I really wanted was the chance to investigate the incident to discover for myself if any of my ancestors had been in any way involved.

"My supposition seemed to intrigue the old librarian, and she stood there for a moment, evidently lost in thought. After a moment, it appeared as if an idea had suddenly come to her. She turned back to me and, for the first time since our meeting, she had the tinge of a smile on her countenance."

"This incident which you speak of; would it have been something which might have warranted investigation at the time?"

"I asked her if she meant by the authorities and was immediately beginning to wish that I had re-worded my sentence in a less conspicuous manner."

"I meant more precisely by the local press. You see, we house all the old copies of the local newspaper here, going back to when they were no more than a monthly printed sheet. If the incident in question that you are referring to was reported in the paper, then I am quite sure that we will have a copy of it in the archives."

"I have to confess, at the sound of her suggestion I felt my heart skip a beat. It made perfect sense that, unless my family had somehow managed to cover it up, the death of Amy might well be a story with enough local interest to warrant publication. The old librarian could obviously see the excitement etched into my face, so she closed the main door and re-locked it without asking me whether I wished to stay or not."

"This time she signalled for me to follow her as she led me to a large wooden door, secreted behind some free-standing shelves, off to one side of the library. She unlocked the door with an old-fashioned wrought iron key, similar to the type which I possessed for the manor's front door. Once inside she switched on the overhead light, and led me down a steep flight of stone steps into a stone-built cellar. There was only one small window at the far end of the room, which appeared to be at street level, as all I could see from it were several pairs of feet passing back and forth.

"There were rows upon rows of metal shelving, which appeared to have been constructed with the purpose of housing the many leather-bound volumes which filled them to the point of overflowing. I estimated that it would easily have taken a month of Sundays to go through all of them, and I prayed that Miss Wilsby had some sort of filing system to make the task more palatable. We walked into the middle of the room before the old librarian stopped in her tracks, and held out her arms, as if she wished to introduce the ledgers to me by name."

"These marvellous old tomes were once housed in the local town hall. I am sad to say that they were kept in a very shoddy state, clearly not befitting their importance. I volunteered to keep them here when the town hall was bombed during the war. It was only meant to be as a temporary measure, you understand, but once the town hall was re-built no one ever question my returning them, so here they stayed. I personally badgered the council for the funding to have them re-bound, as they were in a shocking state, not to mention in no particular order, unlike now.

"It was obvious to me that the librarian was extremely proud of her achievement so I took the cue and complimented her on it, which had the desired effect of eliciting a look of appreciation from her."

"These are not my personal property, naturally; however, as I have put so much time and effort into their maintenance and restoration, I feel that it affords me the right to personally vet anyone who wishes to come down here. I'm sure that you understand, Mr Ward."

"I agreed wholeheartedly, for I believe not to have done so would have been foolhardy in the extreme. These volumes were obviously her most prized possessions, and as I very much wanted a chance to pour over them at my leisure, I felt that it was best to concur."

"Now then, Mr Ward, have you any idea in which year this incident you mentioned occurred?"

"I thought for a moment. Taking into account the age of my benefactor when he died, and the date of his father's death from the tombstone in the cemetery, plus the fact that I had an inkling from what the gravedigger told me about the sequence of events at the manor, I estimated that it was probably best to start my investigation at the beginning of the century and work my way through.

"I explained my process of thought to Miss Wilsby and was grateful that she still did not seem sufficiently inquisitive to ask me exactly what 'incident' I was referring to, and at that moment I began to question my reluctance to divulge that part of the story myself. After all, the main reason that I needed to check the details in the paper was because I wanted to find out if there was any reference to Amy and her accident. Therefore, it did not automatically follow that if I were to reveal to the librarian the details concerning my initial enquiry, that she could possibly surmise anything about my late-night ghostly encounters.

"But a part of me, for whatever reason, was still reluctant to expand on my search details to the librarian So, I decided, for the present, that I would persevere myself in the hope of success.

"Having mentioned my interest in the turn of the century, the old librarian had already begun sorting through her volumes, searching for the correct one. I started to feel a tinge of guilt that I had not confided in her the true aim of my task. While I was thinking of how best to broach the subject with her, I listened as she began to recite a potted history of her printed treasures."

"Our local paper started life, as I believe I explained earlier, as a monthly fact-sheet, back in the mid-seventeen hundred's. By the early eighteen hundred's it had grown somewhat in size, and was produced bi-monthly. Then, by the end of the last century, towards the period that you are interested in, it had grown into a weekly publication."

"At that moment she began to yank at one of the bound volumes which was lodged beneath three others of the same size. I moved over to lend my assistance, and I managed to lift the three top copies just enough to allow her to remove the one that she had been pulling at. Thanking me for my timely assistance, Miss Wilsby carried the leather-bound volume over to a small table which rested directly beneath the lone window."

"I think that this is what you are looking for, Mr Ward. Every copy for the year nineteen hundred. Four sections, with thirteen copies in each, making a grand total of fifty-two for the year, just as I explained."

"I stared down at the immaculately bound tome and considered the weight of my task; possibly having to wade through several such volumes until I came across the correct date that I was in search of, and then to discover if the story I was interested in actually existed. Even though I had no specific plans for the rest of the day, I did not relish the idea of spending it entirely in this gloomy cellar. Nonetheless I thanked Miss Wilsby for her patience, and sat down at the table to begin my task.

"The old librarian stayed by my side as I began to carefully turn the plastic-covered pages, showing what I believed was due diligence, so as not to risk damaging any of them. Once Miss Wilsby was, presumably, satisfied of my assiduousness, she turned and walked back towards the bottom of the staircase. Before she began to ascend she informed me that the library was about to open to the public, and as such, she would be needed upstairs. She took the opportunity to remind me once more of the time and effort she had personally put into restoring the pages I was now turning. Doubtless just in case I was still in any doubt of the wrath I would experience if I so much as crumpled one tiny edge of a single sheet!"

"Once I was alone, I systematically began to scan each page of each edition in turn. When I was finished with the first book, I returned it to the shelf from which I had watched the librarian remove it. Considering the weight of the volume, I was amazed that the old lady had managed to carry it without appearing to exert any real effort.

"Although each page of each volume had been carefully secured within a plastic film, some had already developed clear signs of aging before being encased, to the point that some of the pages were barely readable. I skimmed through headlines and stories concerning local fetes and shows, competitions and startling stories concerning new inventions and discoveries that were bound to change the lives of people, forever - most of which now seemed obscure and, in some cases, even obsolete.

"I finished with the volumes covering 1901 and 1902, and was about half-way through the 1903 version when the old librarian came back downstairs. I looked at my watch in the poor light and discovered to my amazement that I had already been down there for close to two hours. Until that moment I had not realised how much my shoulders and back ached from me being seated in such a scrunched-up position for so long, crouched over the fine, almost indecipherable, print of some of the text. I stretched up my arms and did my best to relieve the soreness.

"As Miss Wilsby approached my desk, she could obviously see from my expression that, as of yet, I had had no success in my task. I could not help but notice that as she passed the shelving racks the old librarian made a crafty scan of the volumes, doubtless to ensure that I had been replacing them in the proper manner. I rubbed the soreness from my eyes as she drew nearer."

"Are you prospering in your task, Mr Ward?"

"Her voice was cheerful enough and that I could tell that she was not making fun of me. I explained that I had had no luck thus far, but that I was willing to persevere, so long as she had no objection."

"None whatsoever, it's just a pity that you cannot elaborate a little further on the specifics of what you are looking for. My knowledge of these pages is really quite profound, you know. I made a point of studying them in my spare time. Local history has become a bit of a hobby of mine."

"I looked up to face the old librarian, and I believe that she could see in my face that her announcement was about to yield fruit. I decided at that moment that it would be in my interest to make a clean breast of things, as hiding it from the old woman now looked to be a futile waste of time. I inhaled a deep breath and did my best to explain to her that my reluctance in revealing the details of the story I was looking into had only been as a result of my not wanting to sound as if I was the victim of listening to local gossip.

"I am not one hundred per cent sure that she believed me, but even so, I continued to explain that the incident in question, which I was trying to verify, involved the death of a young gypsy girl, who may well have met her fate somewhere in the vicinity of my manor."

"To my surprise, Miss Wilsby did not appear to be at all perturbed by my latest revelation. In fact, I honestly believe that she was more bemused by my, hitherto, reluctance to confide in her. She returned to the shelving and removed a volume from a different stack and carried it over, placing it beside the one I had last withdrawn on the table. I glanced at the spine and saw that it was dated: 1904. Had I really been only one volume away from finding what I was after? I felt that it served me right if that were the case.

"The librarian adjusted her glasses and began to skim through the pages of the latest volume. After a short while she paused for a moment as if she were checking over some details, before she turned the book around so that I too might see what was written on the page.

"The headline was not particularly unusual for the time: 'Man Murdered in Highway Robbery'. But as I began to read, I realised the significance of why the librarian had considered the story appropriate to my quest."

'Witnesses are being sought after a young man was shot and killed, during a daring highway robbery, which took place on the Bodlin road, just outside of town, last Thursday.
Three men with their faces masked, held up a carriage belonging to local businessman, Artemis Hunt, of Denby Manor. Also on board at the time, were the owner's son, Spalding, and his nephew
Spencer. The robbers jumped the driver and demanded money from the three male passengers.
During their escape, one of the robbers turned and shot young Mr Spencer, killing him at the scene.
Mr Artemis has offered a substantial reward for anyone who offers information to the local constable, which results in the capture of these miscreants.'

"Beside my benefactor, whose name I naturally already knew, the other two names on the page immediately rang a bell with me, as I had only seen them the day before, etched upon the gravestones in the church yard. I recalled Amy's message from the séance the previous night, where she stated, through Mrs Jarrow, that it was Spencer's relatives that she was afraid of. Now I began to wonder of my benefactor and his father might be the relatives that she was alluding to.

"I turned back to the old librarian, who had been standing beside me, patiently waiting, while I read. I asked her if she was aware of any other articles which related specifically to the occupants of Denby Manor, regardless of their content. She paused for a while, as if lost in thought, and then she turned the tome back towards her and continued to turn the pages. She appeared to be scanning each page in turn, and I could feel myself starting to grow impatient with her laborious method. However, I reminded myself that without her kind assistance it could take me a lifetime to trawl through the rest of the volumes to find what I wanted. I sat there and watched her, without making a sound.

"The next time Miss Wilsby turned the book around for me to read, she pointed to a tiny article, barely more than a few lines long, which described the death of a young girl who had been knocked over by a carriage during a storm. There was nothing much I could glean from the article, other than the fact that it mentioned that the girl had been living at Denby Manor at the time of her death.

"As soon as I read the passage, I knew that it must be referring to Amy! The article did not mention her by name, but after the details revealed at the séance, it seemed too coincidental not to be the case. I read the meagre passage several times over in the hope of finding some clue as to the victim's identity which I might have missed, in my haste. But, the details were so sparse that I soon realised that there was nothing further I could glean from it.

"The article was tucked away in amongst those concerning the more mundane day-to-day local events, such as church affairs, and changes to some of the town shop's opening hours. Therefore, it struck me that the editor of the paper quite possibly did not feel that the article warranted any special attention. I surmised that a carriage accident at the turn of the century might have been an all too familiar occurrence, which would have explained the lack of enthusiasm for the story.

"Once she was sure that I had finished with the article, Miss Wilsby reclaimed the volume and continued to sift through the pages. This turn took even longer than her last, so again, I waited patiently in silence until she was ready to reveal to me her latest find. This turned out to be a half-page spread for the obituary of Artemis Hunt. I devoured the article like a scavenger at a feast. Unlike the piece on Amy, this editorial went into immense detail concerning the life of the great man, and his successes in business. It elaborated on the fact that he had known a fair amount of heartbreak during his life, with the death of his parents whilst he was still a boy, plus the loss of his younger sister several years previously from typhoid, which she had contracted whilst on a trip to India.

"The article continued to praise Artemis for the fact that he allowed a young second niece once removed, named Elisabeth, to stay at the manor during the school holidays while her parents both worked abroad. Furthermore, he apparently took his nephew, Spencer, under his wing after his mother had passed away, and he apparently brought him up as his own son, right up until he was tragically killed by robbers who attacked their carriage, earlier in the year. The article mentioned that he had been succeeded by his son, Spalding, who would now inherit the family business, along with Denby Manor.

"I was curious to note that although Artemis died at home in bed, it was still thought necessary for a full post-mortem to be carried out. However, the result of the procedure, I read further down the page, only confirmed what his doctor had diagnosed; that he had died from heart failure, the cause of which was unknown. The article went on to elaborate about his funeral, and how the entire town turned out to pay their respects."

# NINETEEN

"Once I had finished reading the obituary, I asked the librarian if she remembered any more stories in the paper that might be of benefit to me. This time she did not need to consider the question as she already appeared to know the answer."

"There's only one, from a couple of years later as I recall. It concerned the untimely death of your late benefactor's wife. Would you like me to find it for you?"

"I confirmed that I would be very grateful if she could, and asked if there was any way that I could make a copy of the article concerning Artemis' demise. Even though I had read it from cover to cover, I did not want to leave the library and think of something which came to me later, resulting in my having to come back and bother Miss Wilsby again."

"We do have a copier in my office, Mr Ward, but I am afraid that we charge a shilling per copy."

"I paid over the money, and offered my assistance in carrying the weighty volume back upstairs to her office. But she would have none of it, and instead instructed me to look for the book which covered 1907, which was the one she believed covered the last article I wished to look at.

"I watched the librarian climb the steps at the far end of the room, and, to be fair to her, she did not appear to stumble or struggle at all. She kept the large volume tucked securely under her arm, and walked up with a straight back and a firm step. I set about trying to locate the edition I wanted, and once I had found it, carried it back to the table.

"I carefully leafed through, scanning each page individually, until I came across an article entitled: 'Young wife passes away in sleep'. I began to read, and sure enough, the piece concerned a Phyllida Rosemary Hunt, Née Cotton, which was the name I remembered from the last gravestone in the cemetery. The report claimed that the deceased was indeed the wife of my late benefactor, and that she died peacefully in her sleep, whilst six weeks pregnant with her first child. The article was not particularly long, so I read this one twice also. There was certainly no hint of anything suspicious concerning the lady's death, so much so, that, according to the report, a post-mortem was not deemed necessary. The article mentioned that Spalding, the grieving widower, was not prepared to make a statement at the time, but simply wished to be left alone with his grief.

"Just as I finished my second read-through, the librarian started to make her way back down to the cellar. I waited until she arrived back at the table before I swung the book around and showed her the report, which she confirmed was the one that she had suggested that I look for. She handed me my photocopy, which was a tad grainy, but still readable, and before I could offer my assistance once more, she turned and replaced the weighty tome she had made my copy from back on its shelf. I closed my latest copy, and followed suit.

"Once we were back upstairs in the main building, I noticed several sets of eyes following the pair of us as Miss Wilsby led me back to the main desk. Evidently we had emerged from a doorway that most patrons had not been granted access to, and their curiosity was clearly getting the better of them. There were two young girls and a middle-aged man stationed behind the counter. One of the girls looked up and offered me a smile, which I returned. The other two looked engrossed in their work, so I turned my attention back to the old librarian and offered my hand in gratitude, which she accepted, graciously.

"Once outside, I realised at once how dull and overcast the day had grown. I looked at the time and saw that it was already close to lunch time, and, as I had missed breakfast, I could feel my stomach starting to rumble. I found a corner café with several free tables, and took a seat by the window so that I could watch the comings and goings of the passers-by while I ate.

"I ordered a bacon sandwich and a cup of coffee, and while I was waiting for my meal, I took out the photocopy Miss Wilsby had made for me, and began to read through it once more. The way the report had been compiled, it sounded as if Artemis Hunt was an incredibly benevolent individual, with a kind and generous nature. The fact that he had opted to adopt his orphaned nephew, and that he was willing to have his young niece come and stay during the school holidays, did not sound to me like the sort of person who deserved to be the recipient of the wrath of someone's ghost.

"However, judging by what was revealed at the séance, Amy was quite categorical in her assertion that it was 'Spencer's family' that she was afraid of, and that could only mean Artemis, and his son, Spalding. Furthermore, whenever Amy appeared at my scullery door, she persisted in her assertion that 'they' were trying to take her baby. But there was no mention in the paper about her ever having a baby to begin with.

"When my lunch arrived I carefully placed the paper with the article to one side, so that I did not spill anything on it whilst I was eating. Being as famished as I was, my sandwich tasted even more delicious than I had anticipated. I wolfed the first half down in a couple of bites, and had to force myself to chew it properly to avoid the risk of choking. Once I had finished it I took a sip of my coffee which was still a little too hot for me, so I put the cup back down and returned to my photocopy.

"The information in the article concerning Amy's accident had been so sparse that there was really nothing concrete in it for me to learn from. Likewise, the report of Spencer's shooting gave few details of any note, other than the fact that he had been shot by robbers whilst in the carriage with Artemis and Spalding. I did wonder why it was that only Spencer had been attacked that night, but again, due to the lack of information in the paper, there was no way for me to know for sure what had occurred.

"It was possible that Spencer may have put up some resistance, and received a bullet for his trouble. Or perhaps all three of them decided to fight back, but the other two surrendered once Spencer had been shot. Then of course, the other thing that was starting to bug me was that Amy had mentioned Spencer's family during the séance, which, in itself, seemed to me an odd way of speaking. Why had she not mentioned them by name? Presumably she knew them by name, as she was living in Artemis' house at the time!

"For that matter, why was she living at the manor? Spencer was a relative, as was the little girl, Elisabeth, so there was good reason for them to be there. But why Amy? Was she perhaps a servant? Maybe she was Artemis' mistress?

"I stared at the piece of paper, scanning over the words, although not actually reading them anymore. I felt as if somehow, I was missing something crucial. Somewhere amongst those words was the clue to the next part of my investigation. In truth, I was merely clutching at some very flimsy straws, and I knew full well that the library had been my last hope of finding out anything else about Amy and about the reason why she was haunting me.

"I still felt as if I had more questions than answers, and I was growing increasingly frustrated at the prospect of never being able to find out the truth. Perhaps the strangest part of all, to me anyway, was that if Amy's ghost had been haunting my late benefactor for all these years, how was it that he never felt the need to confide in anyone? I could not imagine what it must have been like, especially if, as I suspected, her nightly visits were as disruptive to his sleep, and his mental state, as they had been to mine. Above which I had only had to suffer her torment for a couple of nights, whereas he must have had to endure them for years!

"I wondered if his resolve was perhaps just that much firmer than mine, that he had in fact learned to take Amy's torments in his stride without allowing them to take such a toll on his sanity. Or had they had the opposite effect, and sent him mad? If so, how had he been able to hide his condition form everyone? The Jarrows for one, who had seen him every day for years! I considered that being the loyal servants that they appeared to be, would his insanity be something that they felt that they should not divulge?

"I folded the paper and placed it in my shirt pocket, before lifting my mug and draining the last of my coffee. I had left if for so long that now the remnants had gone cold. I considered ordering another one and turned around in my chair to see if I could catch the waitress's eye. When she looked up from another customer I waved to her and she nodded her understanding. When she was free she walked back over to me with a cheerful smile on her face.

"I was just about to ask for a refill, when I noticed her name badge pinned to her uniform; 'Lizzie'. For a moment I just sat there with my mouth half-open. She must have thought that I was some sort of village idiot for staring at her name badge so intently, without actually saying anything. After a second or two she asked me if everything was alright, and her words brought me back down to earth. I ordered my second coffee, automatically, without even realising I was uttering the words. As she walked away to fetch my order, I retrieved the folded paper from my pocket and began to read through it, line by line, for the umpteenth time.

"There was something in the report which had stuck in my mind, although at the time, I was none the wiser as to why. Then I found it again. The report mentioned a young distant niece staying at the manor at the time of Artemis' death. The article gave her name as 'Elisabeth'. I vaguely remembered Jefferies mentioning to me that when his parents had recited their story about seeing Amy swimming in the lake, she had been with a young girl who was staying at the manor.

"Was it possible that the young girl, Elisabeth, was in actual fact my father's older sister, Liz? I tried to do a rough calculation in my mind, and worked out that she would in fact have been about eight or nine when Artemis died, and, if that were so, then she might possibly be the only other living soul who knew anything about what really happened to Amy, and why she would be haunting the manor.

"I was in a sudden daze, my head spinning from the possibility that the answers to all my questions could actually be in reach. In that moment, I cursed myself for not having kept in touch with my aunt over the years. The only time my parents had taken us to meet her we were both so young, Jane was practically still a baby, and all I remembered about her was being warned by my mother as we arrived not to speak unless I was spoken to. I also recalled my aunt as not being a particularly affectionate or benevolent individual, and in my mind, I seemed to remember her shouting at me when I spilled my orange squash whilst reaching for a biscuit.

"Even so, that was a long time ago, and was only a child's perception, so I could not rely upon it now. However, now that I came to think of it, I remembered Jane being in tears when she called Aunt Liz to tell her about our parents' accident, and the old woman just slammed the phone down on her. Either way, regardless of her attitude towards me now, I had to at least try to see her, because once she was gone, so possibly was my only chance of finding out the truth.

"The waitress returned with my coffee, and I asked if might pay my bill straight away, and also if I could have some change for the telephone. She obliged my request with her usual smile, and when she came back with my change I left her a tip and stood up to leave. I heard her calling after me that I had not touched my second coffee, so I muttered something about being in a hurry as I closed the door behind me.

"Once I was out in the street I raced across the road to the telephone box, which typically, was occupied. I looked around for an alternative, but there was none in sight. I waited for the lady inside to finish her call, pacing back and forth like a tiger in a cage. It was only a five-minute wait, but to me at the time it seemed like an eternity. I almost managed to wrench the door out of the poor woman's hand as I held it open for her to leave.

"Once inside I called directory enquiries and gave them my aunt's name, stating that she lived somewhere in the Northumberland area. I was fairly sure that she had never married, so it was a relatively safe bet that she would still be under her maiden name of Ward. The operator came back with three possibilities and informed me that, according to their rules, she could only give me one number per call. I pleaded my case as best I could, managing somehow to keep the irritability out of my voice, and eventually she relented and allowed me access to all three numbers. Using the back of the photocopy I wrote down each of the numbers in turn, and thanked the operator for her understanding.

"The first number I dialled was picked up by a young lady, far too young to be my aunt, and once I confirmed with her that she was indeed the only Elisabeth Ward at that address I quickly explained the reason for my call so as not to worry her and rang off. My second attempt continued to ring unanswered for more than twenty rings, so I replaced the receiver and decided to give the third option a go. This time the phone was answered by, what sounded like, a middle-aged lady, who, when I made enquiries about my aunt, informed me that she no longer lived there, and that she had moved into an old people's home, about six months earlier.

"The lady on the phone was initially cautious about giving me any further information, but once I had convinced her that I was in earnest, she located the telephone number of my aunt's home and allowed me to have it. I thanked her, profusely, before ringing off. My call to the old people's home was answered by a very young-sounding girl, who confirmed for me that my aunt was indeed one of their residents, and that she was sure that she would be very grateful to see me as she had not had any visitors since arriving. I hastily scribbled down the home's address, which, typically, was on the other side of the county, and informed the young girl that I hoped to be there within a couple of hours before I put the phone down.

"On my way to my car, I realised that the sky had turned a heavy dull grey and was so overcast that it felt as if it were far later than it actually was. The wind, too, was bitter and biting, and I could see people on the street huddling into their coats to keep out the cold. I did not relish my journey, but I knew that I could not postpone it, as Jenifer would be arriving the next day and I wanted to be in full possession of the facts before she arrived, so that I could make a definitive decision about how to proceed concerning the manor."

## TWENTY

"I sat in my car, plotting the route to my aunt's care home. My estimation to the young girl of approximately two hours seemed a little hopeful as I traced the various 'A' and 'B' roads I would need to follow to reach my destination. I checked the time on the dashboard, and it was a little after one o'clock, so I started the engine and set off, just as it began to rain.

"The going was fairly slow, as I had feared that it would be using so many single-lane roads, but the map offered me little alternative other than to take a massive detour to reach the nearest motorway. Several times along the way I found myself stuck behind slow-moving vehicles which took up the entire road, making it impossible to pass them until they were ready to turn off.

"At one point in the journey, I realised that I had been concentrating so hard on where I was going and making sure that I did not miss a vital turning, that I had not noticed that I was about to run out of petrol. Fortunately for me, I came across a small independent filling station, tucked away, slightly off the beaten track where two 'B' roads converged. Outside the kiosk, in plastic buckets, they had a variety of flowers for sale, so I purchased a couple of bunches to take to my aunt as a sweetener. I filled the tank up so that I would not have to worry about running out again for the rest of my journey. The last thing I needed was to end up stuck out in the middle of nowhere in the middle of the night.

"The rain was growing heavier by the minute, and, although my windscreen wipers were on full power, they could barely cope with the downpour. Some of the roads I ended up on were virtually dirt-tracks, and with the rain they were well on their way to becoming quagmires, which would be impassable if the rain persisted with its present intensity.

"I finally pulled into the old people's home at a little after half-past three. I parked up as close to the entrance as possible, to save me getting drenched on my way in. I held my aunt's flowers above my head as I decided that some protection was better than none at all, and made a dash for the door.

"Once inside, I gave my name to the receptionist, and as it turned out she was the young lady I had spoken to on the phone earlier, so she was fully aware of my pending arrival."

"I informed your aunt that you were coming in to see her, she said that she was looking forward to seeing you."

"I could tell at once from the girl's facial expression that the second part of her statement was definitely a lie. Not that I was particularly surprised. After all, I had never attempted to contact my aunt before, or enquire as to her welfare, especially after what she did to poor Jane over the phone. Even so, there was a part of me that wished right then that I had made more of an effort. It was a completely selfish reason of course, because now I needed her to be forthcoming with the information concerning Amy, and if she decided not to help me there was not a thing I could do about it.

"The young girl left her post and escorted me to my aunt's room. As we made our way down the corridor I began to feel slightly queasy, which I put down to a combination of the clinical odour the place emanated, as well as the fact that I found myself growing more nervous about seeing my aunt the closer we came to her room. I noticed that most of the other rooms on route had their doors open, and as we passed I could not help but notice that they were empty.

"The girl must have seen me glancing inside some of them, and she explained that it was almost tea-time, so most of the residents would be in the communal dining room. When I enquired as to why my aunt was not in there also, the girl looked embarrassed, and she made a casual remark along the lines that my aunt preferred to dine alone. I accepted her answer, although once again I was not one hundred percent sure that she was telling me the absolute truth, but I respected her discretion.

"When we arrived at my aunt's room the door was shut, with a makeshift 'Do Not Disturb' sign dangling from the door number. The young girl cleared her throat, and knocked, gently, with the knuckle of her forefinger. At first, there was no reply and she glanced at me, looking slightly embarrassed, before she knocked again, slightly louder."

"Read the sign!"

"The voice that reached us from behind the wooden door, was coarse, and harsh in its tone. The girl glanced at me again, her cheeks reddening by the second. I could feel her embarrassment, and offered a friendly smile in sympathy."

"Miss Hunt, this is Verity from the front desk, I have your nephew out here with me. Remember I told you earlier that he was going to call?"

"The girl spoke through the door, rather than attempting to open it."

"And I told you then that you could inform him that I do not receive visitors, or are you too stupid to understand simple instructions?"

"Verity bit her bottom lip, as if she was not sure how to proceed, so I decided to put her out of her misery and take the initiative myself. I knocked on the door, and did not wait for a reply before informing my aunt that, as I was here now, could she not find it in her heart to spare me a couple of minutes. I mentioned that I very much needed her help, and had no one else to turn to, in the hope that my plea might spark her interest and convince her to see me.

"It seemed to do the trick, because within a couple of seconds she called out for us to come in. Her room was larger than I had imagined it would be. There was a single bed in one corner, with a nightstand which housed a rather ornate-looking lamp. A large wardrobe and chest-of-drawer's combination dominated one wall, and a bookcase, full to brimming over, took up most of the other. In front of the bookcase was a comfy, leather-bound armchair, with a standard lamp behind it. My aunt was sitting at a table by the bay window opposite the door, reading. She did not bother to put down her book as we entered, and acted as if she was unaware that we were there.

"Standing in the doorframe with Verity, I was not sure what to do next. The idea of striding over to her and kissing her on the cheek seemed a trifle too daunting considering her response to my arrival. Luckily poor Verity took the initiative, and announced my presence as if pretending that my aunt was not aware of it. When she mentioned the lovely flowers I had brought, my aunt still did not turn towards us, but instead she sniffed the air with a hint of distain, before announcing that she was not fond of flowers, and instructed Verity to take them away and put them in the communal playroom, where, according to her, all the old biddies sat and played board games and cards all afternoon.

"I handed the flowers to Verity, who took them, gratefully; doubtless she was glad of having a reason to leave the two of us alone. I watched her walking back down the corridor before I crossed the threshold and closed the door behind me. I continued to loiter for a while, hoping that my aunt would eventually invite me to join her at her table. But once I realised that such an invitation would not be forthcoming, I crossed the room under my own volition, and took the chair opposite her.

"We both sat there in silence for a few minutes, while I tried to sum up the courage to speak, let alone broach the subject of Amy. Finally, my aunt closed her book and removed her glasses, leaving them both on the table. She massaged the bridge of her nose between her middle and forefingers, and then she gave me a particularly stern-looking once over. Instinctively, I ran my fingers through my hair. I was conscious of my dishevelled state, considering my hasty exit having woken late that morning. But I did not think that my aunt would be interested in hearing my excuses, so I merely smiled, and attempted to look suitably admonished.

"And to what do I owe this unexpected pleasure?"

"My aunt's words were sincere, but the sentiment behind them reeked of sarcasm. Even so, I was not about to protest, as I needed her company much more than she needed, or wanted, mine. I began by asking her how she was, and whether or not she was happy, in her new environment. My use of the word 'happy' struck a dire chord, and I regretted it almost immediately. My aunt spoke at length about the incompetence of the staff where she was living, and the fact that they seemed incapable of understanding the simplest of instructions.

"I stupidly countered that Verity had seemed very nice and friendly, which was met with an immediate scowl of disapproval. I decided that under the circumstances that it was best to just let her unload her loathing and scathing, in the hope that once it was all off her chest, she might be willing to acquiesce to my request for information. Finally, when there was a lull in the conversation, I decided to chance my arm, and I enquired as to whether or not she had been informed about my benefactor Spalding's demise.

"Upon my revelation, the look she hit me with, proved to me that she had not, before this moment, been aware of the fact. For a minute, she studied me as if I were a page of a book of cryptic text that she was trying to decipher. Although the uneasiness of the silence was unbearable, I knew better than to interrupt her train of thought. Eventually, she slumped back in her chair as if she had suddenly had a breakthrough in her thought process."

"So, I take it that you've inherited Denby Manor!"

"She did not express her thought as a question, but more a statement of fact. I believe that in that moment, even if I had not inherited the manor, I would have admitted that I had, such was the severity of her penetrating stare. When I nodded my response, an odd smile almost creased the sides of her mouth. My shock at the bluntness of her next statement left me reeling, to the point of dizziness."

"Has she been visiting you at night?"

"I did not need to confirm with her exactly who she was referring to. We both knew, and in that moment, I could tell that she was feeling very pleased with herself, as she realised the true reason for my visit. I allowed her ample time to enjoy her little victory before I dared speak again. As it happened, before either of us uttered another word, there was a knock at the door, and, when it opened, another young girl brought in a tray of tea and biscuits on a trolley."

"The girl smiled at me, but before she had a chance to introduce herself, my aunt bellowed at her that she did not want any tea, and that if she did, she would call for it." The poor girl looked so embarrassed that I could feel my cheeks reddening on her behalf. She looked over at me, obviously too afraid to speak after my aunt's outburst, and indicated towards the tray, as if trying to enquire if I might like something. In truth I was gasping for a cup after my long drive, but under the circumstances I shook my head and smiled back at her, which she sensibly took as her cue to leave.

"Once the girl had closed the door behind her, I decided that now the subject was out in the open, so to speak, I needed to take full advantage of the situation, so I asked my aunt straight out if she would mind filling me in on the details concerning Amy, and why she was haunting me."

"So, you know her name already, that's very clever of you. How did you find out?"

"I explained about my visit to the library, and the articles the librarian had shown me. My aunt actually appeared as if she was impressed with my diligence, and I felt as if I had finally made some headway with her. I only hoped that this new-found admiration she felt for me might actually inspire her to tell me what I so desperately needed to know."

"She used to haunt old Spalding, you know. Not that he didn't deserve it, the weasel. I am amazed that he lived as long as he did without going completely insane. Or perhaps he did, towards the end. I hadn't seen him for years, and he looked much older than his years the last time I laid eyes on him."

"I leaned forward on the table, just enough to give the impression that I would be willing to listen to every word she had to say. Part of me was conscious of not wanting to annoy her now that she finally seemed willing to open up to me. But, at the same time, there was so much that I wanted to know, I believed that it would be more beneficial for me to ask her some direct questions.

"I made a mental note not to let my impatience show, as I realised that this could well be my one and only chance of finding the answers I sought. I spoke as softly and as gently as I could, trying desperately to keep the impetuosity out of my voice. I asked if she could explain to me what had gone on at Denby Manor during that summer, and specifically, the circumstances surrounding Amy's death. She sighed deeply, almost as if she could not be bothered. But, underneath her reluctant stance, I saw a glimpse of self-satisfaction, which led me to believe that she would actually take great satisfaction in divulging all that she knew.

"I waited, with baited breath, for her to begin her story."

"When I was born, your grandparents were both medical officers in the military. As a result, they were often posted abroad at short notice, and the thought of dragging a child around with them must have seemed impractical. Therefore, I was often left in the care of nannies, tutors and any distant relative they could convince to put a roof over my head and food in my belly. These duties of theirs continued well into my early teens, and it just happened that, at the time in question which you are concerned with, I was foisted on my distant uncle, Artemis Hunt, at Denby Manor.

"Artemis was not a kind soul by any stretch of the imagination, but he took me in because my parents were willing to pay him an allowance, and money was the one thing that Artemis loved, more than life itself.

"I was shocked, especially having read the obituary report in the paper, which had made Artemis sound like a veritable salt of the earth. When I mentioned this to my aunt, for the first time since our meeting she threw back her head and laughed, with what sounded like genuine gusto."

"Oh, for goodness sake, Jonathan, don't be so naïve. Spalding paid off the journalist to write that story. Artemis was nothing more than a nasty, mean-spirited, wicked, money-grabbing individual who cared about no one else but himself, and his precious business."

"It was obvious to me now that there was certainly no love lost between my aunt and Artemis Hunt, and there was something in the conviction of her tone that made me believe every word she was saying. Therefore, I knew now that I could virtually discount the article from the paper, and the only way that I was ever going to get to the truth, was to hear what she had to say.

"Suddenly, it was not enough just to know about Amy's death, I wanted to know the entire story about everybody who was living at Denby Manor at that time, and what the circumstances were that led to the tragedy. I decided to lay all my cards on the table and rely on my aunt's compassion and understanding to reveal to me all that she knew.

"I explained to her about Jenifer arriving the following day, and her enthusiasm about seeing the manor for the first time, plus my reservations about Amy, and if my aunt thought that it was safe enough for me to let Jenifer inside the place. My aunt leaned forward with a severe look of reprimand in her eyes."

"You listen to me now Jonathan, you'd be a fool to allow your wife within a mile of that accursed house. If you've got any sense whatsoever, you'll call her and tell her to stay in London."

"Her words certainly struck home. I had been thinking along those same lines, especially as the hauntings appeared to be growing in severity with each passing night. I begged her to tell me everything she knew, from start to finish, and I think that she finally recognised the conviction in my tone, as, after a couple of seconds, she let out a deep breath and nodded, slowly."

"That damn house was built by Artemis and his then business partner, a chap called Harrington. Apparently, the idea was to build somewhere large enough to house both their families, as well as to run the business from. It seems an odd idea to me, but I'm sure that to them it all made sense. Anyway, the story I was told was that when Artemis' parents died abroad, he always thought that they would leave him in sole charge of the family business and finances, as he was the eldest. He had a younger sister, Irma, who I believe was in her teens at the time. But, as it happened, everything was bequeathed to be split evenly between the two of them.

"Artemis was not happy, naturally, but there it was, so he had to include Irma in all his business transactions, although I believe she had no real interest in the business, and usually went along with whatever he said. Artemis and Harrington had made a provision between themselves, that if either died without issue, the other would inherit their share of the business, with an annuity being paid to the deceased partner's spouse, if one existed. As it turned out Harrington died young, and as he had not married his share of the business went to Artemis, leaving him with a majority share over Irma. Not that she particularly cared either way, as I said, the business meant very little to her.

"Irma never married, but she did bear a child, Spencer, as a result of a fling she had with a visiting business associate, who had come over from America to discuss some sort of export deal with Artemis. Poor Irma believed that he was in love with her, but the minute she discovered that she was pregnant he left on the first ship available. Or so it seemed.

Subsequently she found out that Artemis had paid the man to go, as a way of putting a stop to there being any possibility of a permanent relationship forming. You see, Artemis' biggest fear was that Irma would marry, which, in those days, meant that he business interests would automatically pass to her husband, and the last thing that Artemis wanted was someone with business savvy taking an interest in his shenanigans.

"Anyhow, rumour had it that this American was known to the police for his own shady dealings, so Artemis threatened to expose him if he tried to contact Irma again. When poor Irma discovered the truth, she packed her bags and left for America to find the man, who she believed was the love of her life. She left Spencer in the care of a local couple, as she, justifiably, did not trust Artemis, and she sailed away, never to be seen again.

"Word reached Artemis several weeks later that she had contracted food poisoning during the crossing, and died as a result before the ship even made it to port. Artemis arranged for her to be buried in America, doubtless because it was a cheaper option than having her brought home. According to the reports at the time, Artemis was all for sending young Spencer to an orphanage. But, when Irma's solicitor contacted him to tell him that she had left her share of the business to Spencer and made him his nephew's guardian until he was twenty-five, Artemis had no option but to keep young Spencer under his wing.

"Over time, Artemis married some foreign girl he had met on a business trip, I can't remember where, but she died giving birth to Spalding. Her parents arranged to have her remains taken back to their country for burial. I don't know if Artemis held out any objection at the time, but that was an end to it. Spalding was looked after by the same nanny Artemis had hired to look after Spencer, although by now Spencer was almost six years old, so he did not need as much supervision as a newborn.

"Once he was old enough, Artemis packed Spencer off to boarding school, and did the same with Spalding when he reached the same age. Spencer and Spalding were quite close, despite the difference in their ages, and Spencer would do his best to protect his younger relative, treating him more like a little brother than merely his cousin. During the holidays they were left mainly to their own devices, as Artemis was always too busy to bother himself with such trivial matters. The two boys were kindred spirits, as Spencer had only briefly experienced the warmth and affection of a mother's love, and poor Spalding had not even had that. But, as time went by, Artemis took his son more and more into his confidence, enticing him with tales of the importance of being a man of business, whilst effectively leaving Spencer out.

"So it transpired that the two boys began to drift more and more apart, with Spalding under his father's influence, growing more like him with each passing day. By the time I came on the scene, Spencer and Spalding acted more like perfect strangers than relatives. They were as opposite as chalk and cheese. Spencer was kind and protective towards me, and always made me laugh with his silly jokes and odd impressions. Whereas Spalding took himself incredibly seriously; even though he was several years younger than Spencer you would have thought him the elder by far. He acted as if he was already a man with huge responsibilities, and no time for juvenile behaviours such as those displayed by Spencer when he was trying to keep me amused.

"It was true that Artemis by now had already promised his son that he would one day inherit his share of the business, which was considerably larger than Spencer's portion. But Spencer, just like his mother, did not seem at all phased by this, and continued to live his life in blissful ignorance to the plotting and scheming of his uncle and cousin.

"One day, we heard talk of a fair coming to town. I think that I was about nine or ten at the time, and I had never seen a real circus. I pestered Spencer into taking me, and at first, he pretended as if he felt that such amusements were beneath him. But he could not keep up the pretence for long, and eventually he announced that he had already bought us tickets as a treat. I was overjoyed, and I think I must have counted every minute of every day until we went.

"I wore my Sunday best dress, and Spencer looked resplendent in a fine dark suit. Surprisingly Artemis even allowed Spencer the use of his personal carriage, which, in itself, was a first. The atmosphere when we arrived was generated with such energy that you almost felt as if the very air itself had a charge of electricity coursing through it. I had never seen so many people gathered in one place before. It seemed like the entire town had turned out for the first day.

"There were animals that I had only ever read about in books, and never dreamed that I would one day see in real life. They had acrobats, and clowns, dwarfs and men on stilts so tall that I could barely see their heads, and a freak show with all manner of strange and peculiar acts. There was a bearded lady, a man who was meant to be half cat with the strangest eyes I had ever seen. Twins from the orient who were joined together at the hip, and a man with three legs.

"They all looked so odd and scary that I remember holding tightly onto Spencer's hand when we first entered the tent. But he assured me that they were just people like us, and nothing to be afraid of, and after a while, with his encouragement, I found the courage to talk to them. They were all so kind and friendly that by the time we left their enclosure I felt a little tearful for them. But Spencer assured me that they were not to be pitied and that they were happy amongst their own kind, and that showbusiness people were a family within themselves, who loved each other just as we did. That made me feel better, and I continued to enjoy the show.

"There were stalls selling all manner of treats, ice-creams, candied fruits, chocolate and warm cider for the adults. Spencer let me have a ride on an elephant, which was led all around the park by a man dressed from head to toe in Indian garb, and although at first I was terrified about being so high up, after a while I began to love it, and felt as if I was the queen of the world.

"One particular tented-off enclosure seemed to be garnering a great deal of noise and excitement, so Spencer led me in and to my astonishment it was a lion-tamer who had four huge specimens, all of which looked big enough to swallow me whole. As fascinated as I was by the beasts, I was more scared by the fact that there were no cages between us and them, and I remember tugging at Spencer's hand urging him to take me back out again.

"When he realised how petrified I was he acquiesced to my demands, and we were just about to turn around to leave, when a young girl appeared from behind the tarpaulin cover and crouched down in front of me to assure me that there was really nothing to be afraid of."

## TWENTY-ONE

"My aunt stared at me with knowing look, and in a moment, I caught on to her unspoken intimation."

"That's right, it was Amy, and as she spoke to me she gently touched my cheek with the back of her fingers, and I felt a sudden calmness surge through my body, which left me feeling completely unafraid of the lions which moments ago had terrified me. This miraculous transformation in me did not go unnoticed by Spencer, but what was even more conspicuous was the way he looked at Amy. It appeared that I was not the only one whom she had managed to cast a spell over.

"Whether she noticed Spencer's obvious enchantment or not, she kept her attention on me, and asked me if I would like a closer look at the lions. I felt myself nodding, excitedly, and without any resistance from Spencer, she took me by the hand and led me down to the inner enclosure. It is still hard for me to describe what was going through my mind at the time. But, somehow, with Amy guiding me, I had absolutely no fear that anything bad could possibly happen to me.

"As we approached the first lion, Amy made a gesture with her hand, and the animal lay down at her feet without a qualm. She placed my hand on the beast's flank, and I could feel its heartbeat as its massive chest rose and fell. It was one of the most incredible experiences of my life, and I shall remember it to my dying day. With another gesture, the other lions too appeared to be utterly entranced by Amy, and one by one they walked over to us and began to rub themselves against us. One of them even licked me, and its tongue was so enormous it covered my face like a huge flannel.

"The crowd that was gathered in the tent began to gasp and then to cheer, and I suddenly realised that I was part of the show, which made me feel terribly exposed and embarrassed. But Amy took my hand once more and placed me in front of her, urging me to take a bow, and enjoy the adulation of the people.

"After the show, as the rest of the people filed out of the enclosure, Amy took me back to Spencer who had been sitting patiently during the performance. I was so full of animated chatter after my experience with the lions, I barely gave the two adults a chance to say anything. Being so young it was naturally not that obvious to me that the two of them had an instant connection, and that I was doing my level best, albeit unintentionally, to prevent them from introducing themselves to each other.

"Amy, for her part, seemed to find my eager babble quite captivating. I heard her tell Spencer that he and his wife must be very proud of me, which, naturally, prompted Spencer to relay a hasty potted version of our true relationship, and I remember thinking how he seemed to be going to great lengths to emphasise the fact that not only was he not married, but also that he was not even courting. Naturally, had I been a little older and worldlier, I would have realised that I was getting in the way of the pair of them conducting a mutual introduction, but as it was, I was far too young and excited by everything that was going on around me.

"That said, I had already been formerly tutored in the art of young ladies' etiquette, so I knew not to be rude and interrupt once I finally allowed the pair of them to start their conversation. I waited patiently, still holding onto Amy's hand, while the pair of them seemed oblivious to all the excitement and merriment that was happening around us. Finally, Amy made some comment about me wanting to see the rest of the fair, and she handed me back over to Spencer. Even at such a young age, I could tell how reluctant that they were to be parted. But I am afraid that my eagerness to see what else was on offer overrode any feeling on guilt that I may have had at being the one who was driving them apart.

"On the carriage ride home, I was fit to bursting, relaying all the wonderful things I had experienced at the fair to Spencer, as if he had not been there right beside me all along. He however was far more subdued than I had ever seen him before, and I found myself having to tug furiously on his sleeve to exact any kind of response from him. The fair was in town for two weeks, and Spencer returned to it every day, but too early for it to be open. I pleaded with him to take me back again, and he promised me another trip before it left town.

"Spencer was always as good as his word, and sure enough, he took me back to the fair the following week. Only this time, once we arrived, Amy joined us and stayed with us throughout our visit. It made the experience extra special for me, because everywhere we went, when the show people saw that Amy was with us, we were treated like proper royalty. I was ushered to the front of the queue every time I wanted to go on a ride. I was being fed so many free treats by everybody that towards the end of the evening I was starting to feel a little queasy, and Spencer had to start refusing their kind offers on my behalf.

"Amy introduced me to all the animals in the show. Not just the lions, although she did take me to stroke them again. But also, a dancing bear, some gorgeous horses, and the elephant that was giving the children rides. The one which I most hesitant about was when she asked me if I wanted to meet the members of the freak show. She laughed when she saw the scepticism in my little face and crouched down to my level to explain that they were all completely harmless and would very much like to make my acquaintance.

"Even so, I can still remember how tightly I held onto her hand as she introduced me to them all. But she was right of course; they were all incredibly friendly and full of compliments for me and the dress I was wearing that day. By the end of the visit it was almost as if their deformities no longer existed, and I was actually sad to have to leave their tent and move on, but I was old enough to appreciate that they had a show to do.

"After the fair, Amy accompanied us back to the manor. Spencer and I had walked over this time, so Amy borrowed one of the carriages from the fair, and we rode in that. Spencer let me sit up front with him and Amy, which made me feel like a proper grown-up, and I arrived home feeling like the luckiest girl in the world. Amy joined us all for dinner, much to Artemis' chagrin. This was the first time, to my knowledge certainly, that Spencer had ever brought a girl home, and I have often wondered if, even on that first visit, Artemis had recognised the special connection between them.

"Spalding, for his part, could not take his eyes off Amy, although he made a hash job of pretending not to notice her. After dinner, Spencer and Amy took me upstairs to tuck me in. I was still buzzing from all the excitement of the day and was obviously in no mood to sleep. Then, Amy began to sing to me. I later found out that it was an old Romany lullaby, and she had such a lovely voice that within minutes I was sound asleep."

"At the mention of Amy's singing, my aunt, once more, noticed me stiffen in my chair."

"Remind me to give you something before you go!"

"Once more, her words were uttered as more of a command, than a mere suggestion in passing. I nodded my response and urged her to continue."

"Where was I? Oh yes, I remember being awoken in the middle of the night by the sound of Artemis screaming his lungs out at someone. I was too afraid to venture out of my nice warm bed to see what all the commotion was about, so I pulled the covers over my head to help to block out the noise, and eventually, I fell back to sleep. The atmosphere at breakfast the following morning was particularly grim. I had hoped that Amy would still be there, but Spencer told me later that she had left soon after I had fallen to sleep. I remember throughout the meal Artemis glaring menacingly at Spencer over the breakfast table, and I surmised that he must have been the one that Artemis had been shouting at during the night.

"Whenever I would catch Spencer's eye, he would wink at me and smile, as if to allay my concerns. Later that morning, Spencer came and found me and informed me that he had proposed to Amy, and that she had accepted. I was so thrilled by the prospect of Amy coming to stay that I found it hard to contain my excitement, and started jumping around, and whooping with delight. But then Spencer informed me that Artemis was not at all pleased with the news, and that was why he had been shouting at him in the middle of the night. Spencer confessed that he had informed his uncle that once he received his inheritance he intended to sell his portion of the business to the highest bidder, and he and Amy would move away to start their married life.

"My mood changed immediately upon hearing this news, and Spencer was not oblivious to it. But he pulled me close and wrapped his arms around me and assured me that once he and Amy had their own house, that I could come and stay with them during the holidays instead of at dreary Denby Manor. This announcement switched my mood straight back to one of sheer joy, and I hugged Spencer back so hard that he complained I was about to break his back.

"The atmosphere in the house from that day was visibly more strained than it had ever been before. Mealtimes especially were conducted in utter silence, with Artemis grumbling and mumbling under his breath and shouting at the servants even more than was his usual custom. Spalding, for his part, would sit there in silence, concentrating on his food, while Spencer would always make a point of throwing me the odd wink just to assure me that everything was going to be alright.

"Then one night, about a fortnight before I was due to return to school, I was woken by the sound of my bedroom door opening. At first, I was naturally petrified, imagining all kinds of bogey monsters and goblins coming to snatch me away. But my terror transformed into immediate relief when Spencer peered from around the door, holding his finger to his lips as if to convey to me that I needed to be quiet. He came over and sat on my bed and asked me in a voice barely above a whisper if I would like to go to his wedding.

"I was naturally overjoyed by the prospect but asked him why he had not waited until the morning to ask me. He explained that because of Amy's Romany traditions, the wedding had to take place at midnight, when the moon was full. He also explained that he did not want his uncle or Spalding to know, just in case they tried to intervene and prevent the nuptials from taking place.

"I quickly dressed in what I felt was my prettiest dress and wore my best Sunday shoes and bonnet. Although it was a beautifully clear night, with a sky full of stars and a huge full moon, due to the lateness of the hour I wrapped a woollen shawl around my shoulders to fend off the cold before I tip-toed down the stairs to meet Spencer outside. We walked for a little way, just until we were out of earshot, and there was a magnificent-looking carriage waiting for us, pulled along by four of the horses from the fair, all decked out in their performance finery.

"When we arrived at the fairground camp all the performers were in attendance, sitting on the ground in a huge circle with a table in the middle. There were lit torches dotted around the circle, illuminating the entire scene, and when we alighted from the carriage, the bearded lady came to greet us and led me to my place in the circle. I felt a little hesitant, sitting on the dirt floor in one of my favourite dresses, but I was so overcome with the emotion of the moment that I complied without any fuss.

"Spencer was escorted to the middle of the circle and he was left to stand alone by the table. I noticed that there were two bottles upon it, one with a dark red liquid and the other with a clear one, which I considered might have been water. I had never attended a wedding ceremony before, but even so, I had heard about them from some of the girls at school, so I knew right away that this ceremony did not follow the traditional form of practice.

"Everyone began singing, but as I could not understand the words, I just hummed along to the tune, which was merry enough, and all those around me were smiling and cheerful, so it was easy for me to be caught up in the merriment of the occasion. After a short while, Amy emerged from one of the tents surrounding our circle. She looked absolutely gorgeous in the moonlight. Her hair had been braided with flowers and she was wearing a stunning floral-print dress, which accentuated her amazing figure far more than I was used to seeing young ladies, at the time, allow themselves to be adorned."

"Again, I could feel a shiver rush up my spine when my aunt mentioned Amy's wedding dress. Surely, that must be the same one her ghost had worn each time she plagued me during her nightly visits. This time, however, I purposely did not allow my apprehension to show outwardly I wanted my aunt to finish her story with the minimum of interruption, so that I could finally get to the truth. My trick seemed to work, as she continued speaking as if she had not noticed any change to my demeanour."

"Well, the ceremony itself began in earnest when Amy broke the circle and entered to stand opposite Spencer. As they stood there, I presumed, waiting for the singing to cease, Amy turned and gave me a wink, which somehow conveyed to my young mind that she was happy to see me in attendance. As the singing came to an end, the crowd around me began to murmur in hushed tones, some kind of ritualistic oration, which again was in a language which I could not understand, so I just sat there quietly, taking in the ambience of the magical event. Spencer and Amy took their cues, and recited their vows to each other, one line at a time, simultaneously, and when they were finished, Spencer produced a ring and slipped it on Amy's finger. Amy held her arm up with the gold band on display, and an almighty cheer went up from all those gathered, including me.

"Next, Amy poured some of the red liquid from one of the bottles into a glass, and then she mixed in some of the clear. She then began swirling the combined mixture until it became a uniform rose-tinted hue, before draining the glass in one swallow. Then she did something which I at least found very odd. She removed her shoes and placed them on the table next to the bottles. She then proceeded to fill each shoe with the liquid from one of the bottles in turn. Once she was finished, Spencer picked up the first shoe, with the red liquid, and drained it, before executing the same procedure with the other one, also.

"After this, they carried Amy's shoes over to an old lady, who I had not noticed until then, who was the only person in the circle who was sitting on a proper seat rather than on the ground. The old lady took both shoes from them, and both Amy and Spencer went down on one knee, so that the woman could kiss them both on their foreheads, before making a strange sign in the air above their heads. Once the old woman was finished Amy and Spencer breached the circle, just as the elephant which I had ridden on at the fair was brought out by its trainer. They both climbed aboard and rode around the camp three times, at the end of which there was another huge cheer from the crowd, and everybody rose to their feet and started dancing.

"I was grabbed by the hand and pulled into the middle of the melee and was immediately caught up in the music and the singing which pervaded the night air. So much so that I did not see anything of Spencer or Amy until the sun started to rise, which was when the celebration officially ended. Even though I had only had a few hours' sleep before Spencer had crept into my room I did not feel the least bit tired, and I believe that I could have continued dancing for hours to come. As it was Amy and Spencer took me back home, and I was sound asleep before we even reached the manor.

"I woke later that morning in my own bed, and for a minute began to question whether or not I had only dreamt about the festivities. But when I came down to breakfast, there was Spencer and Amy sat together at the table, and I knew immediately that it was all true. I rushed over and gave them both a huge hug before sitting down to await the others. When Artemis and Spalding finally arrived, they were both obviously surprised to see Amy sitting at breakfast. But, when Spencer announced that they had been married, I thought that Artemis was going to burst a blood vessel there and then. His face turned a bright puce, and his cheeks puffed out like a hamster storing its nuts.

"At first he did not seem capable of speech; he just kept opening and closing his mouth without any words escaping. Finally, he roared out something about Spencer not being allowed to marry without his express permission, which of course was nonsense, but Artemis was evidently convinced that he was in the right. Just as the first of the breakfast trays arrived, Artemis leapt from his seat, causing the serving maid to upend her tray, spilling kedgeree all over the table. As he stormed out of the room Spalding followed behind, and we did not see either of them again for the rest of that day.

"The fair moved away, and Spencer and Amy took me with them as she bade farewell to her friends and family. They were all so genuinely happy for her and Spencer that it made me feel quite bad for Amy, considering the frozen reception she had received for Spencer's side of the family. But for all that, Amy never let it show. She continued to be the brightest, happiest, most wonderful person I had ever met. Over the next few days, whenever Spencer was summoned by his uncle to a business meeting, Amy would go out of her way to make my remaining days at Denby an absolute joy.

"We would go out on carriage rides together, and sometimes she would pack a picnic for us if she knew that Spencer would not be available for lunch. She was always singing, and spent hours entertaining me, teaching me how to make necklaces out of flowers and twigs, and anything she could find to hand. On warm days we would go swimming in the lake, and she also taught me several different ways to wear my hair, some of which made me feel far more grown-up than my meagre years. She was also a dab hand at music and did her best to teach me the harpsichord. But to be honest, I was more interested in just lying on a couch and listening to her play and sing for me.

"The situation with Artemis seemed to grow a little less fraught over the next few days. In fact, by dinner on the third day after the wedding announcement, both Artemis and Spalding began to pass the odd pleasantry, although I could still feel an underlying hostility in their overall manner. But Amy and Spencer seemed happy enough to ignore such inferences, and as each day passed they fell more and more in love with each other.

"Then, tragedy struck. Artemis had asked Spencer to accompany himself and Spalding to another town a few miles away on business, claiming that it was necessary for Spencer to attend as he might be called on as a part-owner in the business to sign certain documents. But, on their way back to Denby, their coach was attacked by robbers on horseback, and Spencer was shot and killed.

"From that day, Amy was never the same! She would spend most of the day in bed, and at night, I would often hear her wandering the corridors, crying and sobbing. She refused to eat, and even passed out at Spencer's funeral just as his coffin was being lowered into the ground. Fortunately, one of the mourners nearby managed to catch her as she swooned, otherwise she would have ended up inside the hole on top of the coffin.

"There was a terrible commotion the following night when the local constable brought Amy home in the middle of the night, having found her lying on top of Spencer's grave in the pouring rain, singing to him. Unfortunately, though she was in no fit state to realise it, Amy was supplying Artemis with all the ammunition he needed to have her committed to an asylum. He had already taken over Spencer's share of the business, by arguing that he and Amy had not undergone an official wedding ceremony, and as such, they were not legally married, which made him Spencer's heir. But his asylum bid failed when he could not find two independent doctors to sign a release to state that she was indeed insane.

"Poor Amy seemed oblivious to everything that was happening around her. I must confess that there were times when I would try and visit her in her room, and the look in her eyes actually frightened me. Worse still were the occasions when I would try to convince her to come down for meals, and she would look straight at me and say that she was waiting for Spencer to come and fetch her. It was almost as if her life had stopped moving forward, and she was forever stuck in a void between life and death.

"Then, one-day, Artemis received a visit from a solicitor from out of town. He had apparently been abroad when Spencer was killed and had only recently returned to discover the news. He produced a will, signed and dated by Spencer, leaving his share of the family business to Amy. Artemis was naturally furious. He was a man who was used to getting his own way, but he knew that he could not argue with a legally drafted document. He even called in his own solicitor and insisted that there must be some way that Spencer's hasty will could be invalidated. He even suggested that Amy had put Spencer under some kind of gypsy spell to force him to sign his will. But in the end, there was nothing that his solicitor could do about it. The will was legally binding, and Amy was the sole beneficiary.

"The final straw, for Artemis anyway, came when Amy discovered that she was pregnant. At first, no-one, myself included I must confess, believed her. For one thing it had only been just over a week since she and Spencer were married, and as young as I was, I had always understood that it took far longer than that for a lady to be in that state. But Amy insisted that she had known the minute she had conceived, and furthermore, she was convinced that their child would be a boy. Old Artemis dismissed her revelations as nothing more than insanity, caused by grief. But I saw a change in Amy that day, as her sorrow finally gave way to anger and she confronted Artemis with the fact that she was going to do as Spencer had wanted and sell her share of the business to the highest bidder to get away from him.

"Artemis knew that he only had a short time before Spencer would have turned twenty-five and come into his inheritance, and that now on that same day, he would have to turn over his share to Amy. The obvious solution to anyone looking in from the outside would have been for him to just offer to buy Amy out. But I heard from Spalding much later that Artemis had already used up all his available credit on other business ventures, and he had nowhere left to go to secure anymore.

"By now, Artemis must have been growing desperate. Even I could tell that there was a definite shift in his character which was even darker and more sinister than before. Then, he thought that he had struck upon the perfect compromise. If Spalding were to marry Amy, then everything could be settled, to his mind at least. This was Artemis' last-ditch attempt at keeping the business within the family, but Amy was having none of it. When he broached the subject to her, she actually flew into a rage and told him that she hated Spalding as much as she did him, and that she intended to do everything in her power, once she came into Spencer's inheritance, to ruin both of them.

"Artemis, not being the sort of man to take no for an answer, was now out of options. All he could do was sit by and wait for his business empire to start to crumble. For he knew that the minute some business-savvy outsider became his partner, they would doubtless uncover most, if not all, of his dodgy dealings, and expose him for the fraud that he was. It was therefore with some surprise that I received word from one of the female servants that, as I only had a few days left before returning to school, Artemis had arranged for her to take me to the seaside for the day as a treat. This was completely out of character for Artemis, but with the loss of Amy's company over the past week or so I was desperate for some escape, and agreed eagerly with the plan.

"We spent a very pleasant day at the seaside, and Artemis had supplied the maid with ample funds to ensure that we could visit every ride and attraction available. It was not until the late afternoon that the maid informed me that Artemis had also insisted that we spend the night there, before returning home in the morning. There was no point in arguing, and besides, the maid was a pleasant enough creature, so I was quite content to spend a night away from Denby. We were put up at an extremely modest establishment, but the dinner they provided was extremely adequate, and after such an exciting, if not exhausting day, I was glad of my bed.

"The next day, after breakfast, we set off back to Denby. We arrived shortly after lunch, and the cook was ordered to prepare some milk and sandwiches to tide me over until tea. I sat alone at the dining table and ate in silence. It occurred to me that there was indeed a rather strange air about the place. It was nothing specific that I could put my finger on, but nonetheless, the change in atmosphere was almost palatable.

"After I had finished my meal, I decided to go up and see how Amy was. I hoped that she would be suitably enthralled by the tales of my adventure, but when I reached her room, I found it empty. When I asked a passing servant where she was, the girl placed her hand on my shoulder and whispered that I needed to speak to the master. Confused, and more than a little irritated with the girl's elusive manner, I went downstairs and found Artemis and Spalding in the back parlour, working over several stacks of papers as usual.

"When I enquired as to where Amy was, Artemis sat me down and in the gentlest tone I had ever heard him use, informed me that there had been a terrible accident the previous night, and that Amy was dead. I could not believe my ears, but I could tell immediately from his expression that he was in earnest. His explanation was that Amy, overtaken by grief once more, had rushed out into the night to visit Spencer's grave. There was apparently a terrible storm raging as she left, but this did not stop her and, somewhere further along the Bodlin road, she was struck by a passing carriage and did not survive the impact.

## TWENTY-TWO

"My aunt waited for a moment before continuing, doubtless because she wanted to allow me some time to digest everything she was telling me. There was an awful lot to take in, and I still had myriad questions to ask. But I decided to wait until she was finished. Otherwise I would be taking the risk of throwing her off her track, or worse still, of annoying her with my interruption, which in itself might cause her to refuse to continue.

"But for the moment I seemed to have her on my die, and I was grateful for that. Her initial hostility towards me seemed to have lessened somewhat, to the point where she appeared too wrapped up in her story to remember her initial reluctance to speak to me."

"Well, at least that was the version of the truth I was given at the time. Not surprisingly, neither Artemis nor Spalding felt comfortable enough to let me know the truth. For one thing I was far too young, and what's more, had I have been taken into their confidence I would have screamed the truth form the rooftops until someone in charge listened to what I was saying.

"As I mentioned earlier this was the day before I was due to go back to school, so it all worked out rather well for Artemis. Amy had been laid out in the local morgue, awaiting burial instructions, and I pleaded with

Artemis to let me go and see her before I left. The truth was I was feeling extremely guilty about the fact that since Spencer's death, because of the entire change in Amy's demeanour, I had hardly spoken more than a couple of words to her. In fact, I had not even bothered to say goodbye before we left for the seaside. Naturally I never imagined that I would not see her alive again, but even so, the guilt still ran deep within me.

"Eventually, Artemis ordered one of the servants to drive me into town to see Amy in state. It was a stupid idea of mine, but I was far too young to realise it at the time. I do not know what I expected to see when I arrived at the sombre building, but I was certainly not prepared for the sight of my lovely Amy, laying on a cold marble slab, covered in a sheet. I was barely in there a few moments before I fled in tears.

"In the end, I went back to school, grateful to be away from the manor, and already dreading the prospect of having to return there during our next school break. As things turned out I became rather friendly with a girl who joined that year from another school, and subsequently I was allowed to go and stay with her and her family whenever my parents could not make it back. I don't think that I ever fully expressed to her parents how grateful I was for their kindness, but I remember doing my level best not to give them cause to not invite me back.

"I was told about Artemis' demise in a letter from my parents. To be honest, it may sound callous, but I did not feel any remorse or sorrow at his passing. Many years later, long after I had been finished and moved into the city to take up a position in the secretarial pool for one of the local government departments, I received a letter from Spalding, begging me to go and visit him. I knew that he had married a year or two earlier, and that his young wife had passed away, mysteriously, in her sleep. But all the same, I still found it odd that he wanted to see me after all this time.

"I wrote back to him, conveying my sympathies for his loss, but I made some excuse about not being able to get away from work in order to make the journey. For one thing, Denby had far too many bad memories for me to contemplate setting foot in there again. But he persisted, with letter upon letter, until I finally caved in and agreed to meet with him. However, I stipulated most precisely, and without any room for argument, that I would not come any closer than the main town, and that if he wanted to meet with me so desperately, he would have to make the effort to accommodate my wishes.

"Reluctantly he agreed, and I arranged some lodgings at an inn in town for us to hold our reunion. I could not believe my eyes when he walked into the entrance hall. He looked so gaunt and weathered that I would never have recognised him in a month of Sundays. I had arranged for us to take tea in the main lounge, but he begged me to take him to my room for the sake of privacy. As you can well imagine, under normal circumstances, the thought of a well-bred young lady allowing a single man into her private apartment was decidedly frowned upon. But as I had already announced to the owners that we were distant cousins, I agreed to acquiesce to his odd request.

"When we were alone, Spalding finally confided in me about the goings on at Denby all those years ago. Although I must admit that I was curious to know the full details, I was in no way prepared for the severity of his account. To begin with, he admitted that his father had arranged for the robbers to kill Spencer during that staged robbery. Apparently, as a result of some bad investments which he himself had made, Artemis was so desperate to get hold of Spencer's share of the family business that he was prepared to go to any lengths to secure his nephew's inheritance. Little did he know, at the time, that Spencer had already made a will leaving everything to Amy.

"Apparently, when Artemis could not find a judge to overturn Spencer's will, he grew even more desperate, which was when he came up with the idea of marrying Amy off to Spalding. But, when he realised that that too was not going to happen, according to Spalding, his father completely lost his mind. The day I was packed off to the seaside, Artemis also arranged for the rest of the servants to go and see a play in the next town, and he even paid for them to stay at a local hostelry which rented out rooms.

"Once the three of them were alone in the house, Artemis had ordered Spalding to bring Amy down to see him, but she refused to leave her room. So, Artemis screamed at his son to drag her down by her hair if necessary. Spalding was too afraid of his father to disobey, so he half-coaxed, half-hauled her down, pleading with her not to do anything which would exacerbate his father's temper.

"Once they were all downstairs, Artemis informed Amy that he was giving her no choice, and that she would either agree to marry his son or else sign over her portion of the business to him. According to Spalding Amy just laughed in his face, stating that she would rather die first before acceding to either demand. By this point, Artemis' temper had reached boiling point, and he grabbed hold of Amy by the arms and began to shake her, uncontrollably.

"According to Spalding his father had started drinking the previous night, and had not stopped since, and his temper was always at its very worst when he was inebriated. In a fit of rage Artemis began to slap Amy hard across the face, until she was bruised and bleeding. Spalding claimed that he wanted to intervene, but he knew the consequences of such an action so he just stayed there and watched.

"Eventually Artemis could no longer support Amy's weight, and he let her drop to the floor with an unceremonious thud. Then, as she lay there, helpless, curled up in a ball and sobbing, Artemis stood over her and announced that he had been responsible for Spencer's death, and that he would have no qualms about having the same done to her if she refused to cooperate.

"Spalding told me that he would never forget the expression on Amy's face as the realisation of Artemis' confession took hold. Apparently, she did not even try to get up. Instead, she stayed seated on the floor and began to repeat something in a language with neither Spalding, nor his father, could understand. According to Spalding there was such a look of pure malice in her eyes that even Artemis appeared shaken.

"Then, when she had finished her incantation, Amy rose to her knees and pointed directly at Artemis. When she next spoke, Spalding swore that the voice which came out through her mouth was not hers, but one belonging to some creature of the night. She held Artemis' gaze, and stated 'The curse of Ram Templey is now upon you and all your kin, until the end of time. You will live my pain a thousand times over, and even death will be no escape'. Spalding swore that while Amy, or whatever had taken her over, was relaying this terrible curse, that a huge gust of wind tore through the house, upturning furniture and nearly knocking the drunken Artemis off his feet. When the gust finally died down, Artemis turned to Spalding, his cheeks bright red, so much so that Spalding felt sure that the old man was going to have a seizure. But instead, he demanded that Spalding help him to drag Amy back upstairs, and lock her in one of the attic rooms.

"Spalding claimed that by this point, he wanted nothing more to do with his father's scheme. But, being a coward, he felt unable to stand up to the old man, so he grabbed Amy by the arm and together they half-carried, half-dragged her back upstairs. By now Amy was no longer the helpless girl, weakened to the point of exhaustion by grief. Instead Spalding claimed that she fought them all the way back upstairs, like a feral animal trying to prevent itself from being shoved in a sack.

"Once they finally had her safely behind lock and key, Artemis ordered Spalding to fetch the carriage, and told him that they were going to drive out to a nearby village where a friend of his lived. Spalding claimed to have no idea who his father was referring to, but he acceded to his demand without question. They rode on for over an hour, with Artemis screaming at his son to beat the horses harder to spur them on.

"When they eventually reached their destination, Artemis hammered so hard on his friend's cottage door that Spalding felt sure that the timber would shatter. The door was opened by a small-framed, bespectacled man, who appeared to Spalding to be about the same age as his father. Artemis did not wait to be invited. Instead he barged his way past the man, and without pausing for any of the usual pleasantries to pass between them, he informed the bewildered individual that he needed his medical expertise to perform an abortion that very night.

"Spalding was not sure who between them was the more shocked by Artemis' words. It was obvious to him now that his father would stop at nothing to prevent Amy from receiving Spencer's inheritance, even if it involved conducting something as monstrous as what he was suggesting. With Spencer gone, their baby was the only thing that gave Amy the courage and strength to survive, so doubtless Artemis saw it as an easy way to be rid of her for good without having to kill her. The local constable had swallowed the story about the robbers killing Spencer, but another death in the family so soon after that one might be just a tad too much for anyone else to swallow.

"Spalding discovered, much later, that the poor man his father was haranguing was a retired doctor of his acquaintance, who apparently had a rather unscrupulous reputation for performing questionable procedures for a fee. As it was, the doctor was clearly perturbed at being treated in such a manner, and at first, he refused absolutely to join Artemis and Spalding on their return journey. But Artemis, not a man to take kindly to being unheeded, began to threaten the doctor with information he had garnered over the years, about his nefarious practices. Spalding could tell from the reaction of the doctor that he did not want to risk Artemis reporting him to the authorities, so reluctantly, he agreed to his demands.

"By the time the doctor had gathered up his apparatus, and they set off back to Denby, the sky had grown dark and there was a storm brewing overhead. Even so, Artemis still forced Spalding to punish the horses beyond reason, so that they could make haste back to the manor. When they arrived back at the house the storm was already overhead, and the three of them had to fight against the wind and rain to keep their balance as they climbed the stone steps to the main door.

"Once inside Artemis wasted no time, and he yanked the doctor by his coat sleeve up the stairs to the attic. But, to his horror, when he unlocked the door the room was empty. There was a tiny window in one corner, which barely allowed daylight to penetrate the room, even on the brightest of days. Upon closer inspection they found an old bedsheet tied to the handle of the window lock, which hung down just far enough to reach the lower roof. It appeared that Amy had somehow manged to scramble her way out through the tiny opening, and from there, she must have climbed down one of the drainpipes which ran the length of the outside wall.

"Sure enough, when they glanced out of the window, Spalding said that they could just see the figure of Amy disappearing past the end of the drive, which led out onto the Bodlin road. They must have just missed her in the storm. Or, otherwise, she was still hiding somewhere in the grounds, and made a dash for it once she had seen them enter the manor.

"Artemis was livid with rage. He raced back down the stairs, as fast as his unsteady legs could carry him, screaming at Spalding to follow him outside to the carriage. By the time that they were back aboard the storm was at its worst, and Spalding claimed that visibility was so poor that he could not see past the trees that ringed the drive. Artemis, in his incensed state, seemed oblivious to the conditions, and demanded that Spalding lashed the horses so that they could catch up with Amy.

"As they drove past the clump of trees where they had seen Amy disappear, there was no sign of her on the road ahead. Fearing that she might make it to town to raise the alarm before they could catch her, Artemis grabbed the whip from Spalding's hand and commenced to beat the horses, mercilessly, whipping them up into a frenzy. Spalding said that he was finding it almost impossible to hold onto the reins, but that no amount of entreating seemed to have any effect on the old man.

"As they reached a bend in the road they suddenly caught sight of Amy, vanishing into the storm up ahead. With the horses' hooves trying desperately to keep traction on the soggy, waterlogged ground, Spalding claimed that Amy was making better headway than they were. But Artemis was not about to give up. No sooner had Spalding managed to get the poor animals under control, then his father was lashing them again with the whip. Up ahead, Amy had just reached a sharp turn in the road, and Spalding saw her legs slide out from under her. As she lay there, soaked and battered on the ground, Artemis saw his chance, and continued to spur the horses on by lashing them without mercy.

"Amy managed to pick herself up, but she was obviously injured, as she limped, unsteadily, around the bend and once more out of sight. With Artemis beating the mounts for all he was worth, Spalding hit the bend at much too steep an angle. He claimed that he could feel the carriage skidding out of control, as the horses, desperate to escape the lash of Artemis' whip, raced on, dragging the carriage against the direction of their spinning wheels.

"Spalding said that he did not actually see Amy, he just felt the jolt as the carriage bumped over her. When he finally managed to take back control of the horses, he pulled up further down the road. When he walked back through the driving rain, he found Amy, lying in a pool of blood. He knew right away that she was dead!"

## TWENTY-THREE

"I could feel the anticipation rising in me as my aunt's story grew closer to Amy's death. If everything she was telling me now was true, poor Amy had more than enough reason to wish revenge on my ancestors. The fact that I had suddenly appeared out of the blue and taken up residence in the manor doubtless gave the poor girl cause to presume that I was somehow a part of the misery and heartache that she had suffered at the hands of my benefactor, and, especially, his wicked father.

"The other thought which I could not shake was the location at which Amy had been run over. Was my aunt describing the steep bend in the road known locally as the Widow-Maker? I remembered Peterson explaining to me that it was an old town custom to call it by that name, but now I wondered if that custom had started with the death of Amy.

"That poor girl must have been terrified. Alone, and literally out in the rain and the cold on that dark night, running for her very life, not to mention that of her unborn child. Without so much as a friend in the world to turn to for comfort. Her actual family, those from the fair, were possibly miles away by then having moved onto the next town, or else in another country altogether, and the family she had married into, the ones she should have been able to turn to for succour, wished her nothing but harm.

"Despite all the unsettled sleeplessness that she had put me through since my arrival, I found it impossible, having heard what I just had, to feel anything but sorrow and sympathy for her wandering spirit. It was natural that she had not yet found peace, but I did wonder if when she realised that Spalding was gone she might eventually be able to let go, and move over herself.

"While I was lost in my own thoughts, my aunt waited patiently to continue with her tale. I could tell by the way she was looking at me that I was testing her patience by allowing my mind to wander, so I apologised, softly, and tried to look suitably admonished. Even so, she made me wait for another agonising couple of seconds before she continued. I made a mental note to myself not to allow my mind to wander again during her retelling."

"Spalding claimed that he actually felt a deep remorse as he stared down at Amy's dead body, lying in the rain. Whether that was true or not, he was still very much under his father's wing, so when Artemis shouted to him from the carriage to carry Amy's lifeless body back on the wagon, he did as he was instructed. When they arrived back at the manor, Artemis' doctor-friend had vanished into the night, doubtless after having second thoughts about the task before him. According to Spalding, his father never spoke of the man again.

"As it was, they did not need him anymore anyway. Spalding maintained that his father ordered him to go to town to fetch a real doctor, and that, if asked, he was to say that they discovered Amy missing from the house, and as she had been known in the past to go into town in the middle of the night to sit by Spencer's grave, they decided to try and catch up with her and coax her home. Their story was to be that they came upon Amy's dead body on the Bodlin road.

"Although Artemis had never tried to disguise his animosity towards Amy, there was no-one of standing or influence who was willing to say anything to that effect. Therefore, there was no question as to the voracity of their concoction concerning Amy's demise. By the following day, when I returned from my impromptu visit to the seaside, Artemis had already arranged for Amy's body to be removed to the town morgue, as I mentioned earlier, and there was nothing more to be said concerning the matter, and I left for boarding school the following day.

"Spalding claimed that Artemis was only willing to pay for a pauper's burial for Amy, and that he even refused to allow her to be buried in the family plot he had purchased years earlier. But, somehow, Amy's true family got wind of her death, and the day before she was due to be buried, they arrived back in town to claim her remains. Artemis was not in the slightest bit phased by this circumstance; in fact, according to Spalding, he was quite pleased that he would not have to pay out for her funeral after all. But things were not all they seemed, and Artemis was in for some unsettling times.

"Amy's family set up camp just outside the boundary of the manor. Apparently, they paid the farmer who owned the land a handsome sum to be allowed to pitch camp there, and no amount of argument by Artemis would convince the man to renege on the deal. Although the Romany camp was not on Artemis' land, he could still see them quite clearly when he looked out of the attic window. This in itself gave him even more cause to grumble and protest at the sheer impertinence of their lack of respect for his privacy.

"But that was not all they had in store for him. At night, just as they would sit down to dinner, Spalding claimed that they could hear the sound of chanting, just outside the window. But whenever a servant was summoned to investigate, there was never any sign of anyone outside. The chanting continued at the same time of night, for nearly a fortnight, and it would often continue well into the small hours.

"Artemis even claimed, on occasion, that when he rose to use the commode, if he glanced out of his bedroom window, the Romanies were grouped together on his land, just outside the main entrance of the manor. But yet again, when the servants were roused to investigate there was no sign of them, nor any evidence that they had been present as he had described.

"Spalding could tell that the antics from the camp were starting to take their toll on his father. He tried to involve the local constabulary, and when they pointed out that the Romanies were camped legally and with the land-owner's permission, Artemis flew into a rage and threatened to write directly to the Chief Constable. Not that such empty threats held any persuasion over the officers who had called in response to his complaint.

"He even sent Spalding over to their camp to offer their 'leader' a bribe to move on. Spalding recalled that when he entered the camp, he immediately felt a burning sensation start to wend its way up through his entire body. His first instinct was to flee, but as he knew that he would have to face his father's wrath if he did, he remained long enough to make his offer.

"He said that he was led to a large tent, in which sat an old lady, whose age Spalding could not even hazard a guess at. He said that her skin was so lined with wrinkles that it was almost impossible to make out the features of her face. When she spoke to him, her English was barely perceptible, but nonetheless, she managed to convey to him in no uncertain terms that they were there to seek justice for their child, and that no amount of money was going to save him or his father from their destiny.

"Spalding could not get away from the camp quickly enough, and he claimed that the minute he passed outside their boundary, the burning inside him evaporated on the spot. As he suspected Artemis was furious that his bribe had not worked, and he was beginning to grow desperate, as their constant chanting was having a debilitating effect on his health. Then, one day, about a dozen men arrived at the manor to see Artemis. Spalding claimed that they must have been amongst the ugliest and meanest-looking individuals alive, and that those that spoke while they were there, did so in a gravelly monotone, which belied any trace of humanitarianism.

"Spalding said that judging by the men's faces it was obvious that most, if not all, of them had at one time or another made a living as pugilists. He watched as Artemis handed over handfuls of notes, whilst informing their leader that he did not care how they decided to dispose of the intruders, so long as they were gone by that night. When the men left Spalding said that his father looked incredibly pleased with himself, and seemed to relax completely for the first time since the Romanies arrival.

"But that night, as they sat down to dine, the chanting could be heard as usual. Artemis was so enraged that his latest plan had failed that he jumped up out of his chair, almost upsetting the soup tureen which the butler was placing on the table. Instead of calling for his servants to attend, Artemis grabbed a rifle from its stand and raced outside. Spalding thought it best to follow his father, and when he did, he found him stalking the grounds in front of the manor, holding the gun up in front of him, stating that he could see whoever it was hiding in the undergrowth, and that he was quite within his rights to shoot them on sight.

"Spalding said that his father's ramblings were starting to concern him, more so than usual, so he sent one of the servants into town to fetch the doctor. Meanwhile, Spalding and some of the other household staff managed to coax his father back inside, before taking him straight up to bed to await the doctor's arrival.

"The doctor who attended Artemis gave him something to help him sleep, plus a tonic for his nerves to be taken twice daily. Before leaving, Spalding invited the doctor to take some refreshment, and as they sat in the back parlour enjoying a glass of Artemis' finest port, the doctor relayed a tale to Spalding which, instead of garnering the expected laughter, actually made him turn pale.

"Apparently, according to the doctor, he had been called out earlier that evening by the local police constable, to attend to a group of hideously rough-looking men who had been arrested for public disorder, after they were found walking through town completely naked. Once they were safely behind bars, none of them were able to offer any explanation as to why they were in their current state. The doctor claimed that he had never experienced such an event, and that when he left, the men were still unable to fathom why, or how, they managed to end up in such a state.

"Spalding said that he knew straight away that the men who the doctor was referring to had to be the ones who had stood in their front parlour only hours before. Somehow the Romanies at the camp must have managed to hypnotise, or at the very least, cast some sort of spell over the men, which made them act in the way that they had. He said that he found it extremely difficult to understand how such vile looking individuals could otherwise be coerced into such a situation.

"The following morning when Artemis did not come down for breakfast, one of the servants went to investigate and discovered him dead in his bed. According to Spalding, when he saw his father, he did not recognise the man he had known since birth. The expression on the old man's face was frozen in a look of sheer terror. He had died with his eyes and mouth both wide open, as if he were about to let out an almighty scream. But no one in the house had heard any such cry, so presumably he must have died before he could let it out.

"The official medical report stated that Artemis died of a massive heart attack. But no one, other than Spalding, ventured as to what might have been the cause. Spalding mentioned that the local undertakers informed him that they would not be able to close his father's eyes without first breaking his jaw, and that in order to close his eyes, they would have to resort to sewing them shut. Instead, Spalding opted for a closed casket to avoid subjecting his dead father to such degradation.

"According to Spalding, the morning his father was found dead, the Romanies left the site, and were never seen anywhere near Briers Market again. But, although they did not stay to cause Spalding any grief, he claimed that Amy visited him, both in his dreams as well as in spirit, from that night onwards. Even so, he stayed at the manor. He even married a local girl who he managed to get in the family way. But the poor creature died during childbirth along with their son. Spalding was convinced that the death had something to do with Amy's curse, as he remembered his wife mentioning hearing one of the servants singing late into the night, waking her from her much-needed slumber. But when Spalding challenged his staff, they all denied such activity, as he knew that they would. He was convinced that it was Amy's ghost plaguing his wife, just as she had done to him for so many years by then.

"After the death of his wife and child, Spalding claimed that he no longer possessed the drive or enthusiasm to continue in business, so he sold it off to one of his acquaintances and planned to live out his days from the income. I asked him why it was that he decided to stay at the manor, considering all that had happened there, not to mention what, according to him, was still going on. He gazed at me with the strangest look in his eyes, and merely shook his head, before revealing that he somehow knew that if ever he tried to leave the manor, that Amy would stop him. When I asked him to elucidate further he became very agitated, and just kept repeating that he knew her will, and after all these years he had come to accept it.

"I remember thinking at the time that it was a very odd thing for him to say. But to be honest, it was really none of my business, and I could see how unsettled he was by my question, so I let it drop. I called for more tea, as the pot had grown cold, and after another cup Spalding seemed to settle down somewhat, and he continued talking about Amy as if she were still a real person. I must confess I found this part of our conversation the most disturbing, but by that stage I had already decided that I would probably never see Spalding again, so I allowed him to continue, and merely nodded and pretended to understand his reasoning.

"He told me that beside her nightly singing, Amy had a habit of appearing behind him when he least expected it. He had, by this time, reduced the household staff to a fraction of what it had been, mainly to save costs, so the comings and goings inside the manor were greatly reduced. Therefore, he would often find himself alone in one part of the manor or another, when he would feel a presence behind him, and, if he turned suddenly, he would catch the merest hint of Amy just before her apparition disappeared.

"He also claimed that he had demanded that all mirrors be removed from the walls, because again, Amy had a habit of appearing behind him whenever he was checking his reflection. Over time he had almost begun to live the life of a hermit, never venturing out unless it was absolutely necessary. He told me that he believed that Amy preferred it when he was at home, and that as he did not wish to antagonise her, he relented.

"I have to say that listening to him speak towards the end of my visit made me suspect that he had virtually lost his mind, and were it not for the fact that he was a man of means, he may well have found himself being carted off to the local lunatic asylum. I did not doubt his sincerity that he was in fact being haunted by the ghost of Amy, but it was more a question of his acceptance of the fact, and that he did not feel it necessary to try and do anything about it.

"After all, Amy was a lovely girl, and I was extremely fond of her, but she was gone, and if her spirit could not rest then I felt he needed to do something about it, such as bring a priest in to bless the place at the very least, and if that did not work, then why not try an exorcism? Anything had to be preferable to just living there and suffering night after night without hope of release, until death finally claimed him. But he was obviously set in his resolve, and no amount of ideas or suggestions from me were going to shake him.

"I had allowed him to unburden his guilt, and if that gave him any kind of relief, even short-term, then I was pleased that at least I had the opportunity of offering that. By the time he left, the sun was already slipping out of the sky, and when he finally stood up to go, he looked even older than he had when I first saw him that afternoon. He reminded me of a man about to face his executioner, such was the look of hopelessness in his eyes.

"That was the last time I saw him. We never did keep in touch, doubtless because neither of us had anything left to say to the other. I was surprised that he managed to continue to live in that place for as long as he did. But perhaps in the end his mind refused to recognise that he was being haunted. Or maybe he just found some other way of learning to live with it, without letting it trouble him. Still, hopefully he is at peace now, and out of Amy's clutches.

"As for you though, that's another matter. You need to leave that hateful place right now!"

## TWENTY-FOUR

"The sudden directness of my aunt's command took me totally unawares, and I found myself shifting uncomfortably in my seat. She was right, of course. Amy had no reason to be haunting me, despite the obnoxious and inhumane way my distant relatives had treated her. In my mind I was almost convinced that it was the manor that she was haunting, and who could blame her. I just happened to be there at the moment.

"That said, I had no knowledge or understanding of the conventions or dictates that governed the actions of a vengeful spirit. So perhaps my aunt was right, blunt or not, I needed to heed her warning. While I was pondering my options, she shoved herself out of her chair and walked on unsteady legs over to her bookcase. When I offered my assistance, she just waved me away with the back of her hand and continued with her task.

"I sat there in silence, watching her as she rummaged through a mahogany box which was on one of the lower shelves, surrounded by books, magazines and pamphlets. I glanced at my watch and realised with a rising unease that it was almost half-past seven. I gazed out of the window which had been at my side throughout my visit, and noticed for the first time, it seemed, that it was dark.

"I did not relish my journey back that evening. The rain was still beating against the pane beside me, and having to navigate back in the dark as well was certainly no inducement. Added to which, I needed to phone Jenifer. I knew that she would forgive me if I explained that I had to keep our call short, due to my journey ahead, and there was no point in waiting until I made it back to town, because by then she would be sick with worry, as I would be if our situations were reversed. No, I would need to find a phone box nearby, before I set off back to town.

"I did not dare rush my aunt, despite my urgency to leave. She had been very accommodating, not to mention informative, and for that I was extremely grateful. I could not imagine what she was searching for in that wooden box of hers, but whatever it was, I sincerely hoped that she would find it soon."

"Here you are!"

"She announced her find as if she was speaking to the object in her hand itself. From my angle I could not make out what it was, other than that it was quite small, and fitted easily into her hand. She closed the lid on the box, and slid it back into place, before she came back to retake her seat. She leaned over to hand me her find, which I now could see was a plastic cassette case. I took it, gratefully, and turned it around in my hand to see if there was any indication on the outer case as to the contents of the tape inside. When I could find none, I asked her what was on it."

"That's a recording of Amy singing. I'm not sure why I kept it all these years, I never listen to it, and I have no need for such things these days."

"Upon hearing her words, I almost dropped the cassette on the table. It seemed a singularly odd sort of a gift to give someone, especially considering the circumstances. Even so I did not wish to appear ungrateful, so I thanked her for it, and asked her how she had managed to acquire it in the first place. To my knowledge, such formats had not been invented before Amy had been killed."

"Spencer and I would sit for hours listening to Amy sing, she had such a sweet voice. So Spencer purchased a phonograph and bullied her into singing into it so that he could make a recording of her voice. He was so proud of the recording that he used to keep the tube by his bedside. On the night before I was due back at boarding school, I remembered the tube, and I stole it from his nightstand. After all, both he and Amy were already dead, and I did not think that either Artemis or Spalding would be listening to it anytime soon. I kept it with me throughout boarding school, and when I went to stay with my school chum's family for the holidays, they owned a phonograph of their own and allowed me to play it. They too said how much they loved her voice, so we often listened to her singing in their house.

"When tape recorders became popular, I bought one myself and transferred the old tube from the phonograph over to a spool of tape on my new machine. It wasn't perfect, certainly not by today's standards of machine, but it was clear enough for me. Eventually, I had it transferred onto this cassette. I'm not completely sure why I kept it all these years. I suppose it was because of the memory of that sweet, simple girl, and the fact that she had been so kind to me. But I haven't felt the urge to listen to it since Spalding told me about the hauntings."

"My aunt leaned right over the table and tapped the cassette in my hand with her right forefinger."

"You can do whatever you think fit with this, Jonathan. I'm not giving it to you because I think it may be haunted too, nor because I am scared to keep it. I just don't feel the need to have it anymore. I won't lie to you, you know that your father and I were never close. Possibly to do with the differences in our ages or maybe because I was always a little jealous that when he came along, suddenly our parents had far more time to dote on him than they ever did me. Either way, you are still my nephew, and I would never wish you any harm, so take the advice of an old lady and do not let that wife of yours even cross the threshold of that pest-hole. Call her tonight and tell her to stay put in London. Make up any excuse you think will work, and if I were you, I would put up at a hotel tonight and drive back to London first thing tomorrow!"

"I did not need much encouragement. I had already convinced myself that Jenifer was never going to spend a single night at the manor. But now, having listened to my aunt's story in full, I was more determined than ever to not let her so much as set foot inside. Knowing my wife, I would have a battle on my hands because without telling her the truth, which I was loathe to do, I would have to make up a feasible reason that she could not argue with. But that was another problem which I would face when it was necessary to do so.

"For now, I just needed to ensure that she stayed away. I felt really awful having to leave so suddenly, but as soon as I looked back at my aunt, she seemed to understand my concerns without me having to say the words. In fact, she egged me on, as if she were afraid that I had not taken her warning seriously."

"Go now Jonathan, do not waste any time. Call your wife and make sure that she understands the seriousness of the situation. That house has seen enough misery to last a lifetime. Do not add to it by staying there another night yourself!"

"I kissed my aunt's cheek and thanked her for her time and advice. I dropped the cassette in my jacket pocket, still unsure why I had agreed to take it, other than the fact that part of me sensed that my aunt no longer wished to keep it. As I walked down the corridor to the exit, I saw Verity standing alone at the reception desk. She smiled when she heard me approaching and tried to ask me how my visit had gone, but I cut her off in mid-sentence and asked if there was a payphone in the home. She pointed off to one side and told me there was a phone around the next bend.

"When I reached it, I was relieved that there was no one using it. The thought of having to queue up behind a bunch of old fogies with all the time in the world to talk, was not a prospect I relished. I grabbed the receiver and fumbled in my pocket for my loose change. It was then that I remembered that I had used the last of it to buy my aunt her flowers.

"In desperation, I ran back around to the front desk and the ever-smiling Verity. But, when I asked her for change, she apologised sweetly, and informed me that they did not keep a register at the home, as they did not sell anything from there. She even looked in her own purse for me, but she did not have anything small enough. She saw me eying up the telephone on her desk, but before I had a chance to ask if I may use it, she informed me that staff were not allowed to make private calls from there. Then she suggested that I could reverse the charges. I could not believe that I had been so stupid to have not thought of it myself. I thanked her and gave her hand a gentle squeeze of gratitude, before rushing back around the corner.

"I almost leaped for the phone as I saw a couple of old ladies tottering down the corridor. But, as it was, they did not wish to use it anyway, and just gave me an odd glance as they passed by. I dialled the operator and gave her my details, and she dialled my home phone. I listened as each ring went unanswered, my heart in my mouth. Finally, the operator cur back in and informed me that there was no answer and to try again later.

"It occurred to me that Jenifer may have gone to visit her mother after work, but unfortunately I did not have their number to hand. I re-dialled and asked the operator again to try my home. It was just possible that Jenifer was in the bath or taking something out of the oven when the phone first rang, and she did not manage to reach it in time before the operator cut off the call.

"Hopefully, if that were the case, then Jenifer would have realised that it was me trying to get through, and might be standing over the phone right now, waiting for it to ring again. I listened once more to every ring tone, praying for Jenifer to pick up the receiver. But, yet again, after a dozen or so rings the operator came back on, with the same advice as before.

"I checked my watch; it was now almost eight o'clock, and I knew that Jenifer should have been home hours before. I was at a loss for what to do next. I did not want to start the long drive back to Brier's Market without speaking to Jenifer first. I needed to hear her voice and know that she was safe, and more importantly, convince her not to come down the following day. Then it hit me. I ran back around to the main desk to find Verity talking to a rather severe looking, middle-aged woman with half-moon glasses perched precariously on the end of her nose. By the sound of her tone I gathered that she was Verity's superior, and the last thing I wanted was to get Verity in trouble, regardless of how desperate I was. So, when the dour-looking woman raised her head, I made sure that I chose my words carefully.

"I quickly explained who I was and why I was there and made a point of telling her that Verity had already explained to me that the desk phone was not for general use, but I pleaded with her to just allow me to check a number with directory enquiries. Verity, bless her heart, quickly explained my lack of change situation, and the older woman gave me a very sharp glance up and down before she instructed Verity to allow me to make my call.

"I thanked her for her understanding but she had already turned to leave, and did not acknowledge my gratitude. Fortunately, I knew Jenifer's parent's address, but, as I gave it to the operator from directory enquiries a sudden fear struck me that they might be ex-directory. I waited, patiently, and after a moment or two, the operator came back with the number. I quickly wrote it down on a piece of paper which Verity, anticipating my need, slid over towards me with a pencil on top.

"Once I had the number, I ran back around the corner to the phone kiosk. I dialled the operator and gave her the number, asking once more to reverse the charges. After a couple of rings, I heard Jenifer's father answer the phone. Once the operator had verified that he was willing to accept the charges for the call, she put me through.

"I apologised for not being able to pay for the call myself, and for the fact that I did not have time to pass pleasantries as I was in a tearing hurry. But, before I had the chance to ask if Jenifer was there, he said something which immediately made my blood run cold."

"Jenifer called us from the station when she arrived, has she told you her news, she wouldn't tell us before she spoke to you first?"

"I stumbled over my words, my mind racing ninety to the dozen. I asked him to clarify what he meant by Jenifer having called them from the station, although deep down I feared that I already knew the answer. To my horror he confirmed that Jenifer could not wait until tomorrow to see me, and that she had caught the afternoon train to Brier's Market. She had called her parents at five o'clock that afternoon to confirm that she had arrived and said that she was going to take a taxi to the manor, so that she could surprise me."

"He continued talking, something about Jenifer talking about nothing else all week but the house, and how she was looking forward to seeing me. But his words fell on deaf ears. All I could think was that my darling wife had possibly been at the manor all evening, and what was worse, I was still over two hours away from her, with no means of speaking to her to tell her that she needed to get away from that place right away.

"I think that I actually replaced the receiver without saying goodbye to Jenifer's father. Instead I just ran from the home, without even acknowledging Verity for her kind assistance, and jumped into my car. The rain was still pelting down, and I switched on my wipers and lights as I pulled out of the car park. I knew that there was no way under the sun that I would remember the entire route back to the manor, as I had used far too many back roads for that. So, at some point I would have to pull over to reference the map. But for now, I just needed to be moving.

"I drove like a man possessed. Several times I actually found myself screaming my lungs out at the faceless vehicles ahead of me, not caring about the fact that I was usually the one in the wrong, trying to overtake when there was no physical room to pass by, or tail-gating the car in front of me when they were keeping to the speed limit and driving safely. I cursed myself every time I had to pull over to check the map. On more than one occasion I found myself having to re-configure my route due to flooding having closed off the road I intended to use. Even some of the 'B' roads I found myself using should, in reality, have been closed due to the condition of their surface, but still I raced down them, trying desperately to keep my old car under control.

"There were several times along my journey when I was thankful not to be pulled over by the police, such was the callousness of my adherence to the laws of the road. But there were times when it felt as if I was in one of those strange dreams where you find yourself trying to run away from something, and you do not seem to be making any headway. It was almost as if the manor was taunting me, laughing at my futile attempt to reach it before my poor wife became its next victim.

"My one and only saving grace was that I knew that my wife was a sensible and intelligent individual, who, upon finding that I was not at the manor, would have made her way back into town, rather than just sitting on the doorstep in the freezing cold to await my return. My one hope was that she had not allowed her taxi to leave until she had checked to see if I was in or not. Otherwise, I dreaded to think of her having to walk back along that awful Bodlin road, in the dark.

"I could feel myself starting to perspire from fretting. I shifted in my seat to grab a tissue from my pocket to wipe my brow, and instead found my aunt's cassette tape. I held it up and looked at it for a split second before hearing the frantic honking of a car horn up ahead. Somehow, I had managed to drift over into the oncoming lane, so I grabbed hold of the steering wheel in both hands, letting the tape fall to the floor, and just managed to manoeuvre my way back into my own lane before the car ahead sped past.

"On through the driving rain I sped, my windscreen wipers were, by now, having a tough job in dealing with the onslaught. My windscreen was constantly misting up since I had turned the heater down due to the uncomfortable temperature inside the car. Opening a window was, naturally, out of the question, so I decided that I would have to live with the unpleasant condition for the sake of safety, and turned the heat back on, directing it fully towards the windscreen.

"It seemed like an absolute eternity before I finally reached my exit for town. Luckily for me, the streets of the town were devoid of traffic, so I managed to speed through without any holdups. Once I turned off and left the firm surface of the streets, I could feel my tyres fight to keep purchase on the quagmire that the torrential rain had made of the soft ground leading towards the manor.

"As I approached the sharp bend in the road where it appeared that Amy had met her fate, I skidded to a halt as a lorry came around the bend without indicating. I sat there waiting for it to pass, grateful that I had seen it in the nick of time. As I tried to move off again my wheels began to spin, flicking up mud behind me. I took my foot off the accelerator and braked gently, to allow the wheels to find a hold in the soft mud. This time I pressed the accelerator only slightly, using the biting point with my clutch to edge forward until I was satisfied that I was back in control.

"When I turned the next bend, and saw the manor ahead of me, my heart sank. Even form this distance I could see that the lights were on inside which could only mean one thing. Somehow, Jenifer had found her way inside! I sped on, oblivious to the battle my tyres were having trying to maintain their traction. By the time I turned onto the pathway which led through the trees, I had to use every ounce of my driving knowhow to keep control of my car.

"As I emerged from the dense clump of woodland that ringed the driveway I could see the manor in all its glory, looking every bit the ogre I had come to regard it as, just waiting for me to draw close enough for it to be able to swallow me up for good."

## TWENTY-FIVE

"I pulled up directly in front of the stone flight and leapt out of the car. I paused for a moment and looked up. There, at one of the upper windows, I could see a faint silhouette. Somehow, I knew that it was Amy, waiting for my return. I took the steps two at a time, and as I reached the front door and found that it was locked, a strange sense of comfort washed over me. Perhaps Jenifer was not inside after all. Maybe I had left the lights on by mistake when I left that morning, or Jarrow had somehow set the generator to kick-start at a certain time so that I would not return in darkness.

"My feelings of trepidation began to slip away as I considered the fact that perhaps it was not Jenifer inside, after all. In fact, the more that I thought about it, the more likely it seemed to me that the Jarrows were there, waiting for my return to offer me dinner. The fact that I had missed one of Mrs Jarrow's sumptuous breakfasts may well have inspired them ensure that I had a least one proper meal inside me that day.

"Or perhaps, after last night's séance, they wanted to make sure that I was ok. Mrs Jarrow especially had seemed very concerned for my well-being when they were leaving the previous evening. Maybe they had come over to insist that I spend my last night at their cottage, instead of being alone at the manor. A very thoughtful offer, and so typical of their caring nature, and were it not for the fact that I had to find Jenifer, wherever she happened to be in town, I would have gladly taken them up on it.

"An ear-splitting roll of thunder crashed through the night sky behind me, as I fumbled with my keys. Once I heard the lock snap open I rammed the door, letting it fly open and crash against the coat stand behind it. I stood there in the entranceway for a moment and glanced around me. Everything looked exactly as I had left it that morning, with one notable exception. The small overnight case that Jenifer's parents had given to her last Christmas stood against the front parlour wall, with her raincoat draped over it. For a split-second I was frozen to the spot, my mind a turmoil of possible scenarios as to how Jenifer could be inside the house. Had the Jarrows let her in after all, and then just left her there? Did I leave the front door unlocked that morning? Was there a spare key left outside under a plant pot, which I was not aware of?

"None of that mattered now! Jenifer was somewhere inside the house and I had to find her and get her to safety as soon as possible. Before it was too late! I started calling out her name as I ran into each room in turn, turning on lights in those that were still in darkness. I tried the kitchen and the scullery, but still there was no sign of her. As I ran back out into the hallway I could see someone from the corner of my eye, standing at the top of the stairs. Through the railings I just caught sight of the floral print dress, and I knew that it was Amy, waiting!

"But where was my Jenifer? Was she trapped upstairs, being kept prisoner by Amy's malevolent spirit? I needed to get past her so that I could reach my wife, and at that moment I did not care what she had in store for me. My only concern was to reach Jenifer and protect her as best I could.

"As I rounded the bottom of the staircase, I paused for a moment to catch my breath before facing Amy. But as I looked up, it was not Amy, but Jenifer standing there. I could not believe my eyes. My lovely wife was wearing one of Amy's dresses.

"There were far too many questions in my mind to wait for answers. As I watched, Jenifer began to saunter down the stairs towards me, holding out the hem of Amy's dress with one hand and turning slightly as if she were in some bizarre fashion parade. It was grotesque! The sight of my beautiful wife in Amy's dress was utterly hideous to me."

"What do you think, pretty nice, huh. There's a whole trunk full of gorgeous dresses up there, real period stuff, why didn't you tell me over the phone, I might have come down sooner."

"All I could think of at that moment was that only a couple of nights ago Amy's ghostly figure had drifted down those very stairs, wearing that same dress, as I lay helpless on the stone floor, unable to move. I felt a wave of dizziness waft over me, and I blinked my eyes to clear the awful vision from my head. But when I opened them again, I saw Amy standing at the top of the stairs, wearing the same dress that my wife was presently parading for my entertainment. The look in Amy's eyes as she stared down at my beautiful Jenifer was filled with pure evil, as if she were somehow furious with her for daring to borrow her clothes.

"I acted instinctively. Lunging forward I grabbed hold of Jenifer's hand and half-pulled her down the remaining steps. I knew that she was oblivious to the menacing apparition which loomed behind her, and I wanted her to remain in ignorance. My only thought was to take her as far away from the manor as I could, as quickly as possible.

"As we made for the open front door, I could hear Jenifer's protests. My actions must have seemed quite inexplicable to her considering we hadn't seen each other for a week, and now that we had, instead of taking her in my arms and holding her as I wanted to, I was dragging her out into the storm, with her wearing nothing but a thin summer dress which was not even hers.

"I desperately wanted to explain my actions, to make Jenifer see my reasoning behind them. But to do so would mean telling her all about my experiences in the manor since my arrival, and not only was there insufficient time at that present moment, ideally, I would rather keep all knowledge of the darker side of the manor to myself. There was no tangible reason to involve my Jenifer in anything to do with that accursed place.

"Jenifer continued to offer justifiable objections as well as a token resistance as I led her down the stone steps to the car. A massive streak of lightening lit up the night sky, causing it to resemble daylight for a split second, before plunging it back into darkness. As we reached the car I kept hold of Jenifer's wrist with one hand, and searched for my car keys with the other. I was too afraid to let go of her in case she was somehow sucked back into the manor, and the door slammed shut behind her, trapping her inside forever.

"The rain was hammering down on both of us, and Amy's dress was starting to cling to Jenifer's slim frame like a second skin. There wasn't time for me to take my coat off to cover her shoulders at that precise moment, as again, it would involve me letting go of her arm, and I needed to keep her close to me as my fear of some kind of spectral intervention was too strong to be ignored.

"When I finally managed to open the door I ushered Jenifer inside, with her protesting all the way. As I slammed her door shut, the look she gave me through the window told me all I needed to know about how much I trouble I was in. But that was the least of my concerns. I ran around to my side of the car, and for some reason I cannot fathom, I took one last look at the manor.

"The front door slammed shut. Doubtless as the result of a strong gust of wind, but in my mind, it was almost as if the house was telling me to get out! That my presence was no longer required or desired. Then my eye caught a glimpse of something at one of the upper windows. I knew what it was before I even looked up, and, when I did, sure enough there was Amy glaring down at me. Her hands placed firmly on her hips, and, although I could not see them from this distance, her eyes conveying that same malevolence I had witnessed back on the staircase.

"Another clap of thunder roared overhead, followed almost immediately by a further streak of lightening. At that moment the lights inside the manor flickered and went out, plunging the entire façade into darkness. I slid behind the wheel, my clothes soaked by the rain, and wiped the back of my hand across my face to try and clear the excess water from my eyes. Instinctively I snapped my safety belt into its buckle, before turning the key in the ignition. I looked over at Jenifer who was staring back at me, with an expression that appeared to be a cross between infuriation and incredulousness."

"Are you going to tell me exactly what is going on Jonathan, or am I meant to just sit here and guess?"

"I could hear the understandable undertone of anger in her voice, but at the same time, she also sounded as if she were concerned for my sanity, and who could blame her? My actions thus far that evening had not been those of a sane man, and I made a promise to myself that once I had her safely away from that place that I would do my best to rationalise my actions without mentioning Amy.

"The car started on the first turn, and I slipped it into gear and pulled away slowly to allow the tyres to gain maximum purchase on the waterlogged ground. I could hear Jenifer speaking to me, or more precisely, at me, as I pulled away. I checked my rear-view mirror, and felt the weight start to lift from my heart as I watched the manor diminish.

"As I turned out of the drive, I took the bend too sharply and I could feel the tyres skidding beneath the vehicle. Jenifer grabbed hold of the dashboard in front of her to prevent herself from slamming into the window. Once I had the car back under control, I apologised, and told her to secure her seatbelt, but she was obviously too miffed to take note of my instruction. I could hear her complaining about her suitcase which we had left back at the manor, and the fact that she was soaked through to the skin, and not even wearing her own clothes. But I kept my focus on the road ahead and muttered something about buying her something to wear in town the next day.

"Once we had cleared the trees which now masked the manor from sight, I pressed a little harder on the accelerator. I think that subconsciously I just wanted to put as much distance between us and Denby in as short a time as possible. I had the wipers on full speed as the rain lashed the windscreen mercilessly. Above us the thunder and lightning roared and flashed, respectively, almost as if they were chastising us in unison for having left the manor. Even with my headlights on full beam, the weather was making it increasingly difficult for me to see more than a couple of feet ahead.

"With my concentration completely focused on the road, I did not notice Jenifer as she lifted her bottom to remove something sharp which she complained was digging into her. Nor did I observe her removing the cassette from its plastic box before slipping it into the player in front of her.

"As we approached the blind bend of the Widow-Maker I began to slow down, and was just about to hit the horn when I happened to glance in the rear-view mirror. There was Amy staring back at me, her face contorted into a scowl of pure malice, her eyes burning with hatred and animosity.

"As Amy's sweet, dulcet voice started to emanate from the speakers, my foot slipped off the brake pedal and rammed against the accelerator. The car shot forward, and in that split-second I glimpsed the lights from the oncoming lorry as it swung around the blind bend.

"I spun the wheel to avoid a collision, but it was too late. I heard the wail of the lorry's horn, mingled with the screech from both sets of brakes, as my back wheels lost traction on the road and pulled us back over the side of the sheer drop. As our car began to tumble down the bank I reached over to try and protect Jenifer from the force of the impact, but the stupid seat belt locked in place, and kept me tight against my seat."

"I rushed through the darkened manor with my heart in my mouth, frantically calling for Jenifer. I tried the switch in every room, but the lights refused to come on. I surmised that the generator needed restarting, yet again, and I shouted out to Jarrow to start it up for me. But he made some excuse about having to pick his wife up from work, and left, slamming the front door behind him.

"I screamed after him, but it did no good. Outside, I could hear the rain slamming against the outside of the manor. I reached out along the mantlepiece in the back parlour and found my torch. But as I shoved the button forward the bulb did not light. I shock the holder several times and slapped it against the palm of my hand, but it was all to no avail.

"I threw the recalcitrant object in the air and heard the glass front smash against the stone floor. Just then, I heard voices coming from the next room. I manoeuvred my way around the furniture and edged along the hallway until was at the entrance of the next room. I stared inside, and through the gloom I could see Peterson and Jefferies sitting at the table, discussing land rights and leases. I had no idea why they were there, as I certainly did not remember inviting them. But for the moment I didn't care. I needed to find my wife, and nothing else mattered at that moment.

"I stood in the darkness in the middle of the hallway and called for Jenifer, once more. Suddenly, I heard her reply from upstairs. I ran up the stairs, two at a time, and followed the sound of her voice as it led me to the attic room at the farthest corner.

"With the moonlight shafting in through the tiny skylight window, I could see her standing beside the trunk which was full of Amy's clothes. As I entered the room, she held Amy's floral-print dress against her and asked me what I thought. I was so relieved that she had not actually put the garment on that I grabbed it from her and threw it back into the chest. Before she had a chance to rebuke me, I wrapped my arms around her and held her so tightly that she began to complain of not being able to breathe.

"I reluctantly released my hold slightly, but still kept her close, and asked her how long she had been at the manor, waiting for me."

"Forever, you took so long to get here that I fell asleep and died."

"Still hugging her close to me, I laughed over her shoulder at her clumsy phrasing, and corrected her that what she meant to say was probably that she had fallen into a dead sleep. I closed my eyes and kissed the top of her head, entwining her lustrous golden hair around my fingers. When I opened my eyes, I could see that her hair had changed colour, and that it was now of a much darker hue. I wondered if she had dyed it during the week that we were apart and released my hold on her so that I could take in the full effect of her new transition.

"But it was Amy's eyes that stared back at me with that same, sweet, pleading gaze that she always wore whenever I was summoned by her to the scullery door. She held on to me, tightly, clasping me to her waif-like frame."

"Please help me, they're trying to take my baby!"

"I turned and ran down the stairs and out of the house. As I reached the path I saw my aunt sitting on her chair, in the middle of the driveway, reading. I ran over to her and asked her what she was doing there and invited her to come in out of the cold and rain. But she just looked at me as if she was irritated by my offer and turned her attention back to her book. I wondered how it was possible that she could even see the words clearly with no light, but she appeared to be having no trouble, and looked totally wrapped up in the novel.

"I wanted to grab her by the arm and force her into the house to save her catching her death, but she seemed completely unperturbed by my presence. I crouched down next to her to supplicate with her to move, but she merely turned her head to look at me once more and, with a look of genuine concern etched across her face, she demanded that I run away and leave the manor, before it was too late!"

"I pleaded with her to tell me what she meant but she refused to elaborate further, and continued with her reading. When I turned back around, there was hag-Amy, floating down the stone steps towards me, her arms outstretched as if in anticipation of another embrace. I turned back to warn my aunt, but she was gone!

"I ran for the trees, not daring to look behind me for fear of realising how close hag-Amy might be. My legs felt as if they were made of lead. Each step took more effort than the previous one until finally, I could no longer lift them off the floor. I compelled myself to keep moving, but in the end, unable to take another step, I fell forward. I tensed my body in anticipation as the floor accelerated towards me. But I did not hit the ground as I expected to; instead I kept on falling into a bottomless pit of blackness.

"Eventually, through the blackness, I could hear voices. My sister Jane's was the only one that I recognised, the others were completely unfamiliar to me. The voices seemed to drift in and out of my subconscious and I never fully understood what it was that they were saying. I could feel myself drifting in and out of wakefulness. On several occasions I saw Jenifer's face, hovering above me. She would smile her loving smile, and wink at me, cheekily, and tell me that everything was going to be alright, and that I should go back to sleep.

"But I also saw Amy's face, uncomfortably close to mine, with me unable to move or turn away. Even though she looked tranquil and sad, with that familiar longing gaze of hers, there was always an underlying feeling of terror that would course through me whenever she appeared.

"There were other, unfamiliar faces, which would appear to me from time to time. I could hear questions being asked of me, and sometimes I would try and answer, but it was as if the strange faces could not hear me, so in the end I stopped trying to communicate with them altogether. That's when Jenifer would appear to me again. I would reach out to embrace her, but she would always usher me away, and tell me in her sternest voice not to try and follow her, but to go back, and if I refused, she would get angry with me and refuse to come to me again for ages, so in the end I learned not to try and go after her.

"Eventually, much to my relief, Amy stopped visiting me altogether. I was so grateful, for although on the last few occasions she had not tried to cause me any alarm, I was never fully confident that she no longer wished to harm me. I was sure that it was Jenifer who sent her away. The next time Jenifer appeared to me, with her beautiful golden hair flowing around her shoulders, I could see that she was cradling something in her arms. I tried to lift myself up for a better look, but I could feel invisible hands holding me down.

"Seeing my plight, Jenifer came closer and showed me that she was in fact holding a new-born baby. The child was fast asleep in her arms, and I desperately wanted to ask her whose baby it was, but the words refused to come out of my mouth. I watched Jenifer as she gently rocked the sleeping infant, holding it slightly higher so that I could see its face.

"After a while, Jenifer kissed the child lovingly on its forehead, and looked up at me and smiled, before mouthing what looked like the words 'I love you' before she and the baby faded away from sight. This time I tried to follow, but again, it was to no avail. Something was holding me back, so I closed my eyes and strained with every ounce of energy I could muster to try and break free.

## TWENTY-SIX

"When I opened my eyes again, I could see several unfamiliar faces staring down at me. As my eyes began to focus on my surroundings, I realised that I was in a hospital bed. As I tried to move, one of the doctors placed a hand on my shoulder and told me to remain still. I could see all manner of tubes and wires emanating from machines placed around my bed, all leading directly to me. When I tried to speak, I realised that there was a plastic tube in my mouth, which seemed to pass right down into my throat. A smaller one was inserted inside one of my nostrils, which hampered my breathing.

"Before I had another chance to try and protest, I blacked out. When I came back around, my sister Jane was sitting by my bedside, and most of the tubes had been removed, except for one still attached to my arm. As soon as she saw that my eyes were open, Jane leaned over and kissed my cheek, and stroked it, tenderly. I asked her what was going on, and what I was doing there, and she explained to me that I had been in a coma for nearly three months.

"I tried to fathom the meaning of her words, but they made no sense to me. The last thing I remembered was driving away from the manor in the dark of night, with Jenifer beside me, complaining about her soaking wet dress, and then…I looked at Jane and asked her where Jenifer was. Immediately I noticed her eyes clouding over and, before she could reply, tears began to stream down her cheeks.

"What she told me next made me wish that I had died before ever opening my eyes! Jane informed me that after the crash that night on the Bodlin road, Jenifer and I had been air-lifted to a hospital in London. Apparently, the drive of the other vehicle had died at the scene. Jane fought back the tears as she explained that, due to our injuries, Jenifer and I were both induced into a coma, but that Jenifer succumbed to her injuries and died a couple of days later.

"As she spoke those words, my eyes too began to blur with tears. I could not believe that my darling wife was gone. The thought of never being able to hold her, or kiss her again, made me feel as if my life was already over. Jane held me as best she could with the restrictions placed on us by the apparatus which was attached to my various body-parts. We both cried long, hot tears, until there were none left to cry.

"After a while, Jane squeezed my hand and asked me if there was anything she could get for me. I shook my head. My throat was extremely parched, but right at that moment, I did not care. My gorgeous Jenifer was dead, nothing else mattered, nor would it ever again. Eventually, I found the courage to ask Jane to let me know where Jenifer's body was. It stood to reason that if I had been in a coma for almost three months after she had died, she must already have been buried or cremated somewhere, and I desperately needed to know where.

"Jane nodded to my request, although I could tell how uncomfortable she felt at having to hurt me further with the details. She went on to explain that as the doctors were not sure if I would ever come around from my coma, Jenifer's parents were left to decide how best to honour their daughter's remains. Jane explained that they had Jenifer cremated, and that her ashes were housed in a garden of rest near where she was brought up. Jane told me that she and Mike attended her funeral, and that as soon as I was able, she would drive me to the crematorium, so that I could say my goodbyes.

"She waited a moment or two to allow this new news to settle in with me, before she continued. I thought that my grief was at its lowest ebb, until she asked me her next question."

"Jonathan, did you know that Jenifer was pregnant?"

"The room began to spin around me. I think Jane could see the answer to her question spread across my face without my having to reply. I turned my head away, and after another huge flood of tears, I looked back at my sister, imploring her to tell me that it was not true. But of course, I knew that it was. My sister was not capable of such cruelty as to have made up such a monstrous lie. She explained to me that Jenifer was still only in the early stages of her pregnancy, and that the foetus had not fully formed in her womb, so there was no chance of the doctors being able to save the baby.

"She continued to speak for several minutes, and I managed to catch few words here and there, but for the most part my mind was elsewhere. A jumble of different thoughts and emotions seemed to swim through my brain, without order or substance. I cursed my decision to go and visit the manor to begin with. Had I have stayed at home, had I never even received Peterson's letter, then my Jenifer would still be alive. Then I began to curse my distant ancestor, Artemis, for his wickedness which had brought this curse on our family in the first place. Also, my benefactor, Spalding, for ever leaving that damn manor to me, knowing what I would be inheriting along with the house and grounds. I even blamed myself for having loved Jenifer in the first place, because, if I had never married, or even met her, she would still be alive now.

"True to her word, once I was able to leave the hospital, Jane drove me straight over to where Jenifer's ashes were kept. The garden of remembrance was truly beautiful, and although by now it was only the beginning of spring, the gardeners had managed to create a wonderful array of colour to enhance the overall feeling of tranquillity and serenity, which exuded from the surroundings.

"Jane stayed in the car so that I could be alone with my thoughts when I said my goodbyes. I was glad of that, because I knew what sort of state I would be in when I saw my wife's casket, and I was not wrong. I arranged my flowers in the vase which Jenifer's parents had placed in front of her plot. The engraved plaque which they had commissioned was truly beautiful, if such things can be so described. The words read: To a loving wife, daughter and mother'. The poignancy of the words was not lost on me. For although Jenifer had not lived long enough to give birth to our child, she still had it growing within her when she died, and her parents, understandably, wished to acknowledge their unborn grandchild.

"Once I was able, I bought myself another car so that I could drive out to visit Jenifer whenever I could. I would still go and visit with her parents, who I must say, were wonderful to me. Neither blamed me for the accident, and they both acknowledged how devoted we were to each other. I never felt anything from them other than love. The grief we shared became a bond of its own, one that would last forever.

"In the end, I sold Denby Manor. After all, what else was I going to do with it? To be totally honest the thought of leaving London and moving into the manor with nothing for company but my grief and Amy's late-night visitations did occur to me one night when I was at home, blind drunk and looking through our wedding album. But by the morning the notion had passed.

"Jefferies bought the manor, and he gave me a fair price. The only caveat I insisted on was that I would give the Jarrows their cottage and the land around it, outright. I felt that they deserved it for their years of devotion to my late benefactor. Not to mention the way they tried to help me while I was staying there. I declined Peterson's offer to drive back to Briar's Market to go through the paperwork with him in his office. Instead I asked him to post it to me, which he did, reluctantly. He was obviously not used to contracts of this nature being conducted without being able to go through the paperwork with his client in person.

"I contacted my aunt to offer her some financial assistance from the proceeds of the manor; it seemed only right. But she refused my offer and explained that she had more than enough funds to pay her way at the home until she no longer had need of it. To my shame, I never did go and see her again, but we did speak on the telephone quite regularly. The fact was that she was the only person alive whom I could speak to regarding what happened to me at the manor.

"My aunt, being the pragmatist as always, would often make me lose my temper by telling me that I needed to forget what had gone on before and just move forward with my life. As if I could ever forget what happened to my beautiful Jenifer. Over time I learned to bite my tongue when she acted this way, but there were occasions when she would catch me at a particularly low ebb, and I would grow so frustrated with her that I would slam the phone down. Then, usually within a couple of minutes, my guilt would take hold, and I would call her straight back and apologise. She died peacefully in her sleep about a year after I sold the manor. I felt her loss much more that I would ever have thought, considering we had only become acquainted in the last year or so of her life. But I believe that part of that was that once she was gone, I had no one else to talk to about my experiences.

"I never told anyone else the true story. Not because I feared ridicule, or even because I was ashamed of anything I had done. It was more the fact that part of me was afraid of telling anyone close to me, such as Jane or Jenifer's parents, for example, just in case it somehow opened some sort of spiritual portal, allowing Amy to plague them as she had me. It may sound daft, but after what I had suffered, I was not prepared to take any unnecessary chances.

"Eventually, I went back to work. I suppose that after everything that had happened, I needed the normality of repetitive monotony to keep me sane. To be honest, with the proceeds from the manor I did not really need to return to the bank. I could have taken the opportunity to start a new venture, taken a gamble on something which I had always wanted to do. But in truth, banking was all I knew, and I was not in the mood for wild adventures.

"I managed to talk Jane and Mike into accepting some money to help pay off their mortgage. At first, they both refused, saying that it was too generous, but in the end, they acquiesced when I convinced them that had the situation been reversed, they would have insisted on doing the same.

"My life from that point took on an almost hermit-style existence. I would go to work, go home, sleep and go back to work. At weekends I would visit Jenifer, and when I was invited, Jane and Mike's for Sunday lunch. It occurred to me that there was a certain amount of irony in the fact that the life I was now living, in many ways, mirrored that of my late benefactor. He too had lost his wife and unborn child as a result of Amy's curse, so perhaps we had more in common that I had given credence to.

"One Sunday, having visited Jenifer and placed some fresh flowers in her vase. I decided that I needed a drive to try and clear my head. It was late September, so the nights had already started to draw in, but it was an especially sunny and clear day, with the merest wisp of clouds gliding across an otherwise blue sky. I did not pay much heed as to where I was going. I just needed to be away from all the hustle and bustle of London.

"Eventually, I found myself on the Brighton road. As soon as I realised where I was going, my initial reaction was to turn off at the next exit and head in another direction. But something changed my mind. I have no idea what it might have been. But it felt as if a sudden calmness washed over me and spurred me on ahead. So, I drove past the next turning, and the next, until I was only a few miles outside the town.

"This was the first time I had visited the resort since that last day Jenifer and I had spent together, before my fateful trip. The thought of the memories which seeing the town would resurrect in me gave me pause to reflect, and I found myself intentionally slowing down as I took the final turn which would lead me to the front.

"Once I parked up, I walked in the early afternoon sunshine, listening to the happy families enjoying their day out. Their laughter and enjoyment actually managed to lift my spirits for the first time in as long as I could remember, and it occurred to me that, rather than feeling an inordinate sorrow at remembering this town as the last place Jenifer and I had been together, I should think of it fondly, and consider how much joy and pleasure my wife took form our visit.

"The thought of Jenifer running along the beach towards the pier, excitedly anticipating its many arcades and rides, brought an unexpected smile to my face, and I took in a couple of deep breaths of the fresh sea air, as another reminder of that Sunday afternoon, which now seemed so long ago.

"My mood changed, somewhat, when I saw the old Gypsy's caravan, nestled further along the beach. My memory stirred back to the old woman chasing me across the pier, while Jenifer was enjoying her ride, and the warning she tried so desperately to make me heed. I was struck by a sudden thought. Could the old woman possibly have foreseen what was to become of me by going on that journey? In truth, I had a much greater understanding, if not respect, for the power bestowed on some of the Gypsy clan, having suffered personally as the victim of a Romany curse.

"I remembered once again how excited Jenifer had been at the prospect of visiting the fortune-teller's caravan, and how she had shoved me ahead of her when we reached the wooden steps which led up to the Gypsy's door. Something within me urged me on, and I knew that I had to visit with her again. Even if only to thank her for trying to warn me and apologise for not having listened to her.

"But when I knocked on the arched door, the voice that called back was far too young to be that of the old fortune-teller. I opened the door and ventured into the gloomy caravan. Sure enough, the young girl who sat behind the oval table with the crystal ball in the middle, was the one I had seen that day on the pier, ushering the old lady away from me. What's more, I could see immediately from her expression that she also recognised me, and did not seem pleased to see me.

"She stared straight at me for what seemed an eternity, before she let out a huge sigh and offered me the seat in front of her. As I sat down, the girl took out a cloth and covered the glass ball between us. I thought this a little odd, as, although I had not technically gone there to have my fortune told, she must have presumed that that was the reason for my visit. In which case the crystal ball would be an integral part of her performance, if such a term could apply.

"Before I was given the chance to say anything, the girl spoke directly to me. Not so much as a customer, but in a much more formal tone, and one which immediately made me feel as if she already knew why I was there."

"What is the purpose of your visit here today, Mr Ward?"

"I was immediately taken aback by the fact that she knew my name. I certainly did not remember giving it to the old lady the last time we visited. I was so stunned, that for a moment I could not find an answer worth offering. So instead, I made enquiries as to where the old fortune-teller might be. The girl looked me straight in the eye. Even in the dim light of the enclosed space, I could tell that she was not happy with my question. There were several dried leaves burning in pots which were scattered around the caravan, and the smoke which drifted from them started to make my eyes water, and my throat itch. I cleared my throat and had to rub my eyes several times to clear them."

"My grandmother is dead! Thank you for asking after her health, and it's partly your fault!"

"The young girl's words struck me like the ice-cold shock of having cold water thrown in your face. I sat there for a while staring at her in disbelief. How on earth could I be, in any way, responsible for her poor grandmother's demise? Once the initial shock had worn off, I asked her to explain herself."

"I apologise, Mr Ward, my outburst was unfair. But the fact of the matter is that my grandmother never recovered from seeing your potential future in the crystal. I know she tried to warn you, and to my shame, at the time I did not feel that her actions were befitting of someone of her dignity, which is why, if you recall, I tried to stop her on the pier."

"I was completely perplexed by her explanation. I begged her to elucidate further, as I desperately needed to know what bearing her grandmother's prediction for me could possibly have on her death. I was carrying enough guilt on my shoulders to last me several lifetimes already, and I was not sure that I could bear the weight of any more. But I refused to remain ignorant to the charges levelled at me by the girl's statement, so I pressed on, pleading with her to clarify her accusation.

"Eventually, out of desperation, I pulled out my wallet and without bothering to check how much I had in it, I grabbed all the notes within and placed them on the table, in front of the girl. Unfortunately, the hastiness of my action proved that I had misjudged her intentions. This was not some sort of confidence trick, and the girl's eyes blazed at me with a look of such contempt that I could actually feel myself growing smaller out of shame.

"She snatched up my money and thrust it back at me, letting the notes scatter on the table. Before I could utter a single word, she demanded that I leave the caravan and never come back. I felt so utterly foolish, not to mention ashamed, that I automatically rose to leave. But then on reflection, I had made an honest mistake, and so much misery had befallen me since my last meeting with her grandmother that I was desperate for her help.

"I looked the girl directly in the eyes and explained to her how sorry I was for my indiscretion, and how I was now living with the consequences of having ignored her grandmother's warning the previous year. I begged her to help me understand, or at the very least, explain to me what her grandmother had seen in the crystal. After a few moments, during which her gaze never left me, even for the briefest of seconds, she nodded and I retook my seat."

"My grandmother was a seventh child, of a seventh child, which means that her powers went way beyond those inherent in the rest of us, who have been blessed with the gift of foresight. She had the eye of the Teb'banshi, which allows one to see into the future more clearly than most people can see what's in front of them. I am the only one in our family who has inherited any of her power, and mine is not even a tenth of hers. Although it is more than enough to keep the holiday makers entertained.

"My grandmother's gift was extremely powerful. She did not sit here day after day, dishing stories to the masses because she needed the money. In her lifetime she had made predictions for kings and monarchs of all nations. Her reputation was known in circles so distinguished, that only a handful even know of their very existence."

"It was easy for me to tell from her demeanour, that the young girl was incredibly proud of her grandmother's achievements, and it was evident to me that my lack of appreciation had caused, albeit unintentionally, great insult. Since the girl was not prepared to accept my money, I did not know what else to do by way of atonement. So, for the present, I just listened."

"Some of the predictions she made as a child came true years later. She foretold both world wars, the rise of Hitler, the sinking of the Titanic, the assassination of Kennedy, even the day that the first man would land on the moon!"

"She suddenly looked at me with her brows furrowed. I felt instinctively that I had done something wrong, although I had no idea what."

"I know what you're thinking. If she had such great powers, why did she spend the last years of her life sitting in this caravan like some carnival freak?"

"I shook my head in denial, although the thought had flitted across my mind while she spoke. But before I could fathom what to say to convince her that she was wrong, she continued."

"I may not have the power bestowed on my grandmother, but I have enough to satisfy the kind of people who come in here and are willing to part with a few pounds, expecting to be told that they will all be millionaires one day. After all, that's the limit of their expectations. They only have the capacity to think of happiness in terms of wealth, I see it in their greedy minds. Half of them would trade ten years off their lives for the chance to be wealthy. I can see into their minds, just like I can see into yours, Mr Ward!"

"Her words carried a sting of venom which started to make me wish that I had not visited there in the first place. Yet there was something akin to compassion in her gaze, which compelled me to stay seated and let her finish. If she were capable of seeing into my mind, then she must be able to see the desolation and grief that I was drowning in."

"The reason my grandmother stayed here and performed this ritual was as a means of escape. You cannot imagine what it's like to carry around all the knowledge that she was in possession of. Being constantly bombarded with new discoveries, all through the day and night. Knowing that the person passing by you was going to be killed that night in a random traffic accident, or that someone who happened to be in the same queue as you at the post office was dying with an undiagnosed medical condition.

"And that would only begin to scratch the surface of some of things she would see. Major disasters, epidemics, mass shootings, the list never ended. So, telling fortunes was her way of siphoning off some of the excess. It kept her from losing her mind. She never asked, nor wanted this curse - none of us do. It might sound wonderful to the unenlightened, all they are capable of imagining how they could foresee the winner of the grand national, or the teams that would win them the football pools. But if you told them that one day they might wake up and know, without doubt, when the world was going to end. Do you think that they would be so enthusiastic about acquiring such a gift then?

"What if you could know for a fact what was waiting for you when you died? Even the most ardent atheists still hold onto a shred of hope that there is something better waiting for them when this life ends.

Regardless of whether or not they would ever admit it to anyone. But, if they were confronted with the knowledge whilst they were still alive, how do you think they would react? For that matter, how would religious factions respond to the knowledge that their version of god's laws was incorrect, and one of the alternative religions had got it right all along? Would the Catholics follow the Muslims? Would the Mormons drop everything and convert to Hari Krishna's?"

"She tapped the side of her head as if to emphasise her point."

"The truth is, such knowledge would send the sanest of individuals mad. That's because most people's minds do not have the capacity to deal with the enormity of such knowledge. But my grandmother had often seen into the minds of those society considered to be insane. People who had been locked away, disgraced because they were not considered fit to dwell in society. And do you know what she saw when she looked into their minds?"

"I shook my head, although I assumed that her question had been rhetorical."

"Knowledge. Profound and unrepressed knowledge. The only problem with them was that their minds were just not capable of processing it all, or dealing with the responsibility that came with such information. She used to tell me that when people dismissed such individuals it was only because they were not intelligent enough to comprehend what they had to offer."

"I rubbed my forehead, trying to demonstrate due respect for everything that she was saying. But the heady aroma from the burning leaves was starting to make my head hurt. I held up my hands as if in submission. I expressed my regret at not having appreciated the enormity of her grandmother's burden as sincerely as I could. Then once more I emphasised how desperately I needed to know what her grandmother had seen when she looked into my future that day.

"The girl shrugged her narrow shoulders, and casually flicked back a stray strand of her jet-black hair, which had fallen onto her face. She stared at me with a look of stern indignation for a moment. But then I saw something soften in her eyes, and she leaned closer to speak more intimately than she had thus far during our sitting."

"Alright, it's not my business to keep the truth from you, my grandmother would not approve. Since I was a child and my grandmother saw the gift in me, she always warned me about the Teb'banshi and the power that it bestowed. She had recognised it as a child, and since then, her life had never been the same. She told me what to do if I ever saw its reflection in the crystal. She knew that it was too late for her, but she hoped to save me at least.

"The Teb'banshi is older than any other magic or wisdom the world knows. It emanates from the darkness, and when it is seen, both the one who sees it and the one who has caused it to be seen are cursed. Our culture tells of wizards and sorcerers who over the centuries have tried to understand and command the power of the Teb'banshi, but only a select few ever witness its power unleashed, and those that do, usually do not live to tell others. When my grandmother gazed into the crystal to see your future, she saw the Teb'banshi, hovering over your aura, because you carried its mark, and that is why she tried to warn you. She risked her own life and the wrath of the Teb'banshi to warn you, and you ignored her!"

"I could feel another shiver run down my spine as she spoke. I remembered the terrified look in her grandmother's eyes when she confronted me on the pier that day. Now it all started to make sense. At least, that part of it did. I could see the young girl starting to tear up, doubtless as a result of discussing her grandmother with me. But still I had to know why, if the power of this force was as strong as the girl said it was, her grandmother risked so much to warn me about it."

"My grandmother told me that there was a bond of love between you and your wife, the strength of which she had only witnessed on a few occasions before. That was why she decided to risk the wrath of the Teb'banshi, and warn you. She hoped that with fair warning you might be able to evade the evil she could see in your future. But as a result, she did not survive the experience. When I brought her back here from the pier, I could see in her face that the lifeforce within her was draining away, extracted by the terrible power of the Teb'banshi. She died soon afterwards."

"I was mortified by what the girl was telling me. She evidently believed that her grandmother sacrificed her life to try and save mine. Right at that moment, it did not matter to me whether I believed in gypsy fortune-tellers, or Romany curses. It merely came down to an old woman willingly giving up the rest of her life for a complete stranger, based upon the love which she believed existed between him and his wife. I felt truly humbled, and I think that the girl either saw it in my face, or perhaps, saw it in my heart, because she slid her hand across the table and gave mine a gentle squeeze. When I looked up at her, she was smiling through her tears."

# TWENTY-SEVEN

Jonathan lifted his beer mug to his lips, and drained the last dregs of his beer. Meryl signalled to him for a refill, but he declined with a weak smile and a shake of his head. He gently rubbed his eyes between his forefinger and thumb, to prevent another flood of tears. It was then that he noticed that Meryl, as well as several of the band members, also had tear-stains down their faces.

His story had reached its end, and for the first time in as long as he could remember, Jonathan felt as if a huge weight had been lifted from his shoulders. He had never put much stock in the saying about 'a problem shared is a problem halved', but just relating his story to the others made him feel as if he was finally laying down his burden, and in its place, he felt a wave of calm wash over him.

Jonathan wiped his mouth with the back of his hand to clear the remnants of foam from his beer away, before he continued to speak. There was not much left to say, but he felt that his audience deserved an ending, having sat with him and listened to his story.

"I still see my Jenifer in my dreams. As old as I am now, she always looks as young as she was the last time I saw her. Sometimes she is cradling our baby in her arms, and I pray that it is a sign that they are waiting for me. I won't lie, I have often considered suicide, but I suppose that when it comes to it, I am not that brave. I have always found it odd that so many people refer to it as the 'coward's' way out. As far as I'm concerned, it would take more courage than I possess. Even so, I pray nightly that god in his mercy will take me soon.

"Amy still comes to me, too. Sometimes she has her angelic face on, and she sings to me in her dreams. But other times she haunts my nightmares, and chases me through an endless stream of corridors and passages, shrieking at the top of her lungs. I suspect that, from what that young fortune-teller explained to me, the curse I inherited will always be with me, although now, I have no one left to protect from it, so it's welcome to take me, whenever it sees fit!"

Jonathan heaved himself out of his chair, and began to button his coat in anticipation of the cold weather that awaited him, outside. Meryl tried once more to persuade him to stay for another drink. But she could tell that his mind was made up to leave. She imagined that, now he had completed his terrible story, he probably wished to be alone with his thoughts.

Mike offered Jonathan his hand and the two men shook, as did Fred, from the band.

Melissa and Julie hugged and kissed him on the cheek, and when he reached Barry, the drummer, he too wrapped his arms around the old man and hugged him tightly, telling him to look after himself.

Meryl walked Jonathan to the door, and saw him outside into the cold. She hugged him for the longest time, and informed him that he was always welcome and that from now on, she would save him his favourite seat, and that there would always be a free pint waiting for him at the beginning of the night.

Jonathan thanked her, wholeheartedly.

Meryl watched until he had reached the far end of the road, and turned out of sight.

# EPILOGUE

Meryl never saw Jonathan again after that night. She hoped that it was not embarrassment that was keeping him away, having bared his heart and soul to them all. Another theory which crossed her mind was that perhaps he now associated her pub with the reminder of that song, and as a result, with everything which had happened to him.

Finally, she started to make enquiries from some of her other regulars as to where he lived. She intended to pay him a visit and ensure she told him again that he was always welcome back at her establishment, and that there would be a free pint waiting for him every night.

When she discovered the name of his street, Meryl went to pay him a visit one afternoon when business was slow. The road in question was not particularly long, but she still counted over forty houses lining it. She waited for the first of Jonathan's neighbours to venture out, rather than randomly knocking on doors. The neighbour, although very pleasant and helpful, had only lived on the street herself for a short time, and did not know who Jonathan was.

In the end, having spoken to another two equally uninformed individuals, she finally found someone who had known him for some time. Meryl was dismayed to discover that Jonathan had died. According to the neighbour, a middle-aged lady with a strong Mediterranean accent, his sister had discovered him a few days after he passed away, when he had missed Sunday lunch at her house, something which he never did.

Whilst talking to the lady, Meryl calculated that Jonathan had died the same night he told his story at the pub. Apparently, he was found in his favourite armchair, clutching a picture of his late wife.

Meryl hoped that he was finally with her and their and child, and most of all, at peace.

Lightning Source UK Ltd.
Milton Keynes UK
UKHW011134200820
368549UK00007B/976